COPYCAT

COPYCAT

Betty Rowlands

This first world edition published in Great Britain 1999 by
SEVERN HOUSE PUBLISHERS LTD of
9–15 High Street, Sutton, Surrey SM1 1DF.
First published in the USA 2000 by
SEVERN HOUSE PUBLISHERS INC., of
595 Madison Avenue, New York, NY 10022.

British Library Cataloguing in Publication Data

Rowlands, Betty
    Copycat
    1.   Detective and mystery stories
    I.   Title
    823.9'14 [F]

    ISBN 0-7278-5499-2

Typeset by Palimpsest Book Production Ltd
Polmont, Stirlingshire, Scotland.
Printed and bound in Great Britain by
MPG Books Ltd, Bodmin, Cornwall.

Prologue

"This one is going to be a doddle." Miguel Rodriguez – Roddy to his friends and 'Lucky' Roddy to a select few on account of the way his jobs always went like clockwork – filled the glasses of his two partners in crime from the bottle of rioja at his elbow. It was not by any means the finest vintage his firm supplied as he was well aware that neither Morris nor Crowson had particularly well-trained palates. Still, it was decent enough for him to nose appreciatively before taking his first mouthful. "Salud!" he exclaimed as he raised his glass and the others responded with "Cheers!"

Given the choice, they would both have preferred to be toasting the new enterprise in pints of lager, but Roddy's expertise in all matters concerning wine and his contacts among wealthy wine-lovers had been the key to several highly successful jobs, so who were they to knock it? They drank it as Roddy had taught them, rolling it round their tongues and savouring – or pretending to savour – its smooth, subtle fruitiness.

"So tell us the details, boss," said Crowson.

Morris, whose main functions were to act as look-out, give a hand where necessary in carrying the loot and drive the getaway car, squinted at the paper spread out on the polished table. "I see you've got a plan of the place," he said. "How d'you manage that?"

"Just another bit of the Rodriguez luck," said Roddy. "The owner is having some work done on the building and this was lying on his desk while we were in his office discussing his order. He had a message the foreman wanted a word with him, so he went out telling his secretary to pour me another drink. Next thing he rang through asking for some bit of paper he needed, so off went Fiona leaving me on my own for five minutes. Plenty of time to run it through his photocopier – and have a good look round." He held up his glass to the light, admiring the rich colour of the wine and smiling at the recollection.

There was hardly a woman of his acquaintance who was not completely bowled over by that smile. Slightly mysterious, as if prompted by some secret thought he was not prepared to share until the moment was right, it hinted at warm, passionate nights under a velvety Mediterranean sky, with guitars throbbing in the background. Coupled with his frank, open manner, his natural courtesy and impeccable background, it was also a valuable commercial asset. Customers and suppliers alike agreed that Miguel Rodriguez, proprietor of the highly reputable company of wine merchants that bore his name, was a man with whom it was a pleasure to do business.

Crowson and Morris, who were more likely to associate Mediterranean nights with lager-drinking contests than dreams of romance, were impervious to the Rodriguez charm. In private they referred to him as "that Spanish smart-arse" whom they admired for his skills and organising ability but who, despite his having been born, brought up and educated in England, was nevertheless a foreigner and therefore not entirely to be trusted. They kept their eyes on him, observed his every movement and listened intently to every word as they waited for their instructions.

Roddy drained his glass and placed it on a coaster of beaten Spanish silver, handling it carefully with the slender, sensitive fingers whose speed and dexterity in other fields had proved their worth to the trio on more than one occasion. "Right boys, time to get down to the nitty-gritty. Here's how it goes. The owner's off to Gleneagles tomorrow for a golfing holiday and the house will be empty except for the married couple – a Mr and Mrs Frampton – he employs to run it. There's an external security system of floodlights controlled by sensors, but I've located a point where I can get right up to the house without setting them off. And guess what, that point is immediately below the office window, which is where the main control boxes for both the internal and external alarm systems are located. That's my point of entry."

"Won't it set off the alarm when you go in?" asked Morris.

"There's a thirty-second time-lag to enable anyone entering legitimately to turn it off by entering a code."

"I guess that'll be no problem for you, boss." Crowson spoke with justifiable confidence. Roddy's ingenuity in circumventing even the most sophisticated of security systems had reduced a number of victims to despair at the thought of the money they had invested with so little success.

"As it happens, it might have been tricky," Roddy admitted. "It's a set-up I haven't encountered before – but luck was with me again. There are control boxes beside the two main entrances, front and rear. The Framptons were in town shopping when we got to the house and of course they'd set the system before going out, but Fiona was with us and she opened up and keyed in the code while I was standing just behind her. I don't suppose it entered either of their heads that I was making a note of it."

"Brilliant!" said Morris, tossing off the last of his wine. "Okay, so once you're in, it's up to us, right?"

"Right. I've already shown you where to park your vehicle. Now, this room is where you head for." Roddy indicated their target on the plan and reached for a second sheet of paper. "Here's a list of the pieces I want and their precise location in the room. Nothing heavy, just be careful with the breakables and put the painting in a separate bag to protect it – it's only tiny even though it's worth a fortune. You should be in and out in three minutes at the outside. Oh, and don't forget, the usual rules apply. No one gets hurt. The Framptons sleep some way away and there's no reason they should hear a thing, but if you should be disturbed you know what to do."

There had been no reason to repeat the order, but he never failed to do so. It was part of his credo that so long as no one got physically hurt, there was no harm done. All his victims could well afford to lose a few of their treasures. In fact, although he was well aware that the others were in it solely for the money and expected to be handsomely rewarded for their share in the enterprise, to him it was the excitement, the risk, the thrill of pulling it off that really counted.

The meeting broke up and Crowson and Morris slipped quietly out of the penthouse flat by its private entrance. Left alone, Roddy carefully removed all traces of their presence before reaching for the phone. The night was still young, and Pepita was waiting for his call.

One

"This week has got to be one of the dullest on record," grumbled Mandy Parfitt, civilian Scenes of Crime Officer based at Gloucester police station. "And today's jobs are the dullest of all," she went on, flicking through a sheaf of reports. "Stolen car found abandoned, foiled break-in with nothing taken and a mower pinched from a garden shed. What've you got, Sukey?"

Susan Reynolds – Sukey to everyone except her ex-husband, Paul, who had refused to use the soubriquet on the grounds that it sounded childish – handed her colleague a mug of tea and sat down at an adjacent desk to check her own assignments for the morning. "Nothing wildly exciting," she said with a sigh. "Three cars broken into on the Ramsen estate during the night, radio and a laptop nicked from one, leather jacket from another, window smashed on the third but nothing taken. The villains were probably disturbed."

"Sounds like a Hodson job," Sukey remarked. "Which ones are currently out of the nick?" The numerous members of the Hodson clan were depressingly familiar to police and magistrates alike.

"Can't be sure off-hand," said Mandy with a shrug. "I wonder if anyone got a good look at whoever did that lot."

"If they did, they'll probably keep stumm. The Hodsons don't take kindly to being fingered by their neighbours. Sometimes," Sukey added with a sigh, picking up her mug of tea, "I wonder why we bother with this sort of incident."

"That sounds like a pretty negative approach," said a new

5

voice. The two SOCOs glanced up as Sergeant George Barnes entered the room. "Do I detect a hint of gloom in my section this sunny Spring morning?"

"Not gloom, just frustration at the poor quality of today's villains," Sukey explained. "We haven't had a really challenging case for weeks."

"Well now, what do you fancy? A bit of aggravated burglary, armed robbery – or maybe a nice juicy murder like the 'body in the sauna' case?"

"Ugh, no, anything but that," said Sukey with a shudder. Although she had not actually discovered the victim, it had fallen to her lot to take his fingerprints and the experience had not been pleasant. Still, she could take satisfaction from having at the same time spotted a vital clue on the body.

"How about a really spectacular robbery at a stately home?" suggested Mandy. "Art treasures looted by an international gang, and we're the ones who find the evidence that nails the villains and earns us the undying gratitude of the owner?"

"And a fat reward that would enable us to retire in luxury," said Sukey with a sigh.

"Well, dream on, but in the meantime you'll have to make do with the best the local villains can offer," chuckled George. "On your way, troops."

"Okay, Sarge." Feeling cheered by the nonsense, Sukey put down her empty mug on the scratched top of the wooden desk, reached for her notebook and began planning her itinerary. After all, it was Friday, she'd be finished by four o'clock and the weekend lay invitingly ahead. Her son Fergus would be spending it with his father and – unless there was a serious incident to interfere with their plans – DI Jim Castle was free as well. Excitement – at least of the criminal variety – wasn't everything.

She decided to make the Ramsen estate, where three separate incidents had been reported, her first destination. At one time it had been regarded as a 'sink' estate plagued by drug peddlars, junkies and vandals, many of whom belonged to a large, universally feared and detested family whose adult males had never done an honest day's work in their lives and whose violent and abusive women, children and aggressive dogs made their neighbours' lives a misery. Threats of reprisals had for a long time discouraged any form of resistance until a particular act of vandalism, as a result of which a child was seriously hurt, made the residents decide that 'enough was enough'. With the cooperation of the police they decided to defy their tormentors, set up a Neighbourhood Watch Committee and put together a dossier of incidents which eventually resulted in the culprits being evicted from their council home. Within weeks, the area had taken on a completely new aspect; broken fences were mended, front gardens tidied, and boarded-up windows repaired. Reported crime fell dramatically, but one fly in the ointment remained: the Hodsons, another large and anti-social family, most of whose members had criminal records and were much more difficult to tackle. None of them actually lived on the estate and in fact they were scattered around a number of districts. The older ones made their living in a variety of ways – few of them legal – and the younger ones amused themselves in their spare time with shoplifting, breaking into cars and stealing their contents or – for those with the necessary driving skills – joyriding. Ramsen residents had managed to foil them on several occasions and had recently enjoyed several Hodson-free months.

"Guess we were getting a bit too complacent," admitted the owner of the first car Sukey examined. "I usually take out the radio at night, but I forgot it until I'd locked up—"

"And you thought, 'Let it go for one night'," Sukey sympathised as she brushed the door handle for fingerprints. "It happens so often."

"And I could kick myself for leaving the laptop," the man went on. "It was out of sight in the boot, but they found it just the same. D'you reckon there's any chance of nabbing them?"

"We might, if any of these prints turn out to be on our files

7

– and if we can trace the stolen property back to whoever left them on the car." Sukey lifted a series of prints off the door and began work on the interior.

"Well, I'll leave you to it." Having watched for a few minutes with his hands in his pockets, he turned away and went indoors.

There was no car outside the second address and a woman who answered Sukey's knock informed her curtly that her husband needed it to get to work, he was a very busy man and if she wanted to examine the vehicle she would have to make an appointment. "Anyone would think they were doing us a favour, allowing us to try and find out who broke into their bloody car," Sukey grumbled as she made her report on the phone in her van. "I've left her our number and suggested that her husband call us if he wants us to pursue the matter."

"On our high horse, are we?" The officer in the control room was obviously in teasing mode. "Don't forget all you've been told about public relations."

"There are some members of the public who don't deserve to have relations," Sukey retorted. "I'm on my way now to incident number three."

"Okay. Keep in touch."

The owner of the third car to be targeted the previous night was a stockily built, sandy-haired individual in his forties with a truculent manner and features that reminded Sukey of a pug-dog. "You took your time," he observed, scowling at the ID she held up. "I'm supposed to be at work in half an hour."

"I'm sorry, Mr Blaine, I've had a couple of other jobs to attend to on this estate," Sukey explained, but the scowl merely deepened.

"So I'm told," Blaine sneered. "If your lot were doing what they're paid for, there'd be a lot less of this sort of thing."

"The police can't be everywhere at once." Sukey managed to keep her voice even and her eyes on the damaged quarterlight.

"So what are the public supposed to do – keep watch all night? I was told this was a quiet neighbourhood—"

"It's a great deal quieter than it was before the Neighbourhood Watch was set up, but nowhere's completely crime-free these days, I'm afraid." Sukey walked round the vehicle, looking for other signs of damage. "It doesn't look as if the villains managed to get into your car – do I understand you disturbed them?"

"I've already said so. Don't you people talk to each other? I happened to be awake, heard voices and got up to see what was going on. There were two of them, one had a brick in his hand so I opened the window and shouted at them to piss off . . . which they did, having used the brick to smash the window before they scarpered. Cheeky sods – one even looked up and gave me a V-sign."

Sukey bent over the contents of her case to conceal a smile. She had already come to the conclusion that she was unlikely to find any useful evidence, but decided to leave the disgruntled victim no cause to complain that she had not done her job properly. She began dusting for prints round the door handle.

"You're wasting your time there," he informed her. "They never got around to touching the car. I thought I made that clear to the uniformed schoolboy who came to take my statement."

"I haven't actually spoken to the officer concerned," said Sukey through her teeth. "Do I understand you got a good look at them – good enough to give a description?"

Blaine gave an exaggerated sigh of exasperation. "I suppose you want it all over again? One had a shock of hair like a bloody caveman and the other had a shaved head with a moth-eaten bird's nest on top. Tall and skinny, the pair of them – that seemed to ring a bell with your mate. He asked me if I'd be willing to attend an ID to see if I could pick them out and I said I'd be delighted."

"That'd be great." Sukey packed her equipment away and stood up. It sounded like a couple of the younger Hodsons and she wondered if Blaine would be so keen if he knew of their record of intimidation. "I'm pretty sure I know the family the officer was referring to," she said, "and if you'd be prepared to give evidence—"

"Any time. The old bloke in there" – Blaine jerked his head in the direction of the house next door – "warned me to keep quiet if I didn't want the next brick through my front room window. I told him it'd take more than a couple of teenage yobbos to scare me off." He squared his jaw, doubled his fists and assumed an aggressive stance. "Middle-weight boxing champ in the Royal Marines three years running," he boasted. "Never beaten either, just came to the end of my term."

"It strikes me your neighbours can count themselves lucky to have someone like you around to keep an eye on things," said Sukey and was rewarded with a smile that she found only marginally more pleasant than his normal expression. "I'm sure the police'll be in touch with you soon."

"No problem. I take it it's okay to use the car now?"

"Sure."

Blaine turned on his heel and went back indoors. "Well, thanks for your trouble," Sukey muttered sarcastically under her breath as she returned to her van. She was about to make her report when her call sign came through on the radio. "Sukey, your fairy godmother's been busy," George Barnes informed her. "Break-in at Bussell Manor, near Stroud. Valuable antiques stolen and an employee in need of medical attention. Uniformed in attendance, CID and ambulance called for. Mandy's already on her way and I want you to join her. This is a big one, so make sure you don't miss anything."

"Will do, Sarge." Sukey felt the adrenalin surging through her system at the prospect. "Be there in half an hour."

Two

"How the hell does he do it?" Detective Inspector Jim Castle stood in the galleried entrance hall of Bussell Manor and scratched his head in disbelief. "State of the art, all-singing-all-dancing security system, and he just walks in and out of the place as if all he had to do was unlatch the front door with a credit card."

"Or slide down the chimney like Santa Claus," agreed Detective Sergeant Andy Radcliffe with a wry grin.

"If only Crowson and Morris hadn't given our people the slip," Castle went on in the same disconsolate tone. "We could at least have nabbed them with the loot, and maybe got them to grass on Rodriguez. As it is . . . ." His frown deepened, then faded momentarily as the constable guarding the front entrance popped his head round the door to announce the arrival of the second SOCO. Moments later, Sukey Reynolds walked in, staring about her in a mixture of admiration and awe.

"More like a National Trust house than a private home, isn't it?" she commented. "Who's the owner?"

"A wealthy American called Wilbur Patterson," said Castle. "He bought the property from an impoverished local bigwig and is spending a small fortune restoring it to its original early nineteenth-century grandeur. Seems he wanted an appropriate setting for his collection of antiques."

"Is he here?"

"On his way down from Scotland, spitting fire and brimstone by all accounts and threatening to sue the firm that installed the security system."

11

"Don't blame him." Sukey's practised eye slid round the huge empty space, searching among the suits of armour and the various items of Regency furniture, ornaments and other artefacts, but failing to spot anything resembling a sensor.

"The control panel's behind the door." Radcliffe pointed to a box gleaming with pinpoints of green light mounted on the wall. "The housekeeper swears the system was set as usual and the doors locked and bolted on the inside before she and her husband went to bed last night."

"Have we located the point of entry?"

"Not yet. All we know is that when they got up this morning to open up the house for the workmen, the system was off and the front door unbolted. The first thing they did was to check that room over there." Castle nodded towards a room at the back of the hall where, through the open door, Sukey caught a glimpse of her colleague surveying the scene, fingerprint equipment at the ready. "That's where he keeps most of his collection. I've never seen anything like it in a private house – everything set out and labelled like exhibits in a museum. They realised a number of valuable items were missing and called us. I doubt if Mandy'll find anything useful," he finished gloomily. "There's never been a smell of a clue at any of the previous jobs."

Sukey stared at him in astonishment. "You know who did it?"

"Oh yes, we know who did it," Castle said grimly. "We even knew he was going to do it and approximately when. The trouble is, we didn't know where."

"But how—?" Sukey began, then broke off as she met the detective's eyes. Their expression told her plainly that she was not here to ask questions, but to do a job. While they were on duty, Castle was the senior officer and she a lowly civilian employee. No doubt he would reveal more of the background to the case later on; in the meantime, there was work to be done.

"Where would you like me to start?"

"Have a scout round outside – see if you can find where he got in. You might get lucky and find something."

"Right." She headed for the door, then turned round. "George Barnes said someone had been hurt – was there a struggle?"

"Nothing so dramatic," said Radcliffe. "The housekeeper went into a severe state of shock when she realised what had happened. She's been sent to hospital for a check-up."

"Poor woman. What about her husband?"

"He went with her. We'll have to get their detailed statements later."

Outside, Sukey stood for a few moments admiring the view, as picturesque a prospect as anything the Cotswolds had to offer. Perched on a grassy knoll overlooking the tiny village of the same name that nestled at its feet, Bussell Manor dominated a wide expanse of countryside. On this sparkling April morning, everything was fresh and bursting with new life. Hedgerows erupted in a froth of blackthorn blossom, burgeoning new growth threw a mist of green over patches of woodland, sheep grazed on rolling acres of pasture and the plaintive cries of new-born lambs blended with the joyous song of a thrush perched on a nearby chestnut tree.

She walked a few paces down the drive, turned and stared up at the handsome stone facade topped with a row of stone figures in classical poses gazing out across the valley. They had a proprietorial air, as if claiming everything in sight as their own. They did not, however, offer any help with her present task and she began a systematic tour of the exterior of the house, her practised eyes searching for the smallest clue.

It was not long before she spotted the first indication of the complex security system – small, inconspicuous sensors installed at intervals beneath the string course that ran the entire length of the facade. Their purpose, no doubt, was to activate the exterior lights and possibly also some audible signal inside the building. Assuming that they too were in operation at the time of the burglary, the thief must have found some way of either avoiding or deactivating them.

At the rear of the house she came on a cluster of outbuildings. It was evident from the piles of builders' materials and equipment scattered around that major works were still in progress. A van bearing the name of a local contractor was parked beside a heap of sand and a couple of men in overalls were sitting on a wooden bench drinking mugs of tea and smoking cigarettes. Pop music blared from a transistor radio. She went over and introduced herself.

"I've been asked to try and find the point where the burglars got in," she explained. "Did you by any chance notice whether any of your stuff had been disturbed?"

The two men shook their heads, glancing at one another for confirmation. "Can't say we did," said the younger of the two, a red-faced individual with a genial smile revealing several missing teeth.

"The coppers were already here when we arrived and we were told to keep out of the way and not touch anything till they gave us permission," the older man explained grumpily. "Just when we get some decent weather, we have to sit here on our arses and waste time," he went on, scowling. "I've had to tell the rest of the crew not to turn up. It'd be nice if you could get on with your job so that we can do ours," he added pointedly.

"I'll do my best. What about those ladders?" Sukey pointed to where several were lying on the ground beside a heap of sand. "Are they exactly where you left them?"

"Couldn't say for sure," said the first man. The second merely grunted. Recognising that she was unlikely to receive much help from that quarter, Sukey walked across to the ladders, checking the ground at every step. She turned back towards the house and looked up, noticing that in contrast to the elegant stone of the other three sides some other, inferior material faced with plaster and covered with cream paint had been used for the rear wall. There were three rows of windows; those on the ground floor were protected by iron bars and on the upper two by closed shutters, except for one window on the second floor where the shutters were open. Still picking her way carefully, she moved closer and noticed a dark streak on the plaster immediately below the sill. Directly beneath it she spotted two depressions in the soft earth.

With rising excitement, her eyes glued to the ground, she headed back to the spot where she had noticed the ladders and saw on the muddy, trampled grass distinct traces of sand and several partial shoeprints. None was clear enough to be of any use until, on a small patch of sand that had somehow been separated from the main heap, she found one which was clear enough for identification purposes. She got out her camera and the younger and more amiable of the two workmen strolled over to watch.

"Found something interesting?" he enquired.

"Maybe." Sukey focused the camera and took a couple of shots. "Would you mind staying away from this area, please?"

"Oh, sure." He moved back a few paces, still watching. "You reckon the burglar made that footmark?"

"It's possible."

"Proper little Sherlock Holmes, aren't you?" he said in admiration. "What d'you deduce from that, Watson?" he asked in a mock upper-class voice.

"It looks like a trainer and it's pretty well brand-new." She glanced down at the heavy boots he was wearing. "It certainly isn't one of yours," she commented with a smile. "Do you know if anyone else working on the site wears Reeboks?"

The man guffawed. "You kidding? On what we get paid? Anyway, they're not allowed – we all have to wear these special boots."

"Of course you do."

"My name's Charlie," he added conversationally.

Sukey nodded without responding, put her camera in the pocket of her denim jacket and retraced her steps, this time studying the ground even more closely and trying to figure out how a man carrying a ladder could have managed to plant it against the wall without triggering the lights. From what she knew of such arrangements, sensors were normally angled outwards to avoid being activated by nocturnal animals prowling near the house. A human walking upright would certainly be picked up, but if the burglar had approached on all fours, pushing the ladder along the ground in front of him . . . yes, there were distinct indications that the grass had been flattened along a line leading to the point below the unshuttered window. She took more photographs and made some notes before packing her camera away.

"Finished?" asked Charlie, who had continued to observe her every move from a discreet distance.

"For the time being." She went across to the older man. He had studiously ignored the proceedings so far, but was presumably in charge. "I'm going to arrange for this area to be cordoned off," she informed him. "I'd be grateful if you'd keep clear of it for now."

"If you say so," he said sourly. He lit another cigarette and turned up the volume on the radio.

She made her way back to the entrance to the house and found Castle and Radcliffe conferring with Mandy in the hall.

"Any joy?" asked Castle. "We haven't had much here," he added, his expression still gloomy. "Mandy's dusted around, but we're pretty sure they wore gloves – we've never found any prints at the previous jobs."

Sukey reported her findings and for the first time a trace of a smile softened his aquiline features. "Splendid!" he exclaimed. "We can easily identify the room in question. Andy, you've got that plan of the house the butler, or whatever he calls himself, gave us before he left for the hospital, haven't you?"

"Right here." Radcliffe produced a large sheet of paper and spread it on an ornate chest. The four of them clustered round it while Sukey made some calculations. Five minutes later they were in a well-equipped and furnished office on the second floor. Sukey examined the sash window.

"The catch has been oiled recently," she told them. "Anyone with a Swiss army knife could have opened it from the outside."

A gleam appeared in Castle's greenish eyes and he rubbed his hands together. "Well, that answers our first question," he said gleefully. "Well done, Sukey. Now it's up to you girls to find some evidence to prove that it was our man. Good hunting!"

Three

Absorbed in their task, the two SOCOs were at first only vaguely aware of the approach of a small aeroplane, but as the noise of its engine grew louder Mandy went over to the window and glanced out.

"It's coming down!" she exclaimed. "D'you suppose it's in trouble?"

Sukey joined her in time to see the plane disappear behind a line of trees beyond the outbuildings where Charlie and his disgruntled foreman were eating sandwiches and reading newspapers. "I think it's landed," she said. "It's probably Wilbur the Wealthy, come to check on what's missing."

As if to confirm Sukey's guess, the sound of the engine died; moments later, the figure of a man appeared through a gap in the trees and strode towards the house. He was tall and heavily built, but his movements were athletic and despite his balding crown – easily visible from the women's first-floor vantage point – she judged him to be no older than his mid-thirties. His fawn safari jacket and slacks had an expensive-casual appearance, cut to minimise his tendency to run to flesh, and his face was the colour of weathered brick. Even from that distance, he exuded anger and agitation; he hurried past the two workmen without acknowledging their presence and vanished round the angle of the building.

"There's going to be an explosion any minute!" Mandy predicted gleefully.

The two of them hurried out on to the landing, which gave them a direct view of the front door. They were just in time to

18

see it flung open to the accompaniment of a stentorian voice bellowing, "I don't need an ID to enter my own goddam house!" as the newcomer burst in and headed across the hall towards the room where the collection was displayed. Jim Castle, who had been conducting his own examination there after Mandy had completed hers, met him in the doorway.

"Mr Patterson?"

"That's me." Patterson rocked back on his heels and glowered. "Are you the officer in charge?"

"Detective Inspector Castle." He held up his ID, which received a cursory glance and a grunt. "It seems pretty clear from your excellent labelling system which items were taken," Castle went on in his most emollient tones, unaware of the two pairs of ears straining from above, or of Sukey mouthing "Creep!" as Mandy stifled a giggle.

"We've made this list." Castle handed Patterson a sheet of paper. "It would of course help our investigations if you have photographs of any of the pieces—"

"Sure, sure, no problem," Patterson said impatiently. "Jeeze, the bastards knew what to go for!" he muttered as he scanned the list. "That lot adds up to several million bucks. Let me take a look."

He made a move to enter the display room, but Castle put a hand on his arm. "I'd be obliged, sir, if you'd stay out of there until we've completed our examination."

Patterson jerked his arm free. "I don't take kindly to being ordered around in my own house . . ." he snarled. The watchers held their breath, anticipating a confrontation, but Castle stood his ground and after a moment Patterson, with what appeared to be a mighty effort at self-control, backed down. "So when did this happen?" he demanded, his manner still belligerent. "Any idea who did it?"

"All I can say at the moment is that we think we've found the point where the thief entered the house. Our SOCOs are checking your office – let's join them and they'll explain what they've turned up so far. Oh, by the way, this is Detective

Sergeant Radcliffe," Castle added as the DS emerged from one of several doors leading off the hall. The two men exchanged nods. "He's been checking all the doors and ground floor windows."

"No sign of forced entry, Guv," said Radcliffe.

"Right, let's go upstairs."

The two SOCOs hastily withdrew from their vantage point and resumed their efforts with dusting-brush, tweezers and plastic sample envelopes. When the three men entered the room, Castle explained what they were doing and said, "Sukey, perhaps you'd tell Mr Patterson what you found."

The big American listened in silence as Sukey explained her theory. "I suppose it's feasible," he muttered, half to himself. "That window catch was jammed solid and I had it oiled a week or so ago when the weather turned hot. Just the same, even supposing you're right about the way he dodged the outside sensors, entering the house would have triggered the alarm."

"Unless, of course, the intruder knew how to deactivate it," Radcliffe pointed out. "We found the master control box under your desk. How many people besides yourself know where it is – and how many of them know the code?"

Patterson's show of aggressiveness had been steadily evaporating and was now virtually spent. He slumped into a leather-upholstered executive chair that stood behind the heavy walnut desk and ran stubby fingers through his thinning hair. "My secretary – she should be here any minute, by the way – the Framptons of course—"

"That would be your housekeeper and butler," Radcliffe interposed, checking a page in his notebook.

"That's right. Where are they, by the way? What have they got to say about all this?"

"We've taken preliminary statements from them both. They discovered the theft when they opened up the house this morning and called us straight away, but so far they haven't been able to give us any useful information as they heard nothing during the night. Unfortunately Mrs Frampton has had some kind of seizure, probably due to shock. She's been taken to hospital and her husband has gone with her. We shall, of course, be interviewing them again in due course."

Patterson grunted again. "That goddam security company swore their system was foolproof," he declared. He looked Castle full in the face from piercing blue eyes under thick, bushy brows. "You reckon it was an inside job? Someone tampering with the system? I'm having renovations done – have you checked on the workmen?"

"I'm afraid we haven't had time yet to carry out that kind of enquiry – but of course we shall explore every possibility," Castle added as a 'what the hell have you been doing then?' gleam appeared in Patterson's penetrating eyes. "Indications at present, however, are that someone familiar with the layout of the house somehow found a means of bypassing or deactivating both the internal and external security systems and entered undetected through that window. I'd like you to tell me exactly who has been in the house recently – especially anyone who's been in this room."

"How the hell am I expected to remember? What difference does it make? Folks who come to see me don't normally come in through the window."

"Of course not, sir, but sometimes they leave fingerprints and it helps if we can eliminate people with a legitimate reason for being here," Radcliffe explained patiently.

"Oh sure, sure." Patterson made a slightly helpless gesture. "I forgot about fingerprints. He raised his own hands and glanced from them to the detectives. "Guess you'll want mine as well." For the first time, a faint grin appeared on his florid features.

"In due course, sir. Meanwhile, if you could think of some names . . ."

"Fiona – my secretary – will know. That sounds like her now," he added as a female voice floated up from the hallway, followed by the sound of light footsteps running up the wooden staircase and along the landing. A young woman with a pale face and short blond hair pulled up in the doorway and ran a pair of striking lead-grey eyes over the occupants of the room. Sukey had the impression that she was making a mental image of every unfamiliar face and would be able to describe any one of them in detail if asked to do so.

She addressed Patterson without any greeting or preamble. "How much has been taken?" she demanded.

"See for yourself." Patterson handed over the list.

She studied it briefly, frowning. "Knew what they were looking for, didn't they?"

"Too right," Patterson agreed. "These guys are from the police. They want photographs of the missing items."

"They're in the safe." She pulled a set of keys from her handbag, but Patterson made an impatient gesture.

"Later. Right now they want to know who's been in this room lately."

"What do you mean by lately?" The question was addressed to Castle, whom she seemed instinctively to recognise as the man in charge.

"I'm afraid we can't be precise," he replied. "Let's talk about this week for a start, beginning with the most recent."

"I'll check the diary." She turned to a second, smaller desk in one corner, pulling a face at the grey powder scattered over its surface. "I hope you're going to clear up this mess," she said irritably.

This time it was the SOCOs who were treated to the leaden stare, and Sukey made an apologetic gesture. "I'm afraid we have to leave things as they are for the moment," she said. "We're trying to establish whether any unauthorised person was here by comparing fingerprints."

"Yes, I do know a little about how police enquiries work," Fiona snapped. She was stabbing at keys on a computer; after a moment a list appeared on the screen and Patterson moved over and stood beside her as she scrolled down the names.

"Okay," he said. "There were only two appointments this week. On Tuesday Stuart Lockyer came – he looks after my collection and advises me what to buy. We spent the morning going over a catalogue of a sale at Sotheby's next month. On Monday I had a session with Miguel Rodriguez, my wine merchant. Look," – he swung round and faced the detectives – "these guys aren't just business contacts, they're my personal friends. I don't want them hassled, or made to feel they're under suspicion."

"I assure you, there will be no question of hassling," Castle assured him. "We always make it clear to anyone allowing us to take their prints for elimination purposes that they will be destroyed once we have finished with them – in their presence if they so wish."

"Make sure you do that." Patterson turned back to Fiona. "Who else called in this week?"

They conferred briefly and came up with two more names, those of a representative from the security company and the foreman of the builders who had raised certain queries needing a decision. "That was on Monday, when Mr Rodriguez was here," Fiona commented. "He didn't actually enter the room, though – just knocked and put his head round the door. The two of you went out to discuss the query on site."

Patterson nodded. "That's right."

Radcliffe looked up from his notebook. "Just on a point of interest," he said in a deceptively casual voice, "was anybody left alone here for any reason?"

"No, why should they be?"

"You did call for a file while you were talking to the foreman and I brought it down to you," Fiona reminded him. "When Mr Rodriguez was here—"

"You can cross Roddy off your lists of suspects right now," Patterson told Castle impatiently. "I told you, he's a personal friend."

"Quite so," said the detective soothingly. He turned to Fiona. "You're certain there was no one else who might have had the opportunity to poke around?"

"I can't think of anyone . . . no, I'm sure there wasn't."

"Right then, I think that's all we need to trouble you with for the time being. We'll keep in close touch, of course." He turned to the secretary. "Fiona, if you'd be kind enough to let us have those photographs . . . ?"

To Sukey's amusement, the request was accompanied by a winning smile that transformed his normally severe features and produced an immediate thaw in the woman's glacial expression as she hurried to comply.

"And if you'd allow these ladies to take your fingerprints . . ."

With the preliminaries over, the detectives withdrew and Patterson and his secretary went off to check how the works were progressing, leaving the SOCOs to complete their task in peace. Sukey's brain was buzzing. It was the first time she had been present while Castle was interviewing witnesses and she had found it fascinating to observe him in action. His manner throughout had been impassive, almost detached, as if he was putting his questions out of a polite curiosity and saw no particular significance in any of the answers. Just the same, she could have sworn that the name Rodriguez had caused a momentary, albeit barely detectable, reaction. Recalling Castle's earlier confident assertion that the police knew the identity of the thief, she made a mental note to tackle him on the subject when he came to her house for a meal that evening.

She was still preoccupied with these thoughts as, having packed away their gear, she and Mandy prepared to leave on their next assignments. The two white vans were just moving off when a silver BMW approached at speed along the tree-lined avenue leading to the house. Sukey had a fleeting impression of a cadaverous face and a neatly trimmed dark beard as it swept past and pulled up alongside a small red Peugeot, presumably belonging to Fiona. Out of curiosity, she watched in her rear-view mirror as the driver got out and spoke briefly to the policeman on duty before approaching the front door, which opened before his outstretched finger reached the bell-push. There was a brief glimpse of Fiona's pale, expressionless face as the newcomer stepped inside.

*　　*　　*

At the same time that DI Castle and DS Radcliffe were making their preliminary investigation into the raid at Bussell Manor, Miguel 'Roddy' Rodriguez emerged from the shower and went into the kitchen of his penthouse flat to pour himself a glass of orange juice. He had slept late, as he normally did after a job, and he was feeling particularly pleased with life. The day was bright and sunny, everything had gone according to plan and he had a dinner date with Pepita that evening.

The telephone rang. Crowson was on the line. "What the hell are you playing at?" he demanded furiously.

"Is there a problem? I thought we agreed no phone calls unless—"

"Unless anything went wrong. Well, it might have been okay from your point of view, but we weren't amused at being sent on a fool's errand." Crowson's voice dropped to a menacing growl. "You double-crossing Spanish bastard—"

"What are you getting at?"

"You know bloody well what I'm getting at. Most of the stuff you told us to lift was already gone – as if you didn't know."

"I don't believe it! I checked after opening the place up and it was all there—"

"Sure it was – but not when you left. I suppose you're planning to sell it privately and cut us out."

"You know me better than that. Someone else must have had the same idea and turned the place over after—"

"After you very kindly opened up for him and left us to find the cupboard bare," Crowson snarled. "Don't give me that shit, I wasn't born yesterday."

"I swear to you—"

"Save it. We want our cut and we want it fast, otherwise you're in dead trouble. You've got till six o'clock.

"Look, we have to talk—" Roddy began desperately, but the line had already gone dead.

Four

Later that morning, back at police headquarters in Gloucester, DI Castle stared out of his office window with his hands in his trouser pockets, frowning in concentration. Perched on the edge of the desk, DS Radcliffe watched the hawklike profile, trying to guess what was passing through the inspector's mind, knowing from experience that something about the case was troubling him. Castle's next words confirmed his suspicions.

"You know, Andy," he said moodily, "I have a gut feeling that this slippery bastard is going to get away with it yet again."

"Guv?"

"We know for a fact that Rodriguez had an opportunity to case the house because Patterson invited him there, entertained him to lunch, most likely gave him a conducted tour and showed off his collection before taking him up to the office to discuss the wine order. We know that he was left alone there for a short time, which would have given him a chance to sus out the security system – the main control box is readily accessible and we know he's a bit of a wizard with electronics. But even supposing we find his prints in some, shall we say, unexpected places, it's going to be almost impossible to prove that they got there as a result of any criminal intent. Without some more positive evidence, we won't even have an excuse to bring him in for questioning."

"Hmm, I see what you mean. What about the ladder? Sukey found one with mud and sand clinging to it, which seems to support her theory about how Rodriguez got in. It's aluminium, she might have picked up some fingerprints. Then there's the shoeprint . . ."

"The shoeprint would only be useful if we could prove it matched a pair of trainers Rodriguez is known to have been wearing. As for the ladder, he's far too clever to have carried out that sort of operation without wearing gloves."

"So where do we go from here?"

"I wish I knew."

There was a knock at the door and Sukey entered, carrying a large envelope which she handed to Castle. He almost snatched it from her, extracted some sheets of paper covered with reproductions of fingerprints and spread them out on his desk. "Any joy?" he asked.

"There are one or two still to be identified," she told him, "but I found several that match the ones you gave me." She picked up one of the sheets, indicating the various points where the prints tallied. "They came mostly from the desk and on one of the chairs, but there's a nice thumbprint on the window-catch. There are also several on the photocopier and from their position, I'd say whoever it was used the machine." She put stress on the words 'Whoever it was' and gave him a searching look, but he made no response. Over her shoulder she shot an enquiring glance in Radcliffe's direction, but he merely shrugged and shook his head.

Castle, apparently absorbed in his contemplation of the prints, nodded in evident satisfaction. "The photocopier, eh?" he muttered, half to himself. "I wonder what the blighter was doing with that."

Radcliffe put down a sheet of prints he had been studying and said, "I think you're holding out on us, Guv."

The detective smiled. "Well, yes, I suppose I am, but there's no reason why you shouldn't know. Those prints I gave you for comparison, Sukey, belong to Rodriguez. Only they were obtained in a somewhat, shall we say, irregular manner and for that reason they'd be inadmissible as evidence. I can't tell you any more at this stage," he added, forestalling the questions that she was bursting to ask. She recalled their earlier conversation, when Castle had revealed that he knew a robbery was planned for the previous night and that he knew the perpetrator's identity. *You're going to get a real grilling this evening, my lad*, she said to herself. *There's something very interesting and unusual about this case.*

"So what else did you find?" Castle asked.

"He definitely got in through the window." From the envelope she took out several plastic bags containing samples. "We found traces of sand on the sill and the carpet that appear to match the sand where we found the shoeprint. We think he was wearing black cotton trousers – these are some fibres we found on the sill – and there were also a few grains of sand on the mat by the front door. The samples will need to go to the lab for confirmation, of course."

"So presumably he went out through the front with his loot," Radcliffe speculated.

"That would make sense," Castle agreed. "It would have been awkward to use the ladder with a sackful of goodies, besides the risk of damaging them. I wonder why he bothered to put the ladder away."

"To make it look like an inside job?" Sukey suggested.

"Possibly," said Castle thoughtfully. "Or maybe he was just teasing us. Who knows? Anyway, thanks Sukey – you and Mandy did a great job."

"Thank you, sir. Is there anything else you want me to do?"

"Not for the moment."

"Okay, I'll see if George Barnes has got anything else." If Radcliffe had not been there, she would have added, "See you later," but although both she and Castle were aware that the sergeant, an old friend, knew of their relationship, they made a point of never referring to it in his presence.

"Right." Castle sounded abstracted, as though he had already forgotten her existence. He turned to Radcliffe, "Have a word with Rodriguez, Andy, ask him for his co-operation and so on. Be as diplomatic as you can, offer to send someone round to take his prints, invite him to call in at his convenience, whichever he prefers. We want them officially on record — if we can't nail him for this job, maybe there'll be others."

"You're really convinced he did this, aren't you?

Castle's eyes were as hard as marbles. "Absolutely," he said.

Later that morning, Roddy received a second telephone call. Before he could speak, a man said, "Mr Rodriguez?"

"Yes, who is that?"

"Good morning, sir." The voice, bearing a trace of the local accent, was courteous, almost friendly, giving no hint of the shock waves the next words would send over the wire. "This is Detective Sergeant Radcliffe of Gloucester CID."

"Good morning, Sergeant." Roddy could feel as well as hear the tremor in his own voice. Trying desperately to sound relaxed, he added, "What can I do for you?"

It was such a simple, artless request. Some valuable antiques had been stolen from a house belonging to a Mr Patterson — "I believe he is a client of your company, sir, and that you visited him recently?" — and it would help the police with their enquiries if they could eliminate everyone who had recently entered on legitimate business. His co-operation would be greatly appreciated, someone would call on him at home or if he happened to be in the vicinity of the main police station, whichever was the more convenient for him . . .

The last thing Roddy wanted was to have police calling on him at home. He could hardly refuse to co-operate without arousing suspicion, so going to the nick would seem to be the lesser of two evils. "I can call in this morning," he heard himself saying. He hung up, cutting short the man's thanks.

Back at the station, Radcliffe reported to DI Castle the result of the conversation. "He's coming in this morning to give us his elims."

"How did he react?"

"He sounded pretty jumpy – I thought for a moment he was going to refuse, but I guess he thought better of it. It looks as if you're on the right track, Guv."

"Glad you think so. I hope the Super takes the same line – I'm just off to brief him."

Superintendent Sladden sat with his plump, well-kept hands folded over his stomach and listened gravely to DI Castle's progress report on the robbery at Bussell Manor.

"What makes you so sure this fellow Rodriguez is your man?" he asked when Castle came to the end of his brief recital. "Yes, I know about the pattern so far," he went on before the DI had a chance to reply to the question. "Three jobs within twelve months, all the victims clients of the chap's company, all visited by him by invitation shortly beforehand—"

"Plus a report from the undercover agent that another job was imminent," Castle reminded him.

"Yes, pity that information was incomplete. Didn't you have him tailed?" Sladden ran his eyes once more over the written report that Castle had given him. "Ah yes, and lost him in traffic on Thursday evening. That was . . . unfortunate." He managed by his tone to suggest that ill fortune was not the only factor in the failure of the surveillance operation. "You've no idea where he went after that?"

"No sir. I ordered the team back to his home, hoping they'd pick him up there. They waited till after midnight, but when he hadn't shown up by then it seemed pointless to keep them there any longer and I called them in."

"I'd probably have taken the same decision," Sladden admitted graciously. "Well, Castle, I admit that on the face of it, it looks very much as if this could be this chap's work – but on the other hand, the whole thing could be a series of coincidences. I understand there were other robberies during the same period at houses where he hadn't previously paid a visit."

"That's true, sir," Castle agreed, a trifle wearily. He had

already referred to that possibility during the early part of the conversation, but it was typical of the Super to bring it up later as if it was his own idea.

"And don't lose sight of the fact that it could have been an inside job," Sladden went on. "I take it you'll be checking on the other characters in the cast?"

"Enquiries are already in hand, sir."

"Good show. Keep me informed."

"Of course."

Feeling slightly aggrieved, as was normal after an interview with the Super, Castle withdrew. Shortly after he reached his own office, there was a knock at the door and a young uniformed constable entered with an envelope in his hand. "Elims from Miguel Rodriguez," he said.

"Oh, thanks. Give them to Sukey Reynolds, will you?"

"Sir." The man turned to go, then hesitated. "I don't know if it's relevant, sir, but something rather odd happened a few moments ago. Just as Rodriguez was about to leave, Sukey arrived in a great hurry and went to the security door to punch in the code. When Rodriguez saw her he almost jumped out of his skin and shouted, 'Pepita!' She half glanced round but didn't take much notice, just went through the door and disappeared. He stood there with his mouth open, staring after her as if he'd seen a ghost."

"Did he say anything else?"

"He seemed really shaken. He grabbed me by the arm and said, 'What's she doing here?' I told him she was one of our Scenes of Crime Officers and he said, 'You mean she works for the police?' He seemed horrified and began muttering under his breath. It sounded like, 'How could she, how could she?' He must have mistaken her for someone else and it probably has nothing to do with the case, but I thought it worth mentioning."

"You were absolutely right," Castle told him. "Sometimes these apparently irrelevant details turn out to be of considerable importance." His tone remained matter-of-fact, but as the door closed behind the young officer his smile of approval gave way to an uneasy frown.

There was a ball of lead in Roddy's stomach and burning coals behind his eyes. He sat on the edge of his bed – that same bed where, only two days before, he and Pepita had for the first and only time made love. She had been reluctant at first – not, she had assured him with tears in her eyes, through a lack of desire, but because of a certain loyalty she felt towards a husband she no longer cared for. When at last she yielded they had shared what to him had been the most perfect night that any man could wish for, with – as he had fervently believed – the promise of many more. The memories returned to torment him – the rounded contours of her body, the warmth of her lips, her perfume, the silky softness of her hair, the satin texture of her skin and the touch of her cool fingers caressing his, lingering for a moment on the star-shaped birthmark on his private parts, as she jokingly accused him of having it tattooed. He groaned aloud and sank his face into his hands at the realisation that it had been nothing but a sham, a device to bring about his downfall.

For long, agonising minutes he sat there, remembering nothing of the call from Crowson or of the drive home after the summons to the police station – so anodyne, yet so shattering in its outcome – seeing only the image of the woman he loved as she passed unheedingly before him with all the confidence of someone who knew exactly where she was and what she was doing. The few simple words spoken by the young officer rang in his ears and made a mockery of his dreams. A dozen times he repeated aloud his own response to those words: How could she? How could she?

After a while he raised his head, fumbled in his pocket and pulled out his wallet. From it he drew a photograph of the two of them at a friend's house, the only one of Pepita that he possessed. It had been taken without her knowledge at a party a couple of weeks or so ago and he had treasured it in secret like a schoolboy fan worshipping a picture of a favourite pop star. She had always claimed to have 'a thing' about being photographed and had stubbornly refused to pose for him or allow anyone else to take a shot of the two of them together. Now he knew why. He stared at it, trembling with grief and rage that spilled over into a howl of anguish. *You treacherous bitch, how could you?*

The ring of the telephone brought him back to his senses. A familiar voice said, "Wallis here. You're late checking in. Is everything all right?"

His own voice sounded hoarse and strange as he replied, "No, nothing is all right."

"Explain."

The single word, low-pitched with a hint of a foreign accent, had an ominous ring that sent a shiver down Roddy's back. Already stunned by the realisation that his lover had betrayed him, he experienced a new sensation: fear. Fear at what might happen should this man, whom he had never met but who had come to play such a powerful rôle in his life, believe he had been tricked out of the spoils of his latest scam. His heart thudded in his chest as he recounted the events of the morning: Crowson's threats, the call from the police and the shock of the encounter at the police station.

The silence that greeted his story lasted only a few seconds, yet it seemed an eternity before Wallis spoke. "We must move quickly. Stay where you are and let no one in. You will receive my instructions within the hour."

Five

"Had a good day, Mum?" Sukey's sixteen-year-old son Fergus came bounding into the sitting-room of the little semi-detached house in Brockworth, where she was relaxing with the *Gloucester Gazette*. There was, of course, no mention of the robbery at Bussell Manor; news of that would not have broken in time for the early edition. No doubt it would be the headline story tomorrow. Fergus leaned over the back of her chair and dropped a kiss on her cheek. "Anything interesting?"

"For once, yes. Come into the kitchen and we'll have a cup of tea while I tell you about it."

"It sounds as if Jim's after a really big fish," Fergus commented when she had finished her account of the morning's events.

"I'm pretty sure he is, but he wasn't giving much away."

"Maybe there's been some top secret international undercover operation going on." Fergus, whose concept of police work had a tendency to be influenced by the highly-coloured imaginations of television scriptwriters, was round-eyed with excitement.

"You could be right," agreed his mother with a chuckle. "He's coming for supper this evening – you can have a go at quizzing him then. Not that I give much for your chances, though, he can be a real oyster when he likes."

"We'll see." Fergus put down his empty cup, picked up his school bag and made for the door. "I'm going to have a shower and then I'll give you a hand with the cooking."

"Thanks."

"Oh, by the way, Anita's Mum and Dad are going down to their cottage in Devon for the weekend and they've invited me along. It's okay, isn't it?

"Of course."

"I said I was sure it would be." He clattered upstairs. He was a good kid, Sukey thought as she began sorting out the ingredients for the steak pie she had planned for their evening meal. Not many lads of his age were as ready to give a hand with preparing food as they were to consuming it. The influence of his seventeen-year-old girlfriend, Anita, might have something to do with the phenomenon.

"My, that was good!" With a sigh of satisfaction, Jim Castle laid down his knife and fork.

"Super, Mum," agreed Fergus, who had already cleared his plate and had been waiting expectantly for his mother and their guest to finish.

"Glad you enjoyed it," said Sukey contentedly. "Anyone for seconds?" Knowing full well what the answer from her two hungry menfolk would be, she was already on her way to the kitchen.

"More wine, Jim?" said Fergus, handing over the bottle. "Help yourself, I'm only allowed one small one," he added with a grin.

"Quite right too," said Jim as he topped up his own and Sukey's glasses. "You're lucky to have such a liberal-minded mother. I'd never have been allowed so much as a half of bitter at home till I was eighteen."

"Bet you had a few on the quiet, though!"

"Well . . ." The teenage boy and the forty-year-old man exchanged companionable smiles.

From the kitchen came the clash of dishes and a moment later Sukey re-entered the room bearing the remains of the pie. "Fetch the vegetables, will you Gus?" she said as she cut the crust in two. "I hope you can manage this between you – I've no room for any more."

"Watch us," said Jim, holding out his plate.

It was while Sukey was serving the fruit salad she had prepared for their dessert that Fergus fired his opening shot at Jim. "Mum tells me you're on the track of a serial art thief," he remarked in his most casual tone.

Jim shot a questioning glance at Sukey which she made a point of not noticing. He picked up his wineglass and studied its contents for a moment without speaking, took a mouthful, replaced the glass carefully on its coaster and helped himself to cream. "I wondered when one of you would bring that up," he said quietly.

"Fergus is convinced that whoever carried out the Bussell Manor job is a member of a ruthless international gang," said Sukey. Her tone was flippant, but Jim's expression remained serious and she experienced a momentary flicker of unease. From the moment of his arrival at the house he had given the impression that something was preying on his mind. The way he had taken her face between his hands and given her a searching look before asking, 'Is everything okay, Sook?' made her think he expected to hear of some secret anxiety on which she needed reassurance.

Meanwhile, Fergus pursued his theory. "She says you know who it is, but you won't tell. The police must have got on to him somehow – was there an undercover agent involved? I'll bet there was," he went on as Jim remained silent. "That must be an exciting job. I'd rather like to have a go at it myself one day."

"You wouldn't have been much help in this operation," said the detective, momentarily off his guard.

Fergus pounced. "You mean there was, and it was a woman! *Cherchez la femme* and all that? That must mean your man's susceptible to feminine wiles. I see him as a kind of Raffles character, carrying out these robberies for kicks rather than the money," he rattled on. "Always one step ahead of the police – until he makes one fatal mistake." He paused for breath, his eyes fixed on Jim's face, while Sukey watched the pair of them with mingled curiosity and amusement.

Despite his evident determination to keep his own counsel, Jim could not restrain a smile. "Well, we haven't caught him out in a fatal mistake so far," he said ruefully. "We're all working on it though, your mother included. Watch this space!"

"His lips are sealed!" said Sukey with a chuckle. "I did warn you, didn't I Gus?"

"Well, it was worth a try," her son retorted with a resigned shrug. He got up from the table, saying, "Will you excuse me, I've got some school work to finish and then I'm going to have an early night. Have to make an early start in the morning, Mum – Anita's Dad wants to leave at six o'clock to get ahead of the traffic."

Sukey pretended to shudder at the thought. "You'll have to get yourself up," she said.

"No problem. Good night Jim, have a good weekend."

"You too."

"Good night, Mum."

"Good night Gus. Give me a call before you leave in the morning."

"Will do." At the door, Fergus turned and gave his mother a meaningful look. "See if you can get him to be a bit more forthcoming, Mum. Use your feminine wiles, why don't you?"

"Cheeky!" Sukey picked up the empty wine bottle and pretended to aim it at him. In response, he blew her a kiss and disappeared.

There was a short silence before Jim said, "Shall we clear this lot away?"

"Good idea. I'll make some coffee."

As they waited for the kettle to boil Jim remarked, "Fergus and Anita have been an item for quite a while now, haven't they?"

"Just over a year. It's done Fergus a lot of good – he's matured no end."

"He still seems happy about us." He moved closer, circling her from behind in a gentle but ardent embrace. She put down

37

the two coffee mugs she had just taken from a cupboard and slid round in his arms to face him. His kiss had a surprising urgency and after a while she pulled away from him, her hands on his shoulders and her eyes searching his.

"Something's bothering you, isn't it? Come on, spill it," she urged as he hesitated. "I could tell when you first got here. It's to do with this Bussell Manor case, isn't it?"

"In a manner of speaking," he admitted.

"You were pretty cagey over dinner. Was that because Fergus was there?"

"Partly. I hope he won't go sharing his theories with his friends . . ."

"He won't if I ask him not to. Do I take it that he was on the right track?"

"Yes. That isn't the real problem though. Look, Sukey, as I think you've already gathered, the Bussell Manor job is just the latest in a series that we're pretty certain Rodriguez is responsible for. We have put in an undercover agent, it is a woman and she tipped us off that he and his accomplices were planning a job for last night. The trouble is, she didn't manage to find out where."

"Accomplices? We're talking about a gang?"

"We know he isn't a lone operator and we've run checks on his friends and associates. Most of them are squeaky clean, but there are two characters called Alan Crowson and Jack Morris who have perfectly respectable day jobs in his wine importing company but who turned out to have form for handling stolen goods. We've no direct evidence that they're involved, but it's all we've had to go on so far. Rodriguez is a wizard with electronics and our theory is he gets past the alarm systems – pretty sophisticated ones, you've got to hand it to the bloke – opens the place up and is out of it before the others turn up, take what they're after and disappear. What happens to the stuff after that is a mystery. We've tried all the usual fences but drawn a complete blank. It's pretty obvious it's being nicked to order."

"Order from whom?"

"That's what we don't know. Our informant says Rodriguez – Roddy, she calls him – is a shrewd businessman but in some ways quite immature, adolescent even. He reads tales of derring-do, watches films about swashbuckling heroes, Robin Hood type characters, pirates with hearts of gold, that sort of thing."

"You mean, when he carries out these jobs he's acting out some kind of boyhood fantasy?"

"More or less. His family has a substantial fortune, he lives in a fancy penthouse and it's pretty clear he doesn't need the money. Jo reckons he does it for kicks, like Fergus suggested."

"I'll tell him that, he'll be tickled pink. Who's Jo, by the way?"

"Josephine – that's the name our informant is using for this job. Not her real one, of course."

"I suppose she provided the fingerprints you gave me for comparison?"

"That's right. She also overheard part of a phone conversation that confirmed what she already suspected – because of excuses he made not to see her – that there was something planned for Thursday night."

"I see." While he was speaking, Sukey had made coffee and poured it out. They sat down on opposite sides of the kitchen table and drank for a few moments in silence. Then she said, "The prints you gave me are inadmissible as evidence, of course, and that's why you wanted him to give you some officially, so to speak. Has he been approached?"

"Oh yes, and he's co-operated, with some reluctance according to Radcliffe." Jim put down his coffee mug, his face suddenly serious. "Quite by chance he was at the nick when you got back this afternoon and he spotted you as you went through reception. It caused him considerable agitation."

Sukey frowned. "I wonder why?"

For the moment, Jim avoided a direct answer. "Can you remember someone shouting 'Pepita'?"

"Yes, as it happens I do. I didn't take much notice. Was it this Roddy character?"

"It was."

"But what's that got to do with me?"

Jim got up and fetched his jacket from the hall and pulled out his wallet. He took out a photograph and handed it to Sukey. She stared in blank amazement at what seemed to be her own face looking back at her.

"Who is this?" she asked in bewilderment.

"That's 'Josephine'. Roddy calls her Pepita – it's a Spanish diminutive of the name."

"And when he saw me, he thought I was her. So now he knows, in a back-door sort of way, that his Pepita works for the police. No wonder he got hot under the collar."

"Exactly."

She handed the photograph back and Jim returned it to his wallet. Then he reached across the table and took both her hands in his. "Sook, I'm worried about what he might do . . . I'm afraid for you."

"What on earth are you suggesting?"

For once, Jim's customary sang-froid seemed to have deserted him. He got up and began prowling restlessly round the little kitchen. "I've just got this gut-feeling that there's more to this case than meets the eye. I've already told you I think there's a bigger fish in the background calling the shots and that Roddy is just someone with a skill that's useful to whoever it is. By an unlucky chance, even though it's a case of mistaken identity, he now knows that he's been having an affair with an undercover policewoman, and this information is bound to be fed back."

"And he thinks that policewoman is me. Well, too bad – but I don't see what he can do about it."

"You're not being very bright this evening, Sook. Don't you understand? You represent – or they're likely to see you as – a potential threat to a key operative in a very lucrative scam."

Sukey gaped in disbelief. "You're saying I'm in danger? This is all a bit far-fetched, isn't it?"

"I don't think so. I'd like you to think about disappearing for a few days until we've got this case sewn up."

"Disappear? Where to, for heavens' sake?"

"We'll find you a safe house—"

"But this is crazy! It might be weeks, months even, before—"

"Yes, yes, I know. Just the same, I want you to think about it very seriously."

"I've already thought, and the answer's no. I'm not going to be driven out of my home like a frightened rabbit."

"Then at least let me see about putting some security system in place here."

"Like the kind that Roddy can penetrate in thirty seconds flat? That's a laugh for a start." She picked up the cafetière. "More coffee?"

"No thanks. Sook, I wish you'd take this more seriously—"

At that moment, Jim's mobile phone rang and he broke off to answer. He listened to the caller in silence for a few moments, then said, "Right, go ahead and get a warrant. I'll be with you in fifteen minutes." He put the phone back in his pocket and put on his jacket. "I'm sorry, Sook, I've got to go. We've just had an anonymous tip-off. Someone's fingered Roddy for the Bussell Manor job."

"Brilliant! Does that mean I can sleep easy in my bed tonight?"

"Probably, but it's not over yet, you know. Just be on your guard, make sure all your doors and windows are locked."

"Don't worry."

"I'll talk to you again soon."

As they parted at the front door, she felt a sharp stab of anxiety, not for herself, but for him. She clung to him, savouring his warmth and his strength, realising how much she depended on him, how vital he was to her happiness.

"Jim, you will be careful, won't you?" she begged. "If what you say is right, there could be some pretty ruthless people behind this."

"Isn't that just what I've been telling you?"

Two hours later, just as Sukey was dropping off to sleep, her bedside telephone rang. A disconsolate Jim informed her that the evening's mission had been a failure. "He's done a runner," he said gloomily. "And there's worse to come. Mrs Frampton had a heart attack and died at eight o'clock this evening."

Six

By the time DC Hill reached the fourth floor of the exclusive block where Miguel Rodriguez occupied a penthouse apartment, he had become resigned to having to report a fruitless couple of hours of door-to-door enquiries on returning to the station. The occupants of Langland Tower were, almost without exception, business people who were out all day on their lawful occasions and were never on more than nodding terms with their neighbours. A retired couple at number six proudly informed him that they kept themselves to themselves and were not interested in the comings and goings of the other tenants so long as they were quiet and caused no disturbance around the place. Yes, they confirmed on being shown Roddy's picture, they supposed he lived in the building because they had encountered him occasionally in the lift and exchanged a polite 'Good morning' or 'Good afternoon' as the case might be, but beyond the fact that he stayed in the lift when they left it and was therefore presumably on his way to an upper floor, they had no idea whether he lived in the building or was merely a regular visitor. Apart from the fact that they vaguely remembered hearing the lift go up a couple of times during the previous afternoon at around four o'clock, which was unusual because normally people did not begin returning from work until well after five, virtually no useful information was forthcoming. So it was without a great deal of optimism that the young detective pressed the bell at number eight.

The sound was greeted by an outburst of excited yapping, followed by a querulous female voice saying, "Quiet, Lucy darling, the house isn't on fire," before demanding to know who was there. Hill felt himself being inspected through the spy hole in the door; he held up his identification card and after a few seconds he heard a rattling of chains and the sound of two locks being undone before the door opened to reveal a woman of indeterminate years with unnaturally blond hair and round, soft, carefully made-up features. She was wearing a shapeless Paisley-patterned dress reaching almost to her ankles and beaded velvet slippers, and under one arm she cradled a Yorkshire terrier sporting a scarlet bow on its head.

"Mrs Prendergast?"

"That's right. Miriam Prendergast." She stood aside for Hill to enter and when she spoke again it was to the dog. "It's all right, Lucy, it's a nice policeman come to see us. Remember your manners and say Hullo to him, there's a good girl."

As if in response, the little creature wriggled in the woman's embrace and thrust a damp nose in Hill's direction. He was not particularly fond of small breeds, but sensing that this woman's creed probably included the tenet, 'Love me, love my dog,' he prudently put out a hand and allowed Lucy to lick his fingers. Mrs Prendergast nodded approval. "There, she likes you," she informed him, smiling for the first time and exposing rather large, uneven teeth. "Come along in."

Since his previous enquiries had been summarily dealt with at the front door, it was the first time he had been invited into one of the apartments and he exclaimed in admiration at the view from the wide picture window in the spacious sitting-room. "Yes, it's lovely isn't it?" the woman said. She sat down in an armchair, placed the dog in a basket at her feet and motioned her visitor to a chair on the opposite side of an elaborate gas fire which was switched on despite the warmth of the afternoon. "Now, tell me what I can do for you."

"First of all, could I ask if you were at home yesterday afternoon and evening?"

"I was for part of the time, except when I took Lucy for her afternoon walkies. We can't miss that, can we my love?" She bent down to caress the dog, which raised its tiny muzzle and licked her hand.

"While you were at home, did you notice anything unusual?"

"Unusual?" Mrs Prendergast puckered her pale forehead and pursed her cherry-red lips. "Well, there was the ambulance that took poor Mr Rodriguez to hospital, but I expect you already know about that. Have you any up-to-date news, by the way? I've been quite anxious – such a charming young gentleman, and so good-looking. I've been looking out for his girlfriend, hoping to find out how he's going on, but there's been no sign of her. I expect she's at the hospital, the poor girl must be so worried . . ."

In her impassioned concern for the fate of her neighbour, Mrs Prendergast appeared not to notice DC Hill's start of surprise at this first – and unexpectedly dramatic – lead to the disappearance of Miguel Rodriguez. By the time she had paused for breath he had collected his wits and managed to reply calmly that whilst the police had no details of Mr Rodriguez' condition, so far as they knew he was not in any immediate danger. "You actually saw him being taken away in the ambulance?" he went on. "About what time would that have been?"

"About four o'clock. I was sitting by the window having a cup of tea – oh, my goodness!" She gave an affected little start. "I never thought to offer you any refreshment – what must you think of me? Can I get you a cup of tea? Or would you prefer coffee?"

Sensing that she was a lonely woman, that his visit would probably turn out to be the highlight of her day and that, given encouragement, she might well have some vital information, Hill said politely, "That's very kind of you. A cup of coffee would be very welcome."

Mrs Prendergast practically leapt from her chair, beaming. "It won't take a minute. Lucy, you stay here and keep the gentleman company," she admonished as the little dog, disturbed by the sudden movement, sat up in its basket. She bustled out of the room and Hill got up and moved over to the window, where a chair and a small table indicated the spot where she had probably been sitting when she saw someone whom she had taken to be Rodriguez being put into an ambulance. He sat down briefly in the chair, noting that it gave him a clear view of the forecourt to the building, where ten numbered parking spaces were marked out, plus an additional half-dozen or so for visitors. It was an ideal vantage point for anyone interested in keeping an eye on the comings and goings of their neighbours and Hill suspected that Mrs Prendergast probably spent a considerable amount of time there.

He turned away from the window to study the rest of the room. It was large and furnished in a somewhat florid style, with fussy wallpaper and carpets, large, overstuffed armchairs and a glass-fronted cabinet full of an assortment of china and glass ornaments. A heavy mirror hung over the fireplace, flanked by a number of signed photographs in expensive-looking silver frames. He made a detour on his way back to his chair to take a closer look at them and found to his surprise that they were all of well-known male actors, mostly long dead, all taken when they were in their prime. Above the signatures were written affectionate messages: 'To darling Prendy, with fondest love'; 'To Prendy, with memories of a wonderful first night'; 'For Prendy, my most exciting leading lady.' Among them he recognised Noel Coward, Ralph Richardson and Laurence Olivier. On a shelf below the mirror was a single photograph of a demure young woman, which he judged to have been taken during the same period and was obviously Mrs Prendergast herself.

"Ah, I see you're admiring my picture gallery." Mrs Prendergast had entered silently in her velvet slippers, carrying a tray loaded with delicate china cups and saucers, a small jug of cream and a bowl of sugar. "Yes," she went on with a nostalgic sigh, "They are all I have left now to remind me of my moments of glory. You wouldn't remember Miriam Prendergast, of course – you're far too young." She beamed at him again as if his youth was a point in his favour and handed him a cup of coffee. "Do help yourself to cream and sugar. Those are bourbon biscuits; they're Lucy's favourites, aren't they my darling?" She held out a biscuit to the dog, which accepted it eagerly, before settling back in her armchair and putting her own cup down on a small occasional table beside it. "Now, what were we talking about?"

"You were telling me how you saw Mr Rodriguez being taken to the ambulance – about four o'clock, you said. Did you see the ambulance arrive? Or did you hear its siren?"

"Oh no, nothing like that. I noticed it particularly because it wasn't an ordinary ambulance."

"What do you mean?"

"I mean it wasn't one of the big ones from the regular ambulance service, it was one of those converted private cars. I expect you've seen them around. There's just room for one patient either on a stretcher or in a wheelchair – with a nurse, of course. I was thinking of calling one or two of the private hospitals to see if I could get any news, but of course I'm not a relative so I didn't think they'd give me any information even if I phoned the right one. I'm sure you'll be able to check on him, though. Perhaps you'd be kind enough to let me know how the poor young fellow is."

"I'll make a note of it," Hill promised. Miriam Prendergast beamed again and sipped her coffee. "Was Mr Rodriguez in a wheelchair or on a stretcher, by the way?"

"Oh, on a stretcher. He was lying quite still with his eyes closed."

"You're absolutely sure it was him? It couldn't have been anyone else?"

"Quite sure. I could see his face clearly. Such a handsome young man – very Spanish-looking of course, even though he's so English in his manner." Miriam gave a wistful little sigh and patted her blond curls. "I wonder if he had a heart attack? You'd think he was too young, but you do hear of it happening nowadays to the most unexpected people, don't

47

you, Lucy darling?" She bent down and gave her pet another biscuit. "He always looks so fit and strong – quite the athletic type, I've always thought."

"You know him well?"

"We soon became acquainted." She gave a coy simper. "Of course, I've only lived here a month, and he's such a busy man, but our paths cross from time to time, in the lift and so on. He actually stopped and introduced himself the very day I moved in." It was clear that she was not only willing but eager to talk for as long as her unexpected guest cared to listen. Hill sat back, drank his coffee – which was surprisingly good – and let her talk. Much of what she said would, he knew, be of little value, but there was always the chance that something significant would emerge. It did, just as he took advantage of a lull in her theatrical reminiscences to say that it had been delightful talking to her, but that he really must be going.

"You've been most helpful," he said on his way to the door. "And if you should remember anything else, here's my number."

She took the card he gave her and studied it for a moment before saying, "Oh, yes, there was something else unusual about yesterday afternoon, now I come to think of it. I didn't pay much attention at the time because I was so concerned about Mr Rodriguez."

"Yes?"

"It was about an hour later. Lucy and I were just going out for our afternoon walkies when this van turned up with two men in it. There was a ladder on the roof with the name of a firm of cleaners painted on it, but it wasn't the firm who do the regular cleaning here and it seemed a funny time for them to come anyway."

"Can you remember the name of the firm?"

"I can't be sure, but I think it had the word 'daisy' in it?"

"Daisy?"

"I think so. Anyway, I'm sure it said they were cleaners but I thought it was odd because all the flats in this building are cleaned by the same people who have a contract to do the communal parts – the hallway and stairs and so on. Perhaps one of the tenants was dissatisfied and decided to use another firm. I don't suppose it's important, but I thought I'd mention it."

"Yes, indeed. I'll make a note of it. Goodbye, and thank you once again."

Back at the station, DC Hill checked the Yellow Pages and found a firm called Daisy-Fresh Home Cleaning Services of Andoversford. He telephoned and asked if any of their employees had done a job at Langland Tower at around five o'clock the previous afternoon. He was given to understand by an acid-tongued woman that since their only van had been reported to the police barely an hour earlier as having been stolen, he should have known better than to ask such a stupid question.

"It looks very much as if there's a sizeable organisation at work," remarked DS Radcliffe.

"I had a hunch Rodriguez wasn't working alone," DI Castle agreed. "Not counting Crowson and Morris, of course – they're just a pair of gofers."

"Are you going to pick them up?"

"I sent a couple of men round to search their places, but they didn't find anything. Not that I expected them to – the stuff is probably on its way overseas by now. This is big business, Andy, we could be talking about a money-laundering exercise."

"So what d'you reckon has happened to Rodriguez?"

"He's quite likely on his way overseas as well. A talent like his would be worth preserving."

There was a knock at the door and a young WPC entered and handed a folder to Castle saying, "Report from foren- sics, sir."

"Thanks." Castle opened the folder and glanced at the single sheet of paper it contained. He gave a whistle and rubbed his hands together in glee. "At last, a bit of concrete evidence to link Rodriguez with the Bussell Manor job. A tracksuit and trainers we found in his car during last night's search match the fibres and the shoeprint Sukey picked up. We're on the right track, Andy." He glanced at his watch. "It's almost one o'clock. Let's celebrate with a pint and a sandwich."

Seven

"She's quite batty, of course," said Jim disconsolately. "No earthly good as a witness."

Sukey looked up with a raised eyebrow from the vegetables she was chopping for a stir-fry. "You mean Miriam Prendergast? What makes you say that?"

"Lives in a fantasy world. Out of curiosity I got Hill to check with a couple of London agents and neither of them had ever heard of her. She certainly never starred with any of the actors whose photos he saw in her flat. I'm willing to bet that the nearest she ever got to being a leading lady was in some obscure repertory company half a century ago."

"What about all the signed photographs?"

"Oh, they were genuine enough – after all, actors are only too happy to dish them out to fans. It was the phoney messages that gave the game away."

"How d'you know they were phoney?"

"Hill says they were all written in the same handwriting with the same coloured ink."

"You mean, she wrote them herself? Poor old thing." Sukey finished her vegetable preparation, got out a sauté pan and poured in some oil. "So what about the information she gave DC Hill about seeing Rodriguez being taken away in an ambulance and so on? D'you reckon she made that up as well?"

"No, I'm sure that's all genuine enough. It would never stand up in court, though – not that this case is ever likely to get there anyway."

"But you said you'd issued a warrant for Rodriguez' arrest—"

"We've got to find him first."

". . . and surely the evidence of the tracksuit and trainers is enough to prove he was the one who broke into Bussell Manor?"

"It doesn't prove he nicked anything, and in any event it's not much good if we can't produce him."

"But if in the meantime any of the stolen stuff turns up . . . ?"

"I'm pretty certain it won't. The more I think about it, the more I'm convinced there's a very big and very efficient organisation behind all this."

"Are you suggesting that some shadowy 'Mr Big' arranged for Rodriguez to be spirited away?"

"I'm almost certain of it. His skill at deactivating alarm systems is worth a mint to anyone wanting to add to their art collection without having to part with the true value of the items."

"I still don't see the point of arranging the disappearing act – surely, it would be obvious that it would simply confirm any possible suspicion that he was implicated in the robbery."

"Unless they knew there was a weak link in the organisation that would sooner or later lead to Roddy's arrest."

"Meaning?"

"Don't forget the anonymous tip-off."

"Ah yes." Sukey tipped vegetables into the hot oil and stirred them. "Have you any idea where that came from?"

"None at all." Jim got up and stood beside Sukey at the stove, sniffing in appreciation. "That smells good. What goes with the stir-fry?

"Cajun chicken breasts."

"Great."

"What puzzles me," Sukey went on, "is why there had to be all that cloak-and-dagger stuff. Why couldn't Roddy have simply packed a bag and taken off somewhere?"

"We don't know that he went voluntarily, do we?"

"Are you suggesting he might be in danger?"

"On the contrary, I'm sure he'll be very well looked after. But if there had been any kind of interruption – a visit from a police officer wanting a little more help with enquiries, for example . . ."

"I see what you mean. You can't pester a sick man with questions."

"More likely an unconscious man."

"You think they doped him?"

"It would make sense. Oh yes, as I see it, spiriting Roddy away like that was masterly. Sending people in to clear the flat under the pretence of carrying out a cleaning job was pretty smart as well. They obviously have a very slick set-up to be able to do all that at such short notice."

"What d'you reckon was the purpose of the cleaning job?"

"Obviously, to take away anything incriminating. Maybe Roddy had some of the stolen stuff stashed away there, although I doubt it. It looked as if a lot of his clothes had been taken, and toilet items. His passport wasn't there either, or any other personal documents – no credit cards, nothing. We're trying to contact his family in case they've heard anything – not that I think it's at all likely – but we've had no luck so far, and of course there's no one at his office because it's the weekend."

Jim's gloomy aspect deepened and Sukey fetched a bottle of red wine from a cupboard, took a corkscrew from a drawer and and put them on the table in front of him. "Cheer yourself up with a drop of that," she said. "You know where the glasses are."

It was Saturday evening, the day after the break-in at Bussell Manor. They had just come indoors after spending an hour or so sipping iced drinks on the patio behind Sukey's little semi-detached house in Brockworth while Jim brought her up to date on the progress of the police enquiry. The weather had been fine all day and the soft spring air lay like a warm, light coverlet over the garden and the open fields beyond. With Fergus away with Anita and her parents, the prospect of twenty-four hours on their own stretched invitingly before them. Sukey took the glass of wine Jim handed her, slid an arm round his shoulders and gently kissed his ear. "Don't let it spoil our weekend," she whispered.

"I won't, I promise." He cupped a hand round her head, kissed her on the mouth and ruffled her short, dark curls before releasing her. "You have to admit, though, it is frustrating. If only Nina – that's Pepita's real name, by the way – had been able to let us know where the break-in was going to take place . . ."

"Now come on, we've been over all that."

"I know."

"So let's enjoy the rest of this evening." She gave his hand a gentle squeeze before going back to her cooking.

Later, as they were clearing away after their meal, Sukey said, "So where do you go from here – with the Bussell Manor job, I mean?"

Jim paused in the act of drying the sauté pan. "I thought we were supposed to drop the subject?" he said slyly.

She gave a sheepish grin. "I know, I didn't intend to raise it again, but it's been gnawing away at the back of my mind—"

"Mine too. Well, of course, we'll do all the usual things – ask local art dealers to let us know if they're offered any of the stuff, alert TRACE, make enquiries among known fences and check airports. Patterson seems confident that his insurers will be offering a substantial reward, which may tempt someone out of the woodwork."

Sukey tipped away the washing-up water and dried her hands. "Yes, I've been wondering about Patterson," she said thoughtfully. "Jim, you don't suppose he's in on it, do you? To claim the insurance, I mean?"

"It had occurred to me, but I doubt it. He gave me the impression of being genuinely upset about losing some of his most prized possessions."

"That could have been an act. He was very insistent that his friend Rodriguez couldn't possibly be implicated, remember."

"That's true. I'll be giving it some more thought, but not tonight." He put the pan away, hung up the cloth he had used to dry it, and gently slid his arms round her. She nestled against him, responding eagerly to his urgent embrace. "We are not, repeat not, going to refer to the Bussell Manor job again tonight," he commanded. "Agreed?"

She gave a sigh of mingled desire and contentment. "Agreed."

"So how was your weekend, Mum?"

"Fine thanks. How was yours?"

"Brilliant!" Fergus paused for a moment before adding, "Anita's parents told me to say that if you and Jim would like to rent their cottage some time when they're not using it, they'd let you have it at a special rate."

"How nice of them," Sukey responded warmly, then gave her son a keen look. "Gus, just what have you been telling them about me and Jim?"

"Only that Jim's a great guy and you and he have been an item for quite a while, but they knew that anyway."

"Oh? How?"

"Anita told them, of course."

"Ah, yes." Sukey rinsed out the milk bottles and went to put them on the front doorstep before locking up for the night. She knew, of course, that Fergus was aware of, and sympathetic to, her relationship with Jim Castle, but it came as a slight shock to realise that it had been the subject of discussion outside the family. Then she mentally scolded herself for being so prissy. "Tell Mr and Mrs Masters 'Thanks very much' and I'll mention it to Jim," she said when she returned to the kitchen. It seemed a long time since she had had a holiday and it would be heavenly if she and Jim could have a few days away together.

Fergus upended his canvas holdall, tipped his weekend laundry on to the floor and began loading it into the washing machine. "Any developments in the Bussell Manor robbery?" he asked. "The Sunday papers are full of it."

"Really? We decided not to bother with a paper today."

"Better things to do?" Over his shoulder, he shot a sly, mischievous look at his mother.

"Cheeky!" Sukey landed a gentle thump on his back with her fist before giving him a brief account of the latest developments in the case.

"Wow! It sounds like something out of a spy novel!" he said excitedly. "I wonder what they'll do with the body."

"Oh, Jim doesn't reckon Rodriguez is in any danger. He thinks he's been carried off and hidden away somewhere because they want him for some more jobs."

Fergus considered this theory for a moment, then shook his head and grinned. "That'd be a bit tame, wouldn't it?" he said flippantly. "In a case like this there's sure to be at least one body sooner or later."

Eight

S everal thousand miles away from the semi-detached house in Brockworth where Sukey Reynolds and Jim Castle were spending a blissful weekend, during which they found little difficulty in avoiding further reference to the possible whereabouts and future plans of Miguel 'Roddy' Rodriguez, the subject of their earlier speculation was lying in the shade of a huge umbrella beside a sparkling blue swimming pool, sipping an iced piña colada and reflecting bemusedly on the extraordinary change in his fortunes. He tried to figure out how much time had passed since two strangers in white coats carrying a stretcher had entered his flat claiming to be there to carry out instructions from Mr Wallis, but he was still confused and disorientated. The men had explained that it was considered better for him to 'go away for a while until the heat had died down' and invited him to lie on the stretcher and pretend to be unconscious. When he demanded further explanations they merely said they were there to carry out Mr Wallis's instructions and told him brusquely not to ask questions. Time was short, they said, and would he please get on with it. He remembered reaching for the telephone, determined to get confirmation from Wallis that they were acting under his orders, at which point they had exchanged glances and one of them moved behind him and pinioned his arms while the other produced a syringe. He remembered his shout of mingled alarm and outrage, a brief but futile struggle, and a sharp prick in his arm followed by temporary oblivion.

After that, recollection became blurred, a jumble of

confusing impressions that he could not place in chronological order. He had vague memories of being taken from a car while still on the stretcher and carried aboard a small plane by two men – not the ones who had taken him from his penthouse apartment, but swarthy individuals who remained constantly at his side, spoke to him in Spanish with an unfamiliar accent and gave him warm, sweet drinks that made him sleepy and compliant. After the flight came another car journey followed by a ride in a wheelchair along what seemed to be miles of passages, dimly recognised as airport channels. Solicitous hands that all seemed to belong to beautiful, smiling women installed him in a first-class cabin, fastened his seat-belt, covered him with a soft blanket and at intervals roused him with food and more sleep-inducing drinks.

This morning – or was it yesterday morning, he was still not sure how long he had been under the influence of the drugs – he had for the first time awakened fully conscious to find himself lying in an enormous bed between pale blue sheets that had the cool feel of silk against his skin. Sunlight filtered through shuttered windows; as his eyes adjusted to the subdued light, he made out carved and painted furniture in the Spanish style, and portraits of aristocratic men and elaborately coiffed and gowned women on the whitewashed walls.

There had been a silk dressing-gown on a chair beside the bed. When he stood up to put it on, his feet sank into a soft rug, one of several scattered over a tiled floor. He found the bathroom, appointed in a style that made the Ritz look utilitarian, and took a shower. When he returned to the bedroom, he saw a man whom he vaguely recognised seated in an armchair at the foot of his bed. He remembered asking in Spanish, 'Who are you?' and receiving the reply, 'I am Juan, one of your travelling companions.' On enquiring where he was, he was told, 'You are the guest of El Dueño.' 'Why am I here?' 'El Dueño will explain all.'

El Dueño. The boss. Mr Big. Roddy knew instinctively that Juan had not been referring to Wallis. Somehow he had caught the attention of someone enormously wealthy and powerful whose arm could reach across oceans to pluck him from his home and transport him halfway across the world. Juan had not revealed the exact location, nor even the name of the country where he had been brought.

The heat of the sun was intense, yet there was a freshness in the air that reminded Roddy of visits to the Swiss Alps. He raised his head and looked lazily around him. The villa was definitely not Swiss; it was built in the Spanish style, yet he was certain he was not in Spain either. From the tropical vegetation surrounding the villa, the brilliantly plumaged birds in the garden and above all the majestic backdrop of mountains that looked like pictures he had seen of the Andes, it was more likely to be somewhere in South America. The thought had sinister connotations which he preferred not to consider for the time being.

He relaxed and closed his eyes with a sigh of contentment. He had no idea what drugs they had given him, but for the moment nothing seemed to matter. It was simply bliss to be lying there; it would have been heaven if only Pepita could be with him. Perhaps they'd let him send for her. And then, with the force of a violent punch in the stomach, recollection returned in full. Pepita had betrayed him. She had pretended to love him when all the time she had been working towards his downfall. The memory of her treachery injected a whiff of poison into his newly found paradise. His mind flew back to the moment when he had taken her picture from his wallet and in his blind fury been on the point of ripping it apart. Something had stayed his hand then, perhaps some lingering hope that there had been a mistake, that it was none of her doing that the police were taking so much interest in him . . . but he felt no such qualms now. He would destroy her picture right away, expunge her from his life forever.

He sat up and reached for his wallet; it crossed his mind to feel vaguely surprised that it had not been taken from him, then reflected that at no time had he felt seriously threatened. What lay behind his abduction he had yet to find out, but from the opulence surrounding him it seemed unlikely that they were after his money. He yawned, telling himself that there was no hurry to get to the bottom of it. There was always *mañana*.

He found the wallet and opened it. Everything was in its usual place: credit cards, driving licence, phone card, about fifty pounds in English money . . . but no photograph. He checked everything a second time; it wasn't there, and somehow it became terribly important to find it. From hating Pepita and wanting to tear her out of his memory and his life, he felt a desperate need to see her face again.

"Have you lost something, *amigo*?"

Juan had emerged from the villa unnoticed, moving silently on his soft leather loafers. He was a stocky individual with short black curly hair, olive skin and the appearance of having been tightly compressed before being packaged in his faultlessly cut, pale-blue suit. His eyes were permanently masked behind dark glasses, making it impossible to tell whether or not they reflected the smile that seemed permanently painted on his features. He was smiling now, his full, sensuous lips drawn back from teeth that shone like an advertisement for dental care.

"There was a photograph in this wallet when I left home, and now it's gone," said Roddy impatiently. "Where is it? Have you taken it?"

Juan shrugged dismissively. "What would I want with a picture of your *chica*?" he said blandly.

"How did you know it was my girlfriend?"

Juan gave an oily chuckle, his smile never wavering. "A man does not become so agitated over losing a picture of his maiden aunt," he replied. He helped himself from the jug which Isabella, the taciturn woman with a forbidding expression who apparently presided over the household and complied with Roddy's every request with a murmured, '*Si, señor*,' had placed on a table in the shade.

"Where is it?" Roddy repeated. "I want it back!"

"After she betrayed you?"

"What do you know about that?"

"You told us everything after your arrival here."

"While you had me drugged, I suppose."

Juan merely shrugged, making it clear that he either could not, or would not, give an answer. He sat down on a lounger beside Roddy's and drew a folder from the briefcase he was carrying. "You have created quite a sensation," he said with another flash of enamel. "I down-loaded these from the Internet half an hour ago. See for yourself." He opened the folder and took out a sheaf of papers which he handed to Roddy. "You have been given a nickname – 'The phantom robber'," he went on, rubbing his hands together with glee. "How about that, huh?"

Roddy stared in stupefaction at a reproduction of the front page of one of the more sensational English tabloids. Beneath the solid black headlines, 'Phantom Robber Strikes Again' was a picture of Bussell Manor, described as 'Electronic Wizard's Latest Target'. In a short paragraph at the bottom of the page, readers were informed that the police were seeking a suspect – as yet unnamed – who was alleged to have been spirited away under their noses as they were on the point of making an arrest. Roddy turned to the next page and read on, chuckling at the sensational language the journalist had used to report what was described as 'this clock-and-dagger operation'.

Amusement turned to dismay as he found himself staring at another headline: 'Housekeeper dies after raid on art collection.' He read the report in mounting horror, then threw the folder aside, spilling the contents on the tiled surround of the pool, and covered his face with his hands. "This is terrible, terrible!" he moaned.

"Something is troubling you?" said Juan softly.

"It has always been my rule that no one should be hurt! A woman has died because of my actions – I am a murderer!"

"Nonsense, *amigo*. The woman was sick, she could have died at any time."

"It would not have happened but for me. I am responsible for her death!"

Juan stood up and began picking up the scattered pages. "You must put it out of your mind," he commanded. There was a new, steely edge to his voice and this time Roddy had no doubt that the invisible eyes were fixed on him, their gaze full of menace. "You can study the rest of these later," Juan went on in his normal silky tone. "For the moment, we have other business to attend to."

"What business?" With an effort, Roddy dragged his mind away from the tragedy. His mind suddenly filled with questions. *Was I on the point of being arrested? Wallis certainly seemed very concerned when I told him what had happened. And what went wrong with the raid – was Crowson bluffing or had someone else really been there before he and Morris got to the house?* Aloud, he said, "But what I don't understand is: why should anyone go to all this trouble for me? What does this man, the man you call El Dueño, want with me?" He looked appealingly at Juan, trying desperately but vainly to read his reactions.

"He will tell you himself, when he is ready," Juan said softly, and this time the perpetual smile was no more than a tigerish baring of the unnaturally white teeth. "For the moment, you are to come with me."

Roddy shivered as he stood up to comply. The cool mountain air, that had seemed so pleasant a short time ago, had suddenly acquired a keener, icier edge. Juan led the way round to the front of the villa, where a white Mercedes awaited them. A powerfully built man in a white uniform who, like Juan, wore dark glasses that totally concealed his eyes, sat at the wheel. He got out, held open the rear door and gestured to Roddy to get in. After a moment's hesitation, he complied; Juan slid in beside him, gave a curt order to the chauffeur and they drove off.

The car sped smoothly down winding mountain roads and along broad avenues, past splendid white-walled mansions half-hidden among ornamental fig and flamboyant, vivid scarlet trees. At last they came to a prosperous looking town of elegant apartment blocks and exclusive stores and restaurants, its streets full of sleek cars and even sleeker, expensively dressed people. The driver stopped outside a gleaming glass and stainless steel shop-front and switched off the engine, ignoring signs stating that parking was strictly forbidden at any hour of the day or night on pain of a substantial fine. He opened the rear door and his two passengers alighted and entered the store.

For the next couple of hours, Roddy found himself indulging in the most extravagant shopping spree of his life. In every establishment they entered, they were approached by obsequious assistants who bowed almost to the ground as Juan informed them that El Dueño had given instructions that his friend was to have the very best of everything. He strutted around, smiling his tigerish smile, demanding to be shown – and encouraging Roddy to buy – the most luxurious and expensive items on offer. Designer suits, silk shirts and underwear, hand-made shoes and a Cartier watch were elaborately wrapped and carried to the limousine while the managers agreed with forced, nervous smiles that everything would be charged to El Dueño. Roddy was no gambler, but he would have been prepared to lay considerable odds that no money would ever change hands. There was a price to be paid for the privilege of living and owning a business in this tropical Eden.

And soon, he felt sure, he too would learn the cost of the luxury so arbitrarily thrust upon him. He trembled inwardly at the prospect. On the way back to the villa he thought again of Pepita and the missing photograph. What did they want with it? Cold fingers seemed to brush his spine as the fear crept into his mind that they might mean her some harm. He told himself that it would be no more than she deserved, but he could not deny his true feelings. In spite of everything, she was still the woman of his dreams and the one true love of his life.

Nine

After the excitement of the Bussell Manor robbery and the spectacular disappearance of the chief suspect, the number of incidents reported to the SOCOs on Monday morning was smaller than usual after a weekend and all were depressingly routine.

"The real villains must have gone on holiday," commented Mandy as George Barnes handed her reports of the disappearances of a prize rabbit from its hutch, an ornamental statue from its plinth and a lawnmower from a garden shed.

"Never mind, it's a nice day for outdoor jobs," Sukey consoled her. "What have you got for me, Sarge?"

"Three more cases of handbags stolen from cars parked on Robinswood Hill. They just never learn, do they?" he said gloomily as he gave her the computer printouts. "You'd think, with all the warning notices, people would be a bit more careful."

"It all makes work for the working SOCO to do," said Sukey cheerfully.

"We can tell *you* had a good weekend," said Mandy pointedly, and even George, who was not in the sunniest of moods after spending his weekend decorating the spare bedroom while his wife and baby were staying with his mother-in-law, managed a knowing chuckle.

Checking the cars from which the handbags had been stolen occupied most of Sukey's morning. At midday she returned to the office, where George informed her that no news of progress on the Bussell Manor case had found its way into their department. She had not had a chance to speak to Jim Castle since he left her to return to his flat in Tewkesbury Road on Sunday evening to catch up with some routine paperwork; on the pretext of going to the toilet she slipped along the corridor to his office, hoping to have a word with him, but found it empty. On the way back she bumped into DC Hill, but could get nothing out of him, except that they were following up some new leads, before he hurried off on some urgent errand. Frustrated, she settled down to write her report on her morning's investigations. For the moment there were no more cases to work on and she and George ate their sandwiches and drank their mugs of instant coffee without interruption.

At two o'clock, just as they were beginning to think the entire criminal population of Gloucestershire must have decamped to a neighbouring county, a report came through of a break-in at an address in Tuffley.

"There you are then," said George as he handed it over. "That should keep you going for the rest of the afternoon."

"Thanks, Sarge." Sukey scanned the sparse details. "Nothing missing, by the looks of things."

"You can't have a major art theft every day."

The modest semi-detached house stood at the far end of a short cul-de-sac on what had once been part of a council estate and now consisted entirely of owner-occupied dwellings. The little enclave had an air of modest prosperity, with neat porches, double-glazed windows and stone bird-baths in well-tended front gardens. A police car was parked outside but the road was otherwise empty. Sukey rang the bell and the front door was opened by WPC Trudy Marshall, who greeted her with a cheery smile that lit up her round, freckled face and led her into the front room. A thin, pretty woman in her thirties was seated disconsolately on a couch clutching a mug of tea and contemplating the ruins of her home. At a first glance, it seemed to Sukey that everything moveable, except for the larger items of furniture, had been smashed or overturned.

"Donna, meet Sukey Reynolds, one of our Scenes of Crime Officers," said Trudy. "She's here to look for evidence. Sukey, this is Donna Hoskins. She got back about a couple of hours ago and found this, so she's feeling a bit shook up."

"Understandable," said Sukey sympathetically. "I promise we'll do our best to catch whoever did this."

"Thanks." Donna gave a watery smile. "Would you like a cup of tea?" She spoke with a slight North Country accent. "There's one in the pot."

"No thanks, I've not long had lunch." Sukey put down her bag on one of the few clear spaces on the floor and looked around. "Any idea how they got in?"

"I haven't done a thorough search, but there doesn't seem to be any sign of forced entry," said Trudy. "Donna says the front door was locked as usual when she got home. When she saw what had happened she got scared, ran out of the house and called us from the phone box down the road. I found her shivering on the front step, so the first thing I did was make her a cuppa." She reached across and gently took the empty mug from Donna's unresisting hands. "Want a refill?" she asked.

Donna shook her head. "No thanks."

"Right then. You'll be okay while Sukey and I look around?"

"Of course, but I'd better tell Alan what's happened. Is it okay if I use the phone?"

"D'you mind hanging on for a minute while I dust it for prints." Sukey opened her bag and got busy with brush and aluminium powder. "Is Alan your husband?" she asked conversationally as she worked.

"Partner. I've lived here with him for just over a year."

"What time does he start work?"

"Eight-thirty. He usually leaves about eight o'clock."

"And you got home about what time?"

"Just after one."

"Well, let's hope someone saw something. The police will be asking around among the neighbours."

Donna shrugged. "I doubt if they'll be much help. They're mostly out all day."

Sukey lifted several prints from the telephone handset and labelled them. "You can use this now – sorry, I'm afraid this stuff makes a bit of a mess."

Donna gave another weak smile. "You reckon anyone'll notice?" She got to her feet and picked her way over the scattered debris of books, CDs, videos, magazines and broken ornaments to the telephone. She tapped out a number, waited for a while in silence, then said, "He must have his mobile switched off, I'll try the office." She called another number and after a moment said, "Hullo, it's Donna here – could I speak to Alan, please? What?" There was a pause, during which her expression grew more and more concerned. When she spoke again, her voice was a fearful whisper. "Yes, of course . . . thank you . . . goodbye." She put down the phone and turned to Sukey with dread in her eyes. "He didn't show up this morning, and they've had no message," she said in growing agitation. "I'm sure he said he was going to be working over the weekend, but Maggie didn't know anything about it. D'you think he's had an accident? Perhaps I'd better ring the hospital."

"If it was anything like that, I'm sure you'd have heard." Sukey did her best to be reassuring. "Haven't you any idea where else he might be? When did you last speak to him?"

"Thursday morning when I left home. I've been staying with my Mum in Yorkshire."

"You didn't ring him while you were away?"

"No, we don't normally bother. Mam isn't on the phone." Donna's voice was shaking and she was very close to tears. "Whatever can have happened to him?" Her eyes filled and she made her way back to the couch, sank down and covered her face with her hands. "Whatever can have happened?" she repeated.

"Could he be staying with a friend?" Sukey suggested.

"That's a thought." The cloud momentarily lifted. "I'll try

and have a word with his mate." She got up again and went back to the phone. Out of the corner of her eye, Sukey noticed that she pressed the recall button. After a moment, she said, "It's me again, Maggie. Could I have a word with Jack Morris? What? When did you last see them, then? No, I told you, I haven't any idea where they might be, I've been away . . . yes, of course I will." She hung up and sank back onto the couch in an attitude of utter despair. "They haven't seen Jack either," she quavered. "Neither of them has been in since Friday."

"Maybe they went on a pub crawl and woke up at Jack's place with hangovers," said Sukey, privately thinking that it was an unlikely explanation, but anxious to keep Donna from going to pieces until she could glean a little more information. At the mention of the name Morris, her brain had begun ticking away like a tightly wound clock, but she did her best to keep her voice level as she asked, "Does Alan often work at weekends?"

Donna pulled a handkerchief from the pocket of her denim jacket, scrubbed her reddened eyes and then began nervously twisting the square of cotton between her fingers. "Only now and again, when his firm's extra busy with special orders," she said in a dull voice. "I always go to Mam's when that happens, or when he has to do a lot of overtime. Alan doesn't like the thought of me being stuck here on my own. Ever so considerate, he is."

"Did he happen to work overtime on Thursday?"

"Yes, he did, as a matter of fact." Donna lifted her head and looked at Sukey, her expression suddenly and unexpectedly defensive. "Why d'you want to know? You're not the police, are you?"

"No, sorry . . . only trying to help. I'll get on with my own job."

At that moment, Trudy re-entered the room. "I'm afraid the upstairs is in a bit of a mess as well," she began, then looked at Donna in concern. "What's up, love?"

"Alan's missing, that's what." Donna's tears began to flow again. Trudy sat down and slid an arm round her. Sukey briefly explained the situation.

"I'm sure he'll turn up safe and sound." The young police-woman gave Donna's shoulders an encouraging squeeze. "You just come with me and check around while Sukey carries on hunting for clues."

"All right." Donna put away the soaking handkerchief, got to her feet and looked helplessly about her as if uncertain where to begin. She stooped to pick up a garishly-coloured woollen throw that lay on the floor alongside the couch and almost mechanically began folding it.

In a moment, Sukey was at her side, taking it from her. "Leave the tidying up for the moment," she said. "Don't touch anything – just let Trudy know if anything valuable's been taken."

"Oh, all right."

"I'll take this back to the station with me, if you don't mind," said Sukey. "You never know, forensics might be able get some evidence from it."

"Feel free."

"You'll get it back, of course."

Donna gave an indifferent shrug. "I'm not bothered. I've never liked the thing anyway – Alan's mother gave it to us." She wandered aimlessly out into the hall and Trudy was on the point of following her when Sukey called her back.

"I'm not sure, but I think there may be more to this lot than a bit of wanton vandalism," she said in a low voice. "Look what I've just spotted." She pointed to a dark stain on one corner of the throw. "Unless I'm very much mistaken, that's dried blood."

"Gosh!" Trudy's eyes grew round. "You reckon we're look-ing at a case of abduction?"

"Can't be sure at this stage, but I think CID should know about it."

"It's a mercy Donna didn't see that or she'd have had hysterics."

Sukey rolled up the throw, taking care not to handle the stain. "You keep an eye on her while I take this out to the van and bag it up. While I'm out there I'll contact George Barnes and tell him what we've found."

Ten

When Sukey returned to the station at the end of her afternoon shift, Sergeant George Barnes informed her that she was to report immediately to DI Castle. She found him at his desk, his brow furrowed, doodling on a notepad. When she entered he looked up to greet her, but his expression hardly altered as he waved her to a chair. Without preamble he said, "I understand you've attended a break-in and you think there might be a link between the householder and Miguel Rodriguez."

"Yes, Guv." He continued with his doodling without interruption while she gave him a brief account of what she had found on arrival at Number 8 Vine Close, Tuffley. His features showed no reaction, but she knew from experience that he was listening intently to every word. "The place had been pretty thoroughly trashed, but there was no apparent sign of a break-in and robbery didn't seem to be the motive because the TV was still there, with its screen smashed. That struck me as a bit unusual, but it wasn't until Donna called Alan's firm for the second time and asked to speak to Jack Morris that bells started to ring – I remembered hearing you say that was the name of one of Roddy's sidekicks and that Crowson's first name was Alan, which was how she'd referred to her boyfriend. Of course, she hadn't said what his job was or who he worked for so it could all have been a coincidence, but when I saw the blood on that throw I was sure there was more to the incident than a straightforward break-in and I thought you should hear about it."

"Well done, and full marks for observation," said Castle. He looked up from the pad and for the first time his hawklike features relaxed into a brief smile.

"I'd been hoping to get a bit more out of Donna, but all of a sudden she seemed to get suspicious of my motive in asking questions," Sukey went on. "I'm beginning to wonder whether she knows – or suspects – more about what her man gets up to while she's away than she was going to let on. That would account for her agitation when she found out that he'd gone AWOL."

"You could be right. I understand Trudy offered to take her down to the station so that she could report Crowson as a missing person, but she didn't want to know. Said that on reflection she was sure he'd get in touch with her."

"Does she know about the blood on the throw?"

"Not yet. We've told her we'll come back to her when we've made some enquiries. Trudy made her promise to let us know the minute she hears anything and that's how we've left it. In the meantime, we checked with Roddy's firm and you were absolutely right – the Alan Crowson and Jack Morris who're employed there as delivery men are the same two that Donna Hoskins was enquiring about."

"I imagine they were a bit taken aback to find CID taking an interest."

"Not at all. DS Radcliffe had already been on to them first thing today, asking to speak to Rodriguez. Not surprisingly, he wasn't there. Radcliffe spoke to his partner – a Mr Tomas Rodriguez, a cousin – who told him in confidence that he was concerned because they'd had a fax saying that Miguel had been taken ill over the weekend and was in a clinic where he'd been diagnosed as suffering from nervous exhaustion and had been ordered complete rest."

"Is that the new lead DC Hill mentioned?"

"One of them. Not that it's got us very far. The fax was from a Doctor Laben, who the cousin says he's never heard of, and there was no address of the clinic or any other clue as to where it came from. Tomas is seriously concerned; he's been on to Roddy's GP who said categorically that the story about nervous exhaustion was a load of eyewash. Tomas wants us to do everything we can to find Roddy and, needless to say, Andy assured him we'd be doing just that." Castle gave a wry grin as he added, "He explained that we wanted to check on one or two details about one of Roddy's customers, but of course he didn't let on just how anxious we are to find him."

"So Tomas Rodriguez doesn't know that his cousin is suspected of being the Phantom Robber?"

"No. That's something else we're keeping under our hats for the time being."

"Isn't there any way of tracing the fax?"

"Apparently not – the source has been deliberately with-held."

"So it looks as if your guess was right and Roddy really has been abducted."

"It's looking more and more likely." Castle gave an exasperated sigh, pushed his notepad aside and ran his thin, tapering fingers through his crisp brown hair. "Whichever way we turn we seem to run into the sand."

"You said the fax was 'one' of your new leads. What others have you got?"

"A local dealer called to say that someone he'd never seen before had been in his shop on Saturday offering to sell a clock and a pair of vases. He said he had a feeling the things were dodgy and made an excuse that they weren't his line and his partner would have a better idea of what they were worth, so he told the chap to come back this morning and meanwhile got on to us."

"You reckon the stuff was from Bussell Manor?"

"It could well be – clocks and vases were among the items missing. We've had a man waiting all day at the back of the shop, but the chap never showed. Maybe he smelled a rat – or maybe he wanted to get rid of the stuff quickly and offered it elsewhere."

"You think it might have been Crowson?"

"The shop owner lent us the video from his security camera, but the image is pretty poor. We've asked Mr Tomas to come and look at it tomorrow to see if he can identify the man. If it is Crowson – or Morris – it'll take us a step forward, but it won't be a lot of use if we can't find him."

With a sudden, irritable gesture Castle flung down his pen, got up and went over to the window. He pulled a bunch of keys from his pocket and began tossing it up in the air and catching it, over and over again. It was a nervous habit when he was wrestling with a problem and Sukey knew better than to interrupt his train of thought. After a moment he said over his shoulder, "I've got a bad feeling about this case, Sook."

"Why do you say that?"

He swung round and came back to his desk, perching on one corner, still restlessly tossing the keys. "There's so little to go on. Our chief suspect has disappeared into thin air in very suspicious circumstances. Two of his associates have also gone missing and the blood on that throw seems to indicate that at least one of them didn't go quietly."

"I take it there's no news of Morris either?"

"He lives in Hucclecote and according to neighbours he's a bit of a loner. We've been asking around, but so far we haven't found anyone who can remember seeing him since last Thursday, or who's noticed anything unusual."

"Do we know when the incident in Vine Close took place?"

Castle shook his head. "So far we've drawn a blank there as well – we haven't been able to find a single witness who saw anything suspicious. Whoever attacked and abducted Crowson – we have to assume for the moment that he has been abducted, and probably Morris as well – was evidently looking for something."

"Part of the proceeds of the Bussell Manor job?" Sukey suggested.

"That's the theory we're working on at the moment. I'm

willing to bet that the two are connected and if the video pictures do identify Crowson, that should clinch it. All we have to do now is find him and Morris – but even when we do, I doubt if they'll be telling us much."

"What do you mean?"

"They're small fry, just a pair of gofers who did the fetching and carrying and got paid accordingly. They could have decided that they weren't getting enough. Suppose they got greedy? Suppose that when they went to Bussell Manor to pick up the stuff on Mr Big's shopping list they decided to take one or two extra bits for themselves? If it was Crowson who offered them to Harker – that's the dealer who contacted us – he might have suspected a trap when he was asked to go back another time. What if he went elsewhere, maybe to someone who recognised the stuff and passed the information to someone other than the police?"

The implication was obvious and Sukey felt a twinge of goose flesh run along her spine. "To Mr Big, you mean? That wouldn't make him flavour of the month, would it?"

"Exactly." Castle thrust the keys back into his pocket and stood up. His expression was grim. "That's what's giving me the bad feeling. I think this is going to turn into a murder enquiry."

"Jim talks to you as if you were a real detective, doesn't he, Mum?" Fergus looked up from his helping of shepherd's pie, his eyes sparkling with admiration.

"I suppose he does," Sukey said, conscious of a little glow of satisfaction at the thought. It was Monday evening and they were having supper in the kitchen, as they usually did when it was just the two of them. In response to her son's eager questioning, and having impressed on him that it was in the strictest confidence and he was not to pass any of the information to anyone, not even Anita, Sukey had brought him up to date with the day's events.

"You were talking a while ago about going back into the

force and joining the CID," Fergus went on. "Have you thought any more about it?"

"Yes, and abandoned the idea – for the time being at any rate. Maybe when you've gone off to university – by the way, have you decided where you're going to apply?"

"Mm . . . not really," Fergus responded through a mouthful of mashed potato. "Never mind that for the moment, Mum – tell me more about the hunt for the Phantom Robber and his accomplices. Does Jim really reckon the two gofers have been topped?"

"He thinks it's a strong possibility."

"I said I thought there'd be some bodies, didn't I?" Fergus spoke a trifle smugly and his mother shook her head, frowning.

"We have to hope they'll turn up safe and sound," she reproached him. "They might be villains, but they're human beings."

"Yes, I suppose so." Fergus considered for a moment or two while he cleared his plate. Then he said thoughtfully, "That would help with the enquiries, wouldn't it? – if you could get them to sing, I mean. But even if they did turn up, the heavies would probably have put the frighteners on them so that they'd be too scared to open their mouths."

"You know your trouble, my lad," said Sukey as she took their empty plates to the sink and began serving apple crumble and custard, "You watch too many police series on TV."

Fergus grinned, unabashed. "They're based on real life, aren't they? Or I suppose it would be more accurate to say, 'real death'."

For the second time that day Sukey felt a chill of apprehension. "Let's talk about something else, shall we?" she said.

The following morning, a man out walking his dog spotted the body of Jack Morris among reeds in a creek off the River Severn. An intensive police search led to the discovery a short distance away of a second corpse, identified by a hysterical Donna Hoskins as that of Alan Crowson. Both men had been shot in the back of the head; Crowson showed signs of having been beaten before he died.

Eleven

The summons came the following evening. Roddy had passed an uneventful day swimming or lazing by the pool, trying on some of his new clothes, browsing with only a passing interest through one or two of the wide selection of books he found in his bedroom and eating the food served to him by Isabella. He was about to enjoy his pre-dinner cocktail when, without prior warning, Juan emerged from the villa.

"You are to come with me," he announced, without returning Roddy's greeting. "El Dueño has sent for you."

"Fine," said Roddy cheerfully. "I'll come as soon as I've finished my drink. Would you care to—?"

Juan reached out and took the glass from Roddy's hand. "We go immediately," he said in a tone that made it clear there was no point in arguing.

They travelled in the white Mercedes in which the two of them had been driven from the villa on that memorable shopping expedition. They had the same white-uniformed chauffeur, but this time they were escorted by a powerfully-built man whose eyes were screened by the ubiquitous dark glasses – a swarthy, black-haired android with impassive features and a tell-tale bulge in the jacket of his fawn linen suit. He made no response to Roddy's *"Buenos días"* as he opened the rear door for him and Juan to enter and closed it behind them. He took his place in the front passenger seat and from then on, apart from a muttered instruction to the driver, did not utter a word. The oppressive aura created by his presence reduced even the normally loquacious Juan to virtual silence.

Copycat

The journey lasted about half an hour and at first followed the same route as they had taken the previous day. They swept at speed through the little town while the other traffic seemed to melt away as if the Mercedes was an emergency vehicle with siren shrieking and blue lights flashing. Among the evening crowds thronging the pavements Roddy noticed people watching their progress with what seemed an awed, respectful interest; as they passed through the main shopping centre he recalled the obsequious, fawning manner of the proprietors as his purchases were carried to the limousine by nervous assistants. It all served to reinforce his conviction that the entire population was in thrall to the all-powerful figure whom he knew only as El Dueño. The indications were that he was about to learn the cost of the pampered existence so arbitrarily foisted upon him. He trembled at the prospect.

On leaving the town they followed a tortuous route overhung with lush vegetation, with occasional gaps affording stunning views of forest and mountains which he was in no mood to appreciate. The road ended at a high, white wall topped with metal spikes and pierced with slits like a medieval castle. Massive wrought-iron gates swung open in response to an invisible signal and the big car swept through. A circular drive led past green lawns, dotted with tall trees, brilliant flower-beds and sparkling fountains, to the house of El Dueño.

It was built on the lines of a colonial mansion, with a decorative frieze under the low-pitched roof and a balcony, supported by slender stone columns, which appeared to encircle the building. In the centre of the facade, shaded by an elegant portico, was a pair of massive wooden doors that, as the entrance gates had done, swung noiselessly apart at their approach.

Their mute escort led Roddy and Juan across a lofty entrance hall, up a curving marble staircase and along a corridor. Everywhere were signs of unbelievable opulence; the wry thought crossed Roddy's mind that, if this were the house of some wealthy customer, he would be mentally looking for weak points in the security system. It would, he sensed, present a particular challenge; although no one else had so far appeared he had the impression that hidden eyes were on them every second. Such idle thoughts came to an abrupt end when, halfway along a corridor, they stopped in front of a double door of carved black wood. At the touch of a concealed button a low-pitched buzzer sounded and the doors slid apart. With his heart floundering madly in the region of his solar plexus, Roddy entered.

In his imagination, he had pictured El Dueño as a thickset, bull-necked thug sporting a lot of flashy gold jewellery and smoking a huge cigar. Instead, he found himself shaking hands with a tall, silver-haired, quietly dressed man with velvety brown eyes and aristocratic features, who rose from behind a massive walnut desk to greet him in perfect, barely accented English.

"Señor Rodriguez, it is a pleasure to meet you at last. Please, take a seat." He indicated an upright, upholstered chair facing his and Roddy, somewhat bemusedly, obeyed. "Allow me to offer you a drink," his host continued. "Scotch? Bourbon? Or would you prefer one of your excellent Spanish wines?"

Beneath the urbanity, Roddy sensed a patronising note. Slightly nettled, and for the moment forgetting his perilous situation, he replied, "Thank you. I should prefer Scotch – our wines are best appreciated when drunk with food," and then wondered with some trepidation whether he had got off on the wrong foot.

A momentary lifting of one silvery eyebrow indicated that his remark had been noted as his host, with a snap of his fingers, directed Juan to a well-stocked bar with the remark, "I see you are a man of discernment." Juan poured two generous measures from a heavy decanter into engraved crystal tumblers and brought them on a silver tray before retreating silently to a corner. El Dueño raised his glass and inclined his head towards his guest. "*Salud*", he said gravely. "I trust you are completely recovered from your journey – and your, shall we say, indisposition?" A momentary twinkle lurked in the brown eyes on the final word.

"Oh, er, yes, thank you," stammered Roddy. Despite the courteous reception, he was quaking inwardly. He swallowed a mouthful, and then another. The spirit slid down his throat like smooth liquid fire. That was better. No need to be scared. This was no Mafia-style gangster, but a civilised gentleman. Gradually, his pulse rate began returning to normal.

"I trust you have been well looked after since your arrival in my country?" continued his host.

"Very well indeed. Just the same, I can't help wondering what all this is about. I mean, being drugged and whisked off like a character in a story by Frederick Forsyth and then brought here – what's the purpose of it all?"

"You are no doubt aware that there was a serious risk of your being arrested for the robbery at Bussell Manor, and possibly spending a considerable time in gaol?"

"I knew the police were taking an unhealthy interest in me, yes, but—"

"And your friend Wallis indicated that he was taking charge of the situation?"

"That's what he said – at least, he told me I'd be getting instructions—"

"Which, I understand, you did not immediately obey." For a moment, the brown eyes lost their softness and took on a stony quality, while a hint of steel crept into the almost musical voice. Roddy felt his newly found confidence taking a dive. He reminded himself that, for all the cordial reception, he was a virtual prisoner in this man's citadel.

"I'd never seen the characters who came to get me," he protested lamely. "All I wanted was to check with Wallis that they were telling the truth. They might have been thugs out to rob me." He took another swig of Scotch.

"We will overlook that momentary indiscretion," said his host smoothly. "So long as it is not repeated," he added before taking a delicate sip from his own glass.

"Oh, er, no, of course not."

"You are aware, of course, that the Bussell Manor job was a failure from our point of view?"

"I only know that Crowson claimed most of the stuff he and Morris were supposed to take had already gone. He was convinced I'd double-crossed them."

"And of course, you had done nothing of the kind?"

"Of course not," Roddy insisted. "It has never entered my head – I told Wallis—"

"And Wallis accepted your assurances. I have every confidence in his judgment – had I thought otherwise, you would not be here." The soft voice was suddenly charged with menace and the brown eyes, hard as granite, made the speaker's meaning frighteningly clear. Roddy experienced a momentary stab of sheer terror before he went on in his normal tone, "I merely wanted to gauge your reaction for myself. Now, I owe you some explanation for your presence here." El Dueño paused to take another sip from his drink and signalled to Juan to refill Roddy's glass.

"I would appreciate that." Roddy felt himself relaxing again. "I mean, life here is very pleasant and all that, but what about my business, my partner? He's my cousin, he'll be wondering what the hell's become of me."

"For the moment, he is under the impression that you are suffering from nervous exhaustion and are resting in a Swiss clinic. Bulletins on your progress will be sent from time to time – with your co-operation of course; it will be necessary for them to sound genuine."

Roddy felt himself floundering again. "But why . . . I mean, what use can I be to you . . . ?"

"You are too modest. Expertise such as yours – and I am not speaking of your knowledge of wine – is too valuable to be allowed to languish in gaol. From now on, you will use your mastery of electronic security systems exclusively on my behalf – as in fact you have been doing from the beginning. As a matter of interest, perhaps you can tell me how well protected against intruders you consider this room to be?"

"Pretty thoroughly, I'd say." Out of habit, Roddy had been surreptitiously glancing round for signs of surveillance. "TV camera up there." He pointed to one he had already spotted, disguised as a light fitting and trained on the door. "There's probably another covering the desk . . . yes, there it is, set in a corner of the silver frame of that mirror. I guess there are pressure-pads under some of the rugs, or maybe a heat-sensitive infra-red device linked to an alarm system . . . I'd need a bit more time to sus it out thoroughly, of course."

"And no doubt you would be able to circumvent all these devices?"

"Sure." Roddy spoke confidently, but in his heart he knew that, should the challenge actually arise, the odds would be heavily against success.

"Excellent." El Dueño was rubbing his hands together; for the first time, the man smiled. There was something chilling about the way the lips drew apart and lifted at the corners, while the expression in the eyes did not alter.

"This isn't a trial you're putting me through, is it?" A wild notion had entered Roddy's by now whisky befuddled head that this might be some monstrous joke at his expense. Was this smooth-tongued despot with the humourless smile a sadistic megalomaniac, challenging him to pit his wits against impossible odds and preparing to exact some hideous penalty for an inevitable failure? His newly found confidence ebbed away and he gulped nervously at his drink.

His host seemed to find the question amusing, but made no direct response. He pushed back his chair and stood up. "Come," he said. "I have something to show you." He crossed the room and pressed a switch. A section of panelling slid aside, revealing another room beyond. He beckoned. "Come and see my collection. You may recognise some of the canvasses."

They entered an enormous room whose whitewashed walls were hung with pictures. Roddy exclaimed in astonishment as his eyes fell on a Turner, a Degas, a Boudin and a Toulouse-Lautrec, each of which he instantly recognised as having been taken from one of the houses he and his accomplices had successfully raided. For a moment, he felt a sense of elation, swiftly followed by revulsion as, in a flash, he was brought face to face with a truth from which he had, ever since embarking on his adventures, been trying to hide. The means of acquiring such treasures could, in this as yet unidentified but obviously South American country, be amassed only from dealing in drugs on a massive scale. This man's deadly trade spanned the globe with a web in which he himself was now inescapably enmeshed.

"You appear surprised, my friend." The voice seemed to come from within his own head. He started, almost spilling the contents of his glass.

"I had no idea—" He almost choked on the words.

"And a little angry, perhaps, at the thought of how comparatively little you were paid?"

Roddy shook his head, momentarily speechless. How unimportant the money seemed now.

"You were paid according to my instructions. You were at first, so to speak, on probation. Had things gone well at Bussell Manor, the price would have substantially improved. Crowson and Morris would similarly have benefited – how foolish they were to play such a childish trick and hope to get away with it."

Roddy blinked down into his glass. His brain was spinning and he decided that he had better not drink any more. "I don't understand," he said. "Are you saying that the stuff hadn't been lifted by someone else after all – that they took it for themselves and tried to blame me?"

"Oh, there's no doubt that someone had been there before them. Who it was we don't yet know – he will be found and dealt with in due course." Again, there was the hint of menace that made Roddy shudder. "No, it seems that when they realised there would be no pay-out for them if they had nothing to hand over, they decided to take a few items for themselves and sell them independently. Unfortunately for them, they made the mistake of offering them to the gentleman who was expecting the main consignment. He, of course, reported to Wallis straight away, and Wallis took the necessary steps to ensure that such a mistake could never be repeated. He has, so to speak, terminated their contracts. Perhaps you would care to read about it."

The reptilian smile, the obvious euphemism, left Roddy in no doubt of the price Crowson and Morris had paid for their indiscretion. Even before he saw the stark black headlines 'Bodies Found in River' and read the grim details on the printout that El Dueño took from a folder lying on the desk – the same folder in which Juan had brought Roddy the early reports of the robbery – he had guessed the sickening truth.

"We shall, naturally, arrange replacements for them when necessary." El Dueño took the paper from Roddy's shaking hand and carefully replaced it in the folder, "And in due course I shall have further orders for you, Señor Rodriguez. I am sure *you* will not be so foolish as to disregard them. Now, let us discuss some details." He led the way back through the concealed door, which closed silently behind them.

Roddy returned to his chair on legs that shook and passed a dry tongue over dry lips. "What do you want of me?" he asked in a hoarse whisper.

"Merely to return to England and continue the excellent work you have been doing."

"You mean, open up more stately homes so that your boys can lift more pictures and *objets d'art*? How can I? I'm a wanted man – I'd be arrested the minute I reappeared."

"You underestimate our organisation. A little plastic surgery can work wonders and my friend Doctor Gundlach is a leading practitioner in the field. A new face, a new identity – you will be back in business in a very short time."

Roddy was overwhelmed by a sense of helplessness. He had been given no choice; his enforced departure from England had led to a form of captivity no less secure than if he had been arrested, tried, found guilty and sent to prison. For a few days he had allowed himself to enjoy the pampered life-style into which, willy-nilly, he had been tumbled. He had closed his mind to its source, blotted out all thoughts of the wretched victims who had paid for it in degradation and death. Now, with the realisation that his own escapades – undertaken at first out of sheer devilment and the desire for adventure – had contributed to that vast well of human misery, he felt sickened. And there was no way out; the trap had closed behind him. He had no alternative but to do whatever was required of him.

El Dueño stood up and held out a hand; the interview was over. "I have arranged for a consultation tomorrow morning at Doctor Gundlach's clinic," he said. "And in preparation for your new identity, you are to have some instruction in South American Spanish."

At last, Roddy found his voice. "What is my new identity?" he faltered.

"Your teacher will give you the fullest briefing. Her name is Consuela, and she is very, very beautiful. You will soon forget your English *chica*." The corners of the mouth lifted again and this time, for a split second, the smile crept into the eyes. The effect was almost satanic.

Pepita! In his mental and emotional turmoil, Roddy had temporarily forgotten her. The mystery of the missing photograph flashed into his mind and he was on the point of demanding to know what had become of it, but something held him back. Other questions crowded into his thoughts as well – such as, for example, how his eventual disappearance would be accounted for – but this did not seem the time to ask them. In any case he had no doubt that this man, with his infinite cunning and a vast organisation at his disposal, would have taken every detail into consideration.

On the way back to the villa, Juan, misunderstanding Roddy's thinly concealed agitation, tried to reassure him. "You'll be fine, *amigo*. Doctor Gundlach is the best and

his clinic is the finest in South America. As for Consuela
. . . *hombre!* Some men have all the luck!" He put bunched
fingers to his lips and made kissing noises.

Roddy managed a wan smile. At least, that part of the
adventure sounded promising. He badly needed a woman and,
passionately as he loved Pepita, it was doubtful if he would
ever see her again. With an effort, he thrust to the back of his
mind the gnawing fear that she might be in deadly danger.

Twelve

O n Wednesday morning, DI Castle was summoned to the office of Superintendent Sladden, who demanded to be brought up to date with recent developments. After giving an account of the discovery of the bodies of Crowson and Morris, their subsequent identification and the preliminary report of the forensic pathologist, Castle said, "I can't help feeling, sir, that this latest development supports my feeling that there's a very powerful organisation behind all this. It could be an elaborate money-laundering exercise serving a drugs syndicate."

Superintendent Sladden pondered the suggestion in silence. When a couple of minutes had passed and he had not spoken, DI Castle ventured to say, "I've been wondering, sir, whether it might be an idea to alert the Drugs Squad?"

"Oh, I don't think we've reached that stage yet," said Sladden with a frown. "I'm sure we're quite capable of conducting a murder enquiry without calling in outside help."

"I wasn't thinking so much about asking for their help, just to check whether they have any reason for being interested in Rodriguez."

"Ye . . . es, Rodriguez." Sladden sat back in his chair and clasped his hands behind his head. "You aren't suggesting he had a hand in these murders, are you?" He permitted himself a fleeting, slightly patronising smile.

"No sir, of course not, but surely you must agree that for all three suspects to be eliminated from the scene within what was probably a matter of hours – it has not, of course been possible to establish exactly when Crowson and Morris died, but the pathologist reckons the bodies were in the water for at least twenty-four hours before they were found – surely that has to be more than a coincidence?"

"On the face of it, a connection seems a strong possibility," Sladden admitted, "but it still doesn't prove that their deaths had anything to do with the Bussell Manor job, or any of the other jobs we're talking about either. No," he jerked himself upright and began toying with his heavy onyx desk calendar, "I'm still not a hundred per cent convinced he's our man – oh, I know on the face of it, he might seem to be the most likely candidate," he went on before Castle could protest, "in fact, you could say he's the only candidate at the moment, but the evidence so far is purely circumstantial. A thread from a mass-produced garment, a thumb-print and a few grains of sand that a smart lawyer could easily convince a jury had perfectly innocent explanations – assuming, of course, that the case ever got to court . . ."

"So why the disappearing trick?" Castle asked, a little wearily. Having his theories shot down by the Super was becoming almost routine these days.

"I assume you're taking steps to establish whether this Dr Laben and his clinic really exists?"

"Naturally sir . . . but doesn't it strike you as strange that no address was given and no indication of the source of the fax? Surely that proves something? Mr Tomas Rodriguez is seriously concerned for his cousin's well-being."

"Perhaps the information was withheld at the patient's own request. We don't know what relations are between the two men . . . maybe Tomas has been over-protective in the past and his cousin didn't want him fussing around." The Superintendent was obviously in no mood to be persuaded.

Castle felt his patience wearing thin, but he managed to conceal his exasperation as he said, "You could be right, sir."

The admission was rewarded by a gracious smile. "I'm not trying to trash your ideas, Castle, just making sure you don't lose sight of the fact that there's often more than one explanation for something that at first seems blindingly obvious." Sladden put away in a drawer some papers lying on his desk and pressed a buzzer. It was a signal that the interview was at an end and Castle, feeling more than a little relieved, stood up. As he reached the door, the Superintendent said, with an almost avuncular smile, "Keep up the good work, Castle. You'll keep me posted, won't you?"

"Naturally, sir."

Feeling thoroughly disgruntled, Castle returned to his office to find a message from Sukey. She had been called to check a burned-out car found on Crickley Hill. Destruction had been virtually complete, but the registration number was that of a van belonging to M. and T. Rodriguez Limited.

"There's got to be a link, Sook," said Jim, adding, "Cheers!" as she handed him a glass and a can of beer. "Sladden's right, I admit coincidences can sometimes blow an investigation off course, but there's a whole string of them here, far too many to ignore."

"Mm, I think so too. What has he got to say about the connection between Rodriguez and the burned-out van?"

"He doesn't know about it yet. I'm saving it until forensics have gone over the wreck with a toothcomb."

"I doubt if they'll find much, but you never know." Sukey ran water into the sink and began peeling potatoes. "Bangers and mash for supper tonight," she announced over her shoulder. "I hope that's okay with you. It's one of Gus's favourites."

"Sounds great."

"Jim, why d'you suppose the Super was so reluctant for you to contact the Drugs Squad?"

"Oh, that's easy to explain – he doesn't want the case taken out of his pudgy little hands. He's coming up for retirement soon and no doubt he'd like to go out in a blaze of glory. Nailing the Phantom Robber would be just the thing to set the crown on a distinguished career."

Sukey chuckled. The Superintendent's reputation was well

known in the SOCOs' department. "Wouldn't it just!" she said gleefully.

The front door slammed and Fergus came bounding into the kitchen brandishing a copy of the previous evening's edition of the *Gloucester Gazette*. "Jim, I was hoping you'd be here. Is it true these are two of the blokes you've been looking for in connection with the Bussell Manor job? Mum went all cagey on me . . . said the information hadn't been officially released."

"You were just off to the youth club when the paper arrived and I was afraid you'd say something indiscreet, you were so full of how clever you'd been . . ."

"Clever?" queried Jim with an indulgent smile.

"I said there'd be some bodies, didn't I, Mum?"

"You weren't the only one." Jim's smile faded. "It's all turned very nasty."

"At least, you can be sure now that all three of them were in cahoots over the robbery," Fergus pointed out with an air of great wisdom.

"I wish Superintendent Sladden shared that conviction," said Castle, a trifle sourly. "He's got a thing about coincidences."

"How d'you mean?"

"He doesn't trust them."

Fergus shrugged. Then his eye fell on the sausages that his mother was arranging on the grill and exclaimed, "Ooh, bangers! My favourite! Anything I can do to help?"

"Not for the moment, thanks. Are you going out this evening?"

"Just down to the club with Anita. How long will supper be?"

"About half an hour."

"Okay, I'll go and have a shower."

Fergus clattered out of the kitchen and up the stairs, humming a snatch of the latest Michael Jackson hit. Jim finished his beer and got up to rinse his glass at the sink. "Don't you want another?" said Sukey in mild surprise.

"Not just now, thanks." He came and stood beside her as she turned the sausages under the grill. "Sook, we have to talk."

"What about?"

"You know I said the other evening I was concerned for your safety. This latest turn of events has made me more uneasy than ever. There's a ruthless machine grinding away out there—"

"—looking for more victims? You make it sound like something out of a sci-fi movie," she teased him.

"Be serious, Sook. Those two – Crowson and Morris – were pretty small fry in the set-up, but they might have given us valuable information if we'd been able to get our hands on them, so they had to be disposed of."

"Yes, I can see that, but I don't see what that has to do with me. I don't know anything—"

"Of course you don't, but whoever's behind this thinks you've been having an affair with Roddy, remember? And to their way of thinking, you might well have picked up something that could give us a lead."

"How could I? Anyway, if Roddy's out of the country he's well out of your reach, so what have they got to worry about?"

"We've no proof that he really has gone abroad. We've been making enquiries at all the ports and airports but we've drawn a blank everywhere. Not that that's conclusive – there are ways and means, given the money and the organisation, of spiriting anyone away without leaving any traces."

"Are you saying the fax could be a hoax?"

"Yes and no. We've established through contacts with the Swiss police that there is a real Doctor Laben and he does have a clinic – a very prestigious one patronised by the rich and famous – somewhere near Montreux. Only, the good Doctor denies all knowledge of the fax, maintains he's never heard of Rodriguez and says no patient suffering from nervous exhaustion has been admitted to his clinic within the past week." Jim turned away, picked up an apple from a bowl and began prowling round the kitchen, tossing it moodily into the air. "Whichever way we turn, we seem to run into the sand," he complained. "We're making all the usual enquiries, but so far we haven't turned up a single piece of information that might lead us to the killer – or killers – of Crowson and Morris."

"What about Donna? Hasn't she been able to help?"

"The poor woman's pretty traumatised and we haven't been able to interview her properly yet. One thing we're looking at is whether any of her previous visits to her mother tie in with other jobs that we suspect them and Roddy of carrying out. Not that that would get us anywhere either." Jim dumped the apple back in the bowl and sat down again. "Let's forget that for now and talk about you."

"Are you still suggesting I should go into hiding?"

"I'd be a lot happier if you did – just until we get this lot cleared up."

"You've just said yourself that you haven't got a single lead. It could be months . . . and in any case, if they thought I represented that much of a danger, surely they'd have made a move by now."

"You might be next on the list—"

"Oh, come on, Jim, don't be so melodramatic!"

"So you won't do it?"

"No."

"At least, let me arrange some sort of security system."

"Okay, if you insist." Sukey transferred the cooked sausages to a dish, put it in the oven and began mashing potatoes. "At least, the gang's tame expert is out of the way, so I should be reasonably safe. No, on second thoughts, I've got a better idea," she went on with an impish grin that gave her sharp features the elfin look that always sent his pulse rate rocketing. "Why don't you find me some dishy armed bodyguard to take up residence until you've nailed all the villains?"

He gave a despairing sigh. "Sook, I do wish you'd take this more seriously."

She put down the pan of potatoes and went over to him. "And I wish you'd stop fussing," she murmured with her mouth against his.

Thirteen

Thursday morning brought the usual crop of minor break-ins which occupied Sukey until midday, when she was called to an incident at Robinswood Country Park. A motorist returning to her car after taking her dog for a walk had found it broken into and the radio stolen; when Sukey reached the scene, a young uniformed officer was already in attendance, taking details and doing his best to pacify the victim, a thin, leathery-faced woman in a shabby anorak and shapeless trousers that had obviously seen better days. In one hand she held a stout stick and in the other the lead of a large black labrador.

The policeman greeted Sukey's arrival with obvious relief. "This is Mrs Williams, the owner of the car," he informed her. "I've assured her we'll do everything we can to catch the culprit although I've tried to explain—"

"If you fellows had been keeping a proper eye on things, it wouldn't have happened in the first place," the victim interposed, glaring at him. "What these young hooligans need is a good hiding!" She brandished the stick in a manner which made it clear that, given the chance, she would have not have hesitated to administer the punishment in person.

"We do our best, but I'm afraid we can't be everywhere at once," he said with a placatory smile. "This is Mrs Reynolds, one of our Scenes of Crime Officers. She'll be checking your car for fingerprints. I'll leave her in charge for now." With renewed assurances that the matter would be taken seriously, he closed his notebook and turned to Sukey. "I've given the

94

lady an incident number for her insurance company," he said, adding in a lower tone, "I wrote it down for her, but I'm not sure she's taken it all in. She's pretty wound up at the moment, as you can see. Might be as well to remind her of the procedure when she's calmed down a bit."

"Yes, of course." He got into his car and drove away, while Sukey took her bag out of the van and prepared to start work.

"Upsetting when anything like this happens, isn't it?" she said sympathetically. "Do you often park your car here?"

"Most days, unless the weather's completely impossible," said Mrs Williams. "Bounder loves to tear around up here, don't you boy?" She stooped to pat the labrador as it sat quietly at her feet. "Never had any trouble before," she added resentfully.

"What a super name for him," said Sukey diplomatically. "He's such a handsome fellow, too!"

At this expression of admiration of her pet, the proud owner's severe features relaxed in a smile. "D'you hear that, Bounder – the lady thinks you're handsome. He's a splendid guard dog as well," she boasted. "If he'd spotted whoever did this to our car, he'd have had his teeth in their leg in no time, wouldn't you, boy?" She tickled the dog under its chin and it lifted its muzzle and wagged its tail with a knowing look.

"These people always wait until the coast is completely clear, and then they're into a car and away in no time at all." Sukey opened her case and took out aluminium powder and brushes. "This is a very popular spot and cars left here are often targeted."

"All the more reason why the police should be more in evidence. It really is a disgrace, you can't go anywhere or do anything these days without risking being robbed or attacked, and sometimes it's much worse than losing a car radio." Some of the steam appeared to have gone out of her indignation and she watched with interest as Sukey got down to work. "Have you been doing this job for long?

"Quite a while, yes."

"There was a very nasty incident the other day, just down the road from where I live. I wonder if you worked on that?"

"Whereabouts was this?"

"In Tuffley." If Mrs Williams noticed the way the hand that held the brush momentarily stopped in mid-air, she gave no sign, but rushed on in a sudden burst of pent-up indignation. "They made a terrible mess of the place . . . I felt so sorry for the young woman who lives there, Donna, her name is . . . she always keeps everything so nice . . . seeing it all smashed up was bad enough, but when they found Alan's . . . that's her friend, she used to call him her partner . . . when they found his body it must have been terrible for her. Mind you, I don't really approve of the way these young couples live together . . . I suppose I'm old-fashioned, but I can't help thinking . . . and in any case, I always had my doubts about Alan but I'm sure he didn't deserve to be murdered. Oh dear." Momentarily overcome with emotion, Mrs Williams bent down to fondle the dog again. "It really makes you wonder what the world's coming to."

"You're speaking of the break-in in Vine Close?" said Sukey, trying not to betray her excitement. She was still diligently testing the damaged passenger door of the car for fingerprints, but her mind had switched back to the scene at number eight. Her instinct told her she might be on the verge of learning something significant.

"Ah, I thought you'd know about it." Mrs Williams took a large handkerchief out of her trouser pocket and blew her nose with a flourish. "I live just a few doors away from where it happened. The police came knocking on my door asking if I'd seen anything, but I couldn't help them because I'd been away all over the weekend. Do you know if they've caught anyone yet?"

"Not so far as I know." Sukey waited a second or two before adding casually, brushing away for dear life, "You say you didn't approve of Donna's partner. Why was that?"

"I pride myself on my ability to judge people," said Mrs Williams. "I remember saying to her, when she first took up with him, 'My dear, are you sure you know what you're doing? He's a lot older than you are and I shouldn't be surprised if. . .' well, I didn't like to say so in so many words, but you know, I just had this feeling that he might have a shady past, or even still be mixed up in something not quite, you know, legal." She seemed to have forgotten her loss in her fascination with the possibly dubious history of her late neighbour. "Do you know," she squatted down so that her face was level with Sukey's, "I often wondered whether the reason why he used to send her away to stay with her mother was so's she be out of the way while he got up to something."

Sukey put away her brush, got out her roll of transparent tape and began lifting a couple of promising prints. "Did you mention that to the police?" she asked.

"Oh no, I never thought of it. I wouldn't have said anything anyway – I mean it was none of my business and I'm not one to poke my nose into what doesn't concern me." Evidently, Mrs Williams had forgotten the gratuitous advice offered to Donna that she had mentioned only seconds ago. "Of course, that was before the bodies were found," she went on. "The police didn't ask about anything like that. Perhaps I should have mentioned it . . . what do you think?"

"It might be helpful in their enquiries to know about it. And there might be other things you could tell them . . . maybe things you never thought of as especially important . . ."

"Do you really think so? Good gracious, how exciting! Should I call and tell them I've got some information for them?"

"If you like, I'll mention it when I get back to the station. They'll send a detective round to have a chat with you."

"Thank you very much. Just think, Bounder, we're going to help the police with their enquiries!" She gave a little tug at the dog's lead; this time it gave an excited bark and wagged its tail. "You know," she said earnestly, "He understands every word I say."

"I do believe he does," Sukey agreed. She completed her task and began packing her equipment away. "Well, I've finished here. You're lucky, the damage isn't too bad and the car is okay to drive. You'll be reporting to your insurance company of course – the officer did give you an incident number, didn't he?"

"Oh yes, thank you, he wrote it down." Mrs Williams fished in the pocket of her anorak and produced a crumpled slip of paper. "And you'll be sure and tell the detectives that I'm happy to help them in any way I can?"

"I will indeed. If you'll just give me your address?"

"It's number eighteen Vine Close, Tuffley – I did give it to that young policeman and he wrote it in his notebook. Come along Bounder, we're going home for lunch now." She opened the rear door and the dog jumped in. "Goodbye, and thank you so much."

"No trouble. We'll do our best to catch them."

"You mean the murderer? Oh, I do hope so."

"Actually, I was thinking of the thieves who took your radio," said Sukey with a smile.

"Oh, that. I hardly ever listened to the thing anyway." It was clear that the prospect of being considered a key witness in a murder enquiry had more than compensated Mrs Williams for such a comparatively trivial loss.

Mention of lunch reminded Sukey that she was hungry, but before starting on her sandwiches she called CID and spoke to DS Radcliffe. Having passed on the gist of the information she had gleaned from Donna Hoskins' loquacious neighbour, she added mischievously, "By the way, Andy, you might mention that it would be a good idea for whoever goes to interview Mrs Williams to be a dog lover."

Radcliffe chuckled. "I'll make a note of that. I think I'll send DC Hill – he specialises in dotty old ladies who dote on their pooches."

*   *   *

"What a bit of luck, running into Mrs Williams like that," said Fergus as he filled the kettle for the cup of tea that he and his mother always shared on returning home at the end of the afternoon. "She sounds just the sort who might have noticed something useful."

"Yes, quite a coincidence, wasn't it?" Sukey agreed. "The sort that Superintendent Sladden loves to pour buckets of cold water over," she added with a grimace.

"Have you told Jim? Is he coming round this evening, by the way?"

"I hope so, but I haven't spoken to him today. I left the message with Andy Radcliffe."

"Do you know if there's been any more news of the hunt for the Phantom Robber?"

"You mean Rodriguez? I haven't heard anything. Andy was rushing off somewhere so there wasn't time to ask him. And of course, we don't know for certain yet that Rodriguez is the Phantom Robber. As Superintendent Sladden keeps reminding Jim, all the evidence against him is circumstantial."

"Well, maybe this Mrs Williams will be able to help."

"I'd like to think so. I got quite excited when I first realised that she knew Donna and Alan, but of course gossip and surmise isn't evidence." Sukey broke off to fetch mugs, milk and sugar for their tea. "Still, you never know, something might come out of it. I wonder if Donna or her Mum keeps a diary."

"A diary? What's that got to do with it?"

"Think about it."

The lad paused in the act of spooning tea into the pot, frowning in perplexity. After a few moments his brow cleared. "Of course!" he said gleefully. "That'd make old Sladden sit up and take notice, wouldn't it? What's for supper?

It was gone eight o'clock before Jim phoned to say that he still had paperwork to do and had decided to go straight home when it was finished for a bath and early bed.

"What about food?" Sukey asked anxiously.

"Don't worry, I had a pie and a pint with Andy. By the way, Sook, full marks for putting us on to Mrs Williams. We'll have you in CID one of these days."

"Thanks. Has anyone spoken to her yet?"

"Andy sent DC Hill round to see her, but she was out. He left a card asking her to call in and she phoned a couple of hours later. He's going to see her in the morning."

"What about Donna? Have you been able to talk to her again?"

"Not properly. She's still under mild sedation from her doctor and very reluctant to talk about the tragedy, but her mother's come down from Yorkshire to stay with her and she's promised to try and persuade her daughter to help us. With this new information you've given us, we're hoping we can get something useful out of her."

"I do hope so."

"See you tomorrow, then?"

"Sure." After a moment, Sukey added in a softer voice, although Fergus was out of the room. "Gus will be with his father this weekend."

"Wonderful!" There was no mistaking the throb of eagerness in Jim's voice and Sukey experienced an answering thrill of anticipation as she put down the telephone.

Fourteen

"No need to be scared of him, mate. Looks fierce, but he's soft as a mop really. Like his owner." DC Hill turned to find himself face to face with a stocky individual in oily jeans, holding a plastic carrier bearing the name of a supplier of spare automobile parts in one grimy hand.

"Are you sure?" said Hill doubtfully as he eyed the huge black dog that stood on its hind legs, front paws on the gate of number 18 Vine Close, barking furiously.

"Course I'm sure." The man reached across the gate and tickled the dog behind the ears. The barking ceased and the black body wriggled in delight. "See what I mean?"

"He obviously knows you." Hill was still hesitant and he looked hopefully towards the house for Mrs Williams to come to his rescue, but there was no sign of her. "I'm not sure that he'll let me in."

"Course he will. Soft as a mop, I tell you," the man repeated. He looked Hill up and down for a moment before saying, "You're a copper, aren't you?"

"How did you know?"

The man grinned, showing a row of broken, discoloured teeth. "Smell 'em a mile off, I can. Not that I've anything to hide," he added with a knowing wink. "Me, I always like to keep on the right side of the law. My name's Hitchin, by the way, Frankie Hitchin." He jerked an almost bald head in the direction of the house. "What's the old bat been up to, then?"

"We're hoping she can help us with some enquiries," said

Hill, a trifle stiffly. There was still no sign of Mrs Williams and he was beginning to wonder if someone had made a cock-up over the time of the appointment.

"Ah, that'll be about the murders," said Hitchin knowingly. "Wouldn't take too much count of what she says," he added. "I'm not suggesting she tells deliberate porkies – just a bit given to exaggeration, if you know what I mean. You know what these old women living alone are like."

"Thank you, I'll bear that in mind." Hill made his tone deliberately dismissive, but the man seemed in no hurry to go on his way.

"I think I knew one of the blokes who got topped," he said. "Only by sight, mind you, we never got chatting."

Hill, who had been listening to Hitchin with increasing irritation, suddenly found his interest aroused. "Which one?"

"The one called Crowson."

"Why do you only think you knew him?"

"Never knew his name and it was a pretty ropey photo they published in the local rag. I rent a lockup from a bloke who's got a workshop on the industrial estate just down the road, see. The chap who rented one in the same block looked very like Crowson."

"Why haven't you reported this before?"

Hitchin shrugged. "You know how it is – kept meaning to, but never seemed to find the time. Anyway, I wasn't sure – I mean I never even spoke to the bloke. It was really up to the owner, only he's a surly bugger who wouldn't cross the road to help anyone. Besides, it's up to your lot to come round asking questions, innit?"

"Where is this lockup?"

"I told you, Meadway Industrial Estate. Go to the end of this road, turn right, then left, then left again. The lockups are down at the end. Tell you what, I'll be there until twelve o'clock, working on the Mini." He held up the carrier as if in confirmation of the legitimacy of his errand. "If you like to pop round after you've finished talking to the old dragon – if

102

she ever shows up, that is. I reckon she's forgotten all about you . . . no, I tell a lie, here she comes. See you later."

Hitchin went on his way whistling and Hill turned in relief to greet a panting and very apologetic Mrs Williams. "Constable Hill?" she panted. "I really am sorry to have kept you waiting. I wanted to have something nice to offer you with your coffee . . . you will have a cup of coffee, won't you? And there were so many people in the shop, and they were all talking about those dreadful murders . . . I do hope you haven't been waiting long. It's all right Bounder, you can let him in," she went on, ushering Hill through the open gate.

As if in response to his owner's words, the dog began frisking round Hill's legs and, remembering Sukey's message, he stooped to pat it. "He's a great guard dog, isn't he?" he remarked. "Very intelligent, too, by the looks of him."

"He's the cleverest dog I've ever had," beamed Mrs Williams, completely won over. "Now, come along in and I'll make that coffee I promised, and we can have our chat while we drink it. I've got some nice Madeira cake to go with it."

"It's very kind of you to go to all this trouble," said Hill politely. Privately, remembering Hitchin's warning, he was already having doubts about the potential usefulness of the interview.

The furniture in Mrs Williams' little sitting-room had the same well-worn quality as her garments and the atmosphere had a distinctly doggy smell. Hill sat down in an armchair covered in faded cretonne and accepted a cup of milky coffee and a slice of insipid-looking cake served on a bone china plate. He waited politely while his hostess, puffing slightly, settled herself on a similarly covered sofa with the dog curled up alongside, its muzzle on her lap and its gaze fixed hopefully on the two slices of cake on her plate.

"I'm not being greedy, these aren't both for me, one's for Bounder," she explained, breaking one of the slices into fragments and popping the first into the dog's eager mouth. "He does love his bit of cakie, don't you boy?"

"It's delicious cake," said Hill politely. "Now, Mrs Williams, I understand that you feel you might be able to help us with our enquiries into the attack on the home of Donna Hoskins and Alan Crowson . . . and possibly Mr Crowson's death as well. Sukey – Mrs Reynolds, our Scenes of Crime Officer – said you knew them—"

"Yes, I did, didn't I?" Mrs Williams broke in. Suddenly, she appeared ill at ease. "You know, I've been thinking so hard ever since yesterday about what I said to that young woman – Sukey, you said her name is – I did tell Sukey that I had my doubts about Mr Crowson, but really, I don't *know* anything to his detriment, not for certain I mean, and really it does seem wicked to speak ill of him now the poor man's dead." She broke off to drink deeply and noisily from her cup of coffee.

"Mrs Williams, the man was brutally murdered," Hill pointed out patiently. "It isn't your personal opinion of him I'm after so much as information about his background, who his associates were, that kind of thing. Tell me, how long have you known him?"

Mrs Williams fidgeted with her plate and looked uncomfortable. It was clear that she was beginning to wish she had never become involved in the enquiry. "Well, I didn't really *know* him at all – in fact, I only ever exchanged a few words with him," she admitted reluctantly. "I used to chat to Donna . . . or rather, she used to chat to me quite a lot. Living so far away from her mother, I suppose she saw me as a kind of aunt, someone she could confide in. She's quite naive in a way. That's why I was so concerned when she let that man move in with her."

"He moved in with her? You mean, the house belongs to her?"

"Yes. She's got quite a good job with a big insurance company. That's another reason why I had my doubts about him. I once said to her, 'Are you sure it isn't your money he's after?' but she said, 'Oh no, Alan's got plenty of money of his own, he's got a good job with . . .' I can't recall the name of the firm, they deal in wine . . . Spanish sounding, it was."

"Yes, we know where he worked and of course we're making enquiries there too. Do you by any chance remember the names of any other people that Donna might have mentioned . . . friends of Crowson, people he worked with, that sort of thing?"

"Well, Donna used to talk about a man called Jack – I don't know his other name. I think Crowson shared a flat with him until he moved in with Donna. She didn't like him at all, said he was a bad influence on Alan."

"In what way?"

"She didn't say, really. I think, once he moved in with her, she was hoping he'd see less of Jack – although of course they worked at the same place."

"Now, I believe you mentioned that Donna goes to stay with her mother from time to time." Hill referred to his notebook. "According to Sukey's report, you actually used the words, 'he used to send her away'."

"Yes, well, that was her way of putting it. I remember her saying this last time, 'Alan's working all this weekend so he's packing me off to stay with Mam,' but, now I've had time to think about it, she was probably only joking. Perhaps I shouldn't have said that, I don't want you to think I'm in the habit of speaking unkindly of people. He was probably just being considerate." The troubled expression returned to Mrs Williams' weathered features. "Perhaps I was too quick to judge him."

"It's really only information I'm after," Hill repeated, doing his best to conceal his exasperation. "Now, do you know if this man Jack ever came to the house while Donna was away?"

Mrs Williams fed another piece of cake to the dog and thought for a moment. "I can't be certain," she said hesitantly, "but I remember once when I was taking Bounder for his evening walk . . . this was quite a long time ago . . . I went past the house just as Alan and another man were coming out. I wondered at the time whether it might have been Jack, although so far as I knew I'd never actually set eyes on the man. They got into a car and drove off. I expect they were going to the pub or something. I didn't take much notice."

"Can you remember when this was?"

"Goodness, no . . . at least, it must have been wintertime because it was cold and dark although it was early evening . . . yes, I remember now, people had started to put Christmas lights in their windows so I suppose it was some time early in December."

"And you're sure Donna was away?"

"Oh yes, quite sure."

"Did you tell her when she got back?"

Mrs Williams sighed heavily. "No. I thought about it, wondered if I should mention it . . . but I didn't want to cause trouble between her and Alan so I kept quiet."

"And you can't recall ever hearing or seeing anything suspicious?"

"No, really, I can't."

"Can you remember other times when Donna went away to her mother's?" asked Hill, reflecting ruefully that Hitchin certainly had a point. He finished the lukewarm coffee and put down his cup with some relief; it had been far too sweet and he much preferred it black.

Mrs Williams fed the last morsel of cake to the dog and then, to Hill's disgust, licked her fingers. "I can't remember every time," she said after a moment's thought, "but once . . . it was towards the end of March and Donna was a bit worried because there was some talk of a train strike and she decided to go by bus instead . . . it was, let me see, the weekend before Easter. The strike never happened so she could have gone by train after all, but you never know what to do for the best, do you? Would you like some more cake? Another cup of coffee?"

"No thank you." Hill put his notebook away and stood up. "Thank you, Mrs Williams, you've been very helpful," he said politely.

"Oh, have I?" She beamed and gave the dog a cuddle. "And we thought you might be cross with us, didn't we Bounder?"

"Not at all." In the circumstances, Hill reflected, as he made his escape, he had been fortunate in getting one solid piece – with luck, two pieces – of verifiable information. He went back to the car, checked in at the station on his radio and set off for Meadway Industrial Estate.

The somewhat grandly named development consisted of a line of single-storey concrete buildings on a fenced-off area adjoining a patch of waste land. Several of the units were empty; others, identified by peeling painted boards, were occupied by a small printing works, a vehicle repair shop and a firm selling plumbing equipment. A series of speed humps had been laid at intervals along the access road, which had been heavily colonised by weeds where the tarmac had split. Apart from a few parked cars and a small builder's van being loaded with plastic piping, there were few signs of activity.

At the end of the line of buildings the road swung to the left and ended in a wide turning area. Tucked away round the corner, well out of sight of the entrance, was a block of six garages with metal up-and-over doors. One was open, revealing a jacked-up scarlet Mini with a pair of legs protruding from beneath it. As Hill parked alongside, Hitchin wriggled out from under the car and stood up, brushing grit from his jeans. "Thought you'd be along," he said cheerfully. "Did you get anything useful out of the old bat?"

"She was very chatty," said Hill non-committally. "Now Mr Hitchin, I can see you're very busy and I don't want to take up too much of your time, but if you'd be kind enough to show me which garage was rented by the man you think might have been Crowson . . . ?"

"The one at the far end." Hitchin pointed with a grease-blackened finger.

"You're sure about this?"

"Course I'm sure. You want to have a look inside?"

"Won't it be locked?"

Hitchin grinned. He wiped his hands with an oily rag, fished in his pocket and brought out a bunch of keys. "These locks are a doddle. The chap who rents the one next to mine forgot his one day, but with a bit of jiggling we managed . . ." While he was speaking, he had made several unsuccessful attempts to open the end garage. "Well, I'm buggered," he exclaimed in disgust, banging on the metal door in frustration. "I do believe he's had a new lock put on. I'll bet old Gunning doesn't know about that."

"Gunning?"

"The owner. He's the one with the printing business."

"And the entire block of garages belongs to him?"

"That's right. He'd be able to tell you whether or not it was Crowson who rented this one." Hitchin put the keys back in his pocket. "Anything else I can do for you, mate?"

"Not for the moment, thanks. I think I'll go and have a word with Mr Gunning."

"Best of luck. Like I said, he's a miserable old devil." Hitchin gave a sudden, throaty chuckle. "If that fellow died still owing him rent, he'll do his nut!"

Fifteen

While DC Hill was trying, with limited success, to extract some useful information from Mrs Williams, DI Castle was experiencing similar frustration at the hands of a pale and subdued Donna Hoskins and the dumpy, sharp-eyed woman who answered his knock, announced that she was Donna's mother and, after scrutinising his identification card for several seconds, admitted him with considerable reluctance.

"I'll not have you upsetting the lass," she warned as she closed the front door behind him with exaggerated care, as if to avoid disturbing a sleeping invalid. "She's still devastated by the tragedy."

"I quite understand and I'll do my best not to upset her," he promised. "I'm sorry it's necessary to disturb her, but we need her help if we're to catch the people who killed Alan Crowson."

Mention of the name evoked something that sounded very like a sniff of contempt, but all the woman said was, "If it gets too much for her, you'll have to leave." She led the way into the sitting-room, now restored to an almost aggressive neatness and smelling strongly of furniture polish. "It's the police," she announced and Donna, who was sitting on the sofa staring into space, a brimming cup clasped between her hands, briefly switched her gaze in Castle's direction and gave a languid nod. "Drink your tea while it's hot, lass," the mother went on encouragingly. "She's still under sedation," she informed Castle in a low voice. She waved him to a chair before sitting down heavily beside her daughter and picking up her own cup of tea from a small side table. She took several mouthfuls and put it down again; her failure to offer a cup to their visitor made it quite clear that not only was he not welcome, but also that the interview was going to be brief and under her control. It was not an encouraging start.

"The last thing I want to do is to cause Donna any distress, Mrs Hoskins," said Castle in his most conciliatory tone. "I know that she has suffered a terrible shock and is still grieving over the death of her friend—"

"Friend!" interrupted Mrs Hoskins with an indignant snort. "Friend to no one but himself, that one."

"Mam!" Donna turned moist, reproachful eyes on her mother. "He's dead. You've always said we shouldn't speak ill of the dead."

"I make an exception of him." Mrs Hoskins breathed heavily, sending her ample bosom heaving with indignation. "Moved into your house, never offered you anything but a load of junk furniture you wouldn't give house-room—"

"He gave me lovely presents and paid for everything when he took me out," Donna protested. "I earn more than he did, I didn't want his money."

"It's not the way to go on, not the way you were brought up to," her mother insisted. "A man should support his wife . . . not that he even had the decency to offer marriage—"

"Please, madam," Castle interposed, "I understand your concerns, but I'm not here to probe into your daughter's relationship with Alan Crowson. Donna, I'm trying to find the people who killed your partner and his friend and I think you may be able to help us—"

"Partner!" the mother broke in again. "Partner in crime, most like!"

This time Castle allowed the interruption. "Would you mind explaining what you mean by that, Mrs Hoskins?" he asked politely.

"Whenever she came up to stay with me, she used to worry

in case he and that Jack Morris were up to something – oh yes you did," the mother insisted as Donna took a quick breath as if to contradict her.

"I didn't mean anything criminal," Donna protested. For the first time since Castle's arrival, she showed a spark of animation. "It was just . . . I never trusted Jack and I never liked the idea that he and Alan saw so much of each other . . . that was why I was so keen for Alan to move in here with me . . . he used to share a flat with Jack—"

"But they worked together, didn't they? You couldn't stop them plotting their mischief," her mother pointed out.

"What sort of mischief are you talking about?" Castle was beginning to feel more optimistic, but his hopes were soon dashed.

"Oh, how do I know? Women, drink, drugs—"

"Alan never looked at another woman after he met me!" Donna declared, her languor evaporating at this slur on the man she had obviously adored. "And he never drank a lot, not even when the three of us were out together."

"Your mother mentioned drugs—" Castle began.

"Alan would never touch drugs," said Donna angrily. "You've no right to suggest that, Mam!"

"All right lass, I'm sorry." Mrs Hoskins patted her daughter's hand.

"If I could just go back to what you were saying a moment ago, Donna," said Castle patiently. "You mentioned that the three of you – Alan, Jack and yourself – sometimes used to go for a drink together—"

"That was before Alan moved in here," asserted Mrs Hoskins. "She wouldn't have anything to do with Jack after that."

"Please, madam, let your daughter speak for herself. Donna?"

"It's like Mam said – when I first met Alan, he and Jack shared a flat and, yes, we did go out together now and again, but I never enjoyed it."

"Why was that?"

"I don't know, I just didn't feel comfortable with Jack around."

"Can you remember what the three of you used to talk about?"

"Nothing much, the usual things." Donna put down her untouched cup of tea and made vague gestures with her hands. "Mostly it was the two of them talking and me listening – it was never anything very interesting, though, just football, things that happened at work – half the time I wasn't paying much attention."

"Can you remember if they – or maybe just Alan when the two of you were on your own – ever referred particularly to any other person? Their boss, people they worked with, for example?"

"Not really."

"You're sure?"

"I can't think of anyone, really."

Castle put aside the notebook which he had had little occasion to use so far and leaned forward. He reached out and took the young woman by the hand. "Donna," he said earnestly, "the police are trying very hard to catch Alan's killer, but so far we have very little to go on. Even the tiniest piece of information could be useful. Now, I want you to think very hard and try to remember anything unusual that you heard Alan and Jack talking about when the three of you were together. Or maybe, something you might have overheard, in the pub for example? Did you ever go to the toilet and leave them alone together . . . ?"

There was a long silence while Donna appeared deep in thought and her mother fidgeted impatiently, evidently anxious for the interview to come to an end. At last Donna spoke in a voice totally devoid of animation. "I do remember once . . . like you said, I'd been to the loo, and when I got back they had their heads really close together and I heard Alan say something about someone being 'shit-scared of Wallis'. Then they saw me and Alan stood up and asked me if I wanted another drink."

"And nothing more was said about this chap Wallis?" Donna shook her head. "Do you know who he is?"

"I've no idea."

"What about this person who was supposed to be scared of him?"

"I didn't catch the name."

"Didn't Alan say?"

"I never thought to ask." Donna's voice suddenly cracked and she sat back and covered her eyes with her hands. "What does it matter now?" she gasped between racked sobs.

"There, there, lass, you don't have to answer any more questions." Mrs Hoskins gathered her daughter into her arms, stroking her hair and making soothing noises while indicating to Castle with a jerk of her head that the interview was at an end.

He put away his notebook and stood up. At least he had one small crumb of information to add to the meagre store already on record. "Thank you, I'll see myself out," he said.

On arrival back at the station he was greeted by DS Radcliffe who enquired, in a tone that suggested he was expecting a negative reply, whether he had learned anything useful from Donna Hoskins. Castle gave a brief résumé of the interview.

"Wallis, eh?" Radcliffe mused. "The name doesn't ring a bell."

"Nor with me. Have a word with Tomas Rodriguez and see if he can shed any light. There doesn't have to be a connection, of course—" Castle broke off with a gesture of something like despair. "I can't recall a case where there's been so little in the way of solid leads."

There was a knock on the door and DC Hill appeared. "Can you spare a moment, Guv?"

"Sure Tony, come in."

"I don't want to raise false hopes, but there's a chance we might be on to something," said Hill.

"Even a false hope would be better than nothing," Castle observed. "Let's have it, Tony."

The upshot of DC Hill's report was that, after receiving grudging consent from the surly owner of the garage rented by the late Alan Crowson – on the explicit condition that all damage would be paid for in full – Hill and Radcliffe were despatched to break down the door. Inside, they found a quantity of shabby furniture, none of which appeared to have any resale value . . . and a fragment of gilded wood, apparently broken from a picture frame.

"It does seem as if we're a little further forward," said Jim Castle. "Not much, but at least we've got a couple of things to check out, which is more than we had this time yesterday. Thanks, love," he added as Sukey handed him a glass of wine and offered a dish of assorted nibbles. He sat back in the armchair in her cosy sitting-room with a sigh that held a hint of weariness. "I'm trying not to build too many hopes on any of them getting us anywhere, though."

Sukey sat down beside him and he put his free arm round her shoulders. "Frustrating, isn't it?" she said sympathetically.

"The piece of picture frame has been sent off to forensics," Jim went on. "It's just about big enough to give some idea of the design, and the experts will be able to tell what age it is so there's an outside chance it can be identified as coming from an item from one of Roddy's jobs. That at least would suggest a definite link between him and Crowson. And if it turns out that Donna's visits to her mother coincide with the dates of other robberies—"

"You've already admitted that that would only be circumstantial evidence," Sukey pointed out, reflecting ruefully that since Jim had arrived at the house half an hour ago they had spoken of nothing but events surrounding the Bussell Manor robbery and the subsequent deaths of Crowson and Morris.

"On its own, it doesn't carry much weight, but added to other factors . . ."

"I can't imagine it would cut much ice with Superintendent Sladden."

"You're right there." Jim took a mouthful of wine, put down his glass and helped himself to a crisp. "I wish we could get a lead on this chap Wallis."

"The one who's supposed to terrify some person or persons unknown? I take it you've checked with Roddy's firm?"

"Of course. The name didn't ring a bell with anyone there. Speaking of Roddy," Jim added thoughtfully, "I'd give a lot to know where that blighter is at the moment . . . and exactly what he's up to."

It was time for firm action. "I've just had a brilliant idea," said Sukey.

"You have? Let's hear it."

She put down her own glass and nestled against him, bringing her mouth close to his ear. "Why don't we forget about Roddy and Bussell Manor until Monday morning?" she whispered.

He responded by putting his other arm around her, holding her close. "That's the best idea I've heard in a long time," he whispered back.

Several thousand miles away, Miguel Rodriguez lay in a bed in Doctor Gundlach's clinic. Soon, the final remnants of his identity would be taken from him; his appearance would be altered beyond recognition by all but the few who were closest to him. Pepita would not be deceived, he thought in an upsurge of longing but, like so much else that was dear to him, she had been exorcised from his life forever. He was no longer 'Lucky Roddy', the light-hearted, light-fingered bandit who could open up the houses of the wealthy without leaving a trace of his presence, but who had never, until the tragic death of the elderly servant, caused harm to a living soul. Miguel Rodriguez was shortly to die on the operating table, to be reincarnated as Ramon Alvarez from Santo Domingo in the Dominican Republic, heir to a recently deceased Spanish wine merchant.

115

Within a few weeks, just as soon as his scars had healed – and El Dueño had assured him that under Dr Gundlach's skilled hand they would be virtually invisible – Señor Alvarez would be on his way to claim his 'inheritance' and establish himself in Spain. Thence he was to travel to England, ostensibly to set up an office but in reality to resume the business of assisting in the process of relieving wealthy art lovers of the choicest items in their collections. It would have been a prospect to be relished, but for one inescapable factor that filled him with dread. No longer could he deceive himself that he was his own man, working in partnership with, but not subservient to, the shadowy Wallis. From now on, wherever he went, he would feel the evil might of El Dueño behind him. So long as he played his part well, he would survive in luxury. One step out of line and who knew what fate awaited him?

Don't think of failure. Think of pleasant things. Think of Consuela. Consuela with the glowing eyes and husky voice, who had come to the villa every morning to school him in his new rôle and again in the evening to slip into his vast, silken bed. Her passionate, welcoming body, the smooth pliant limbs interlaced with his, had eased but never entirely assuaged his aching hunger for Pepita. Pepita, whom he had been ordered to forget. He felt a surge of impotent rage as he remembered that even her picture had been taken from him. He had been deprived of everything that was his own: his name, his life, his love. Where was Pepita now? Was she even still alive? He groaned aloud at the thought of what fate El Dueño might have ordained for her.

As he waited to be taken to the operating theatre, the thought came into his mind that it would be better if he should die under the anaesthetic.

Sixteen

It had been the intention that Sukey would be on her own in the house before Fergus returned on Sunday evening from the weekend spent with his father, but at eight o'clock, just as she and Jim were finishing their supper, they heard his key in the door. It was not that the lad was unaware of the nature of his mother's friendship with the man with whom she had once, before meeting his father, briefly discussed marriage. On the contrary, hard on the revelation of his own first sexual encounter with the nubile Anita, he had magnanimously given her his blessing. Just the same, Sukey felt a certain reluctance to make the sexual side of her relationship with Jim too obvious. "He's accepted it, but I don't want to ram it down his throat," she had once said to Jim, and with the sensitivity and understanding for which she had come to love him he made a point of avoiding overt physical contact with her in her son's presence.

Fergus came quietly into the kitchen and dumped his overnight bag on the floor. "Hi folks, had a good weekend?" he asked.

"Yes thanks," replied Sukey and Jim in chorus. "How about you?" Jim added.

"It was okay."

"Did you watch the match yesterday?"

"Oh yes." Uncharacteristically, Fergus showed no sign of wanting to talk about football. His eye fell on their almost empty plates. "Any of that left?" he asked.

His mother got up and inspected the casserole. "Just a

117

smidgeon. You're back early. Haven't you had any supper?"

"Oh yes, but you know what Dad's cooking's like. This evening it was cold ham and chips from the freezer." Fergus fetched a plate and emptied the contents of the casserole on to it. "All right if I finish it?" he said as an afterthought.

"Go ahead. I'm afraid we've eaten all the veg."

"Don't worry, I'll have some bread with it. Don't mind me if you want to get on with your puds." He sat down at one corner of the table and began eating.

"It's all right, we'll wait for you," said Jim. Across the table, he and Sukey exchanged glances and a silent message passed between them. "On second thoughts," Jim went on after a moment, I don't think I've got room for any pudding and I've got some unfinished paperwork at home, so I think I'll be on my way. So long Gus, be seeing you." The lad looked up and nodded, but made no reply.

At the front door Jim said in a low voice, "I don't know about you, Sook, but I get the feeling the visit hasn't gone too well."

"I think you're right. I'll try and find out what went wrong." Sukey reached up and twined her arms around Jim's neck. "Good night, and thanks for a wonderful weekend," she whispered.

"As they say in France, it's I who thank you. Good night, love. See you tomorrow."

When Sukey returned to the kitchen she found Fergus staring moodily at his empty plate. She sat down beside him and put an arm round his shoulders. "Something wrong, son?" she asked.

"Not with me, I'm fine. It's just . . . I'm worried about Dad. He's so quiet and sort of sad these days . . ."

"It's understandable. After all it's only a few months since the tragedy."

"I know, but it isn't as if he misses her all that much. They were barely civil to one another during the last months before she was killed and he hardly ever mentions her."

"Just the same, it was a terrible shock."

Fergus nodded. He sat crumbling the remains of a bread roll between his fingers. "It was a shock for you too, Mum – after all, you were the one who found her."

"Don't remind me." Sukey's mind flew back to that terrible April morning when she had been called to Dearley Manor, the house where her ex-husband and his glamorous and wealthy new wife had lived since their marriage, to deal with what appeared to be a simple break-in but had turned out to be an appalling case of murder. The memory of the bloody, mutilated corpse of the woman who had stolen her husband haunted her for a long time. She often thought wryly that, had she been unable to account for her movements at the time of the killing, she could well have been considered a suspect. Heaven knew she had motive enough.

After his cavalier desertion of her and their son, she had felt little sympathy for Paul on learning from Fergus of the gradual deterioration of his new marriage, but it had been impossible for her to remain aloof as he struggled to come to terms with her violent death. There had even been moments when divided loyalties had put her relationship with Jim under a strain. Thank God those days were past.

Fergus took his empty plate to the sink and inspected the untouched treacle tart that stood ready beside the cooker. "What are we having with this?"

"I thought ice-cream – is that okay with you?"

"Fine." He got out plates and spoons while Sukey fetched the tub of ice-cream from the freezer and cut the tart into slices. "Mum," he repeated as they sat down again, "I worry about Dad, I really do."

"Gus, what are you trying to say?" she asked gently.

"I think he'd like you back."

The words came as no surprise, yet they gave her an unexpected jolt. She had long suspected, from odd remarks Fergus had let drop in the past, that she had only to say the word and Paul would come running back to her, begging to be forgiven, to pick up the threads of their old life together, even to remarry. Despite the comfortable relationship Fergus had built up with Jim, she sometimes wondered if that was what her son hoped for as well.

"Is that what you'd like, Gus?" she asked gently.

He concentrated on his portion of treacle tart and did not reply for several minutes. Then, pushing his empty plate away, he gave a sigh. "In an ideal world, I suppose the answer would be 'yes', but I guess it would never work," he said sadly, and she felt a stab of mingled pain and pride at his mature acceptance of the situation. "And there's Jim, isn't there? He'd be devastated if you chucked him and went back to Dad."

"It isn't only because of Jim."

"I know." Fergus grabbed his mother's hand and gave it a fierce, painful squeeze. His eyes were moist and his upper lip, with its carefully nurtured trace of a moustache, trembled.

"Try not to worry about your father, Gus. He's feeling a bit sorry for himself at present, but he'll get by. With any luck, he'll meet someone else before long."

Fergus brightened. "I think one of the secretaries at the office is quite keen on him, although he makes out there's nothing in it."

"Well, there you are then." Sukey stood up and began clearing the table. "Let's get on with the washing-up, shall we? And don't let's be too late to bed – it's work for us both tomorrow."

Shortly after eight o'clock on Monday morning, DI Castle put his head round the door of the SOCOs' office to look for George Barnes. On seeing the desk empty he turned to leave, almost colliding with Sukey as she returned from the recently-installed drinks machine with a polystyrene cup of tea.

"Oops – sorry!" he apologised. He followed her into the room, giving a quick glance over his shoulder to make sure there was no one within earshot, and whispered, "Did you sleep well?"

She turned a glowing face to him. "Like a baby, thanks. How about you?"

"Likewise." His eyes lingered on hers for a moment. "Did you find out what was bugging Fergus?"

"He's concerned about his father – says he's pretty down in the dumps. It's only natural, of course, but I think it's a bit much for Paul to burden Gus with his problems, especially as he's never been one to bother himself with ours."

"Don't let it get to you love. Gus is a pretty resilient lad, he'll be okay. Takes after his mother, doesn't he?" He gave her hand a surreptitious squeeze and she acknowledged it with a grateful smile. "Have a good day – I'll call you this evening. And will you tell George when he comes in that I'd like a word with him?"

"Will do." There was a sound of approaching footsteps in the corridor. "That's probably him now."

"Something's tickled him, by the sound of it," said Castle as a rousing guffaw heralded the arrival of Sergeant Barnes and Mandy Parfitt, both smiling broadly. "What's the joke?"

"Henry Greenleaf's place has been done over." Barnes handed Castle a sheet from the sheaf of papers he brought with him. "How's that for a bit of poetic justice?"

"Who's Henry Greenleaf and what's so funny about his place being done over?" Sukey asked Mandy as the two men studied the details of the report with evident relish.

"He's a fence, according to George," said Mandy.

"*Suspected* fence," Barnes corrected. "He runs what he describes as an antiques business, but it's really a glorified pawnshop off Barton Street – it looks a dingy little dump from the outside but it seems to support him in a pretty comfortable life-style. His father was a goldsmith from central Europe and the family fled from the Nazis and settled in Birmingham just before the war. His son inherited his business acumen but not his skill."

"You seem to know a lot about him," Sukey commented.

"We ran a check on him some months ago when one of

our officers spotted a suspect in a jewel robbery leaving his premises," Castle explained. "He affected to be very shocked when we told him the man had form, explained that he hadn't been trying to sell anything, had only called in to enquire about a clock, swore he'd never have any dealings with him in future and so on. We've never been able to pin anything dodgy on him – on the contrary, he's always been most co-operative about passing on details of stuff he's been offered that he suspects of being hot. In fact, we've picked up several villains as a result of information he's given us."

"So why do you suspect him?"

"We aren't convinced that he's as squeaky clean as he'd have us believe, which makes us wonder whether for every small-time job he tips us off about, there may be something more substantial that he forgets to mention." Castle handed the report back to Sergeant Barnes. "Keep me posted on that one, George. And there are a couple of other things I want to talk to you about."

"Yes, Guv. If you don't mind waiting a second while I dish these jobs out – can't have our SOCOs standing idle, can we?" Barnes glanced briefly through the rest of the reports before dividing them into two and handing them over. "You've got the Henry Greenleaf job, Sukey. Remember to give him the VIP treatment – the DI's orders," he added with a wink.

"Will do," she promised.

The glow of happiness was still with her as, humming a tune, she set off on the short drive to the turning off Barton Street where Greenleaf ran his business from a single-fronted shop with the legend 'Henry Greenleaf Antiques' in faded gold lettering on a dingy fascia board below the traditional pawn-broker's insignia of three golden globes. When she arrived at the scene, a minor local drama was being played out, watched with delighted interest by a cluster of schoolchildren on the opposite side of the street. A portly man in an ill-fitting grey suit was standing on the pavement outside the shop, wildly waving his arms and gesticulating at the empty spaces on the

122

shelves and the heavy iron bar lying among the fragments of glass from the shattered window, at the same time hurling abuse at a young constable who was trying, bravely but unsuccessfully, to get a word in edgeways. "I run an honest business," Sukey heard the man shout as she locked the van. "I do my best to help the police and where are they when my shop is attacked? Nowhere to be seen. Why weren't they here to protect me when I needed them, that's what I'd like to know."

"If you could just come inside for a minute and give me a few details and a list of the missing items," the officer interposed when the outraged victim momentarily ran out of steam, "our Scenes of Crime Officer," – he nodded in Sukey's direction – "will be able to start work."

Still grumbling, Greenleaf allowed himself to be steered towards the entrance to the shop. "It couldn't have happened at a worse time," he complained. "I'm expecting some important visitors very shortly. What a start to a Monday morning – my place burgled and my assistant hasn't turned up yet. Ah, there she is, and about time too. Gladys, you're late!" he bawled at the thin, middle-aged woman clutching a shopping bag, who had arrived unnoticed and was looking at the damage with her mouth open. "Don't just stand there gawping, get busy sweeping up the mess."

"Er, not just yet if you don't mind," Sukey interposed. "I'd like to have a look round first – it shouldn't take too long. I daresay you'll want to arrange temporary repairs."

"Yes, yes, you see to that, Gladys. And don't forget, Mr Wallis will be here shortly. Did you buy his favourite biscuits?"

"Yes, Mr Greenleaf," said Gladys meekly as she followed the two men inside, while the children, realising that the fun was over, reluctantly moved on.

Before getting down to work, Sukey spent a few moments surveying the scene. It had been a typical smash-and-grab affair leaving little hope that, unless there happened to be witnesses to the crime or identifiable prints on the implement that had caused the damage, there was much prospect of nailing the culprits. She picked up and bagged the iron bar before turning her attention to the items remaining in the window, which included a motley assortment of artefacts and ornaments in china, silver and glass, some of which had been overturned and broken as the thieves reached in to grab what they wanted. Most were scattered over several empty trays that, at a guess, had contained small items of easily disposed of jewellery, but among the shards of glass on the pavement lay the remains of a porcelain vase, probably intended to be part of the loot, that the thieves had dropped in their haste. It might possibly bear the odd fingerprint.

Once more humming softly to herself, Sukey squatted down to gather up the delicate fragments. As she got on with the task in hand, half her mind was still happily preoccupied with more pleasant things. It was not until much later that she realised that there had been something particularly significant about the scenes she had just witnessed.

Seventeen

Sukey had just finished her examination when the constable emerged from the shop. "What a pain in the neck!" he muttered in her ear. "Thinks just because he's shopped a couple of small-time villains he's entitled to round-the-clock police protection." He glanced at the bags of samples she held in her hand. "Find anything useful?"

She shrugged. "We'll have to see. Probably not, but if they didn't wear gloves and we've got their prints on our files, we might get lucky."

"Well, good hunting!" He went back to his car, whistling. As he pulled away, a silver-grey BMW drew up in the space that he had just vacated. One of this morning's important visitors, perhaps. Squatting on the pavement to repack her bag, Sukey noticed the driver bend down as if fumbling with something in the passenger footwell. He had still not alighted from the car when she went into the shop to make her report.

The interior had a fusty, stale atmosphere. The shelves lining three of the four walls were crammed with a bewildering assortment of articles in polished wood, brass, copper, china and glass. No attempt had been made to display the stock in any kind of order; apart from a long-case clock just inside the door it seemed to Sukey's relatively inexperienced eye that there was little of any particular value or likely to appeal to a serious collector. At the far end of the shop was a glass-topped counter behind which stood Gladys, fidgeting with some papers. She looked up with a nervous start as a bell, activated when Sukey stepped on to the mat inside the door, let out a shrill warning. "Did you find any clues?" she asked.

"Maybe one or two." Sukey held up the bags of samples. "I'm taking these back to the lab for testing and someone will be in touch when we get the results. It's okay to sweep up outside and get the repairs under way now."

"Oh right, thank you."

The bell sounded again and both women turned towards the door. Sukey stood aside as a tall, bearded man holding a brown paper parcel under one arm approached the counter. "You appear to have had a spot of trouble," he commented with a jerk of his head towards the shattered window. "I have an appointment with Mr Greenleaf, but perhaps I should come back another time."

Gladys checked an open diary that lay on the counter beside the telephone. "Is it Mr Smith?" she asked in a brisk, businesslike voice that made a faintly comic contrast to her nervous manner of a few moments ago.

"That's right. John Smith."

Presumably, this was the driver of the BMW. Idly watching him, Sukey had the impression that he was slightly tense. John Smith was quite possibly his real name; there were any number in the telephone book, but just the same . . . she recalled the comments DI Castle and Sergeant Barnes had exchanged about Henry Greenleaf, and an earlier reference to important visitors, for one of whom special biscuits had to be provided. She found herself making a careful note of the newcomer's appearance. Was there something vaguely familiar about the thin nose and hollow cheeks? It was impossible to be sure.

Gladys placed a careful tick against an entry in the diary. "Yes, it has been a little upsetting," she said, "but the police are dealing with the matter and I'm sure Mr Greenleaf will want to keep the appointment." She picked up the phone and pressed a key. From somewhere overhead a buzzer sounded. "Mr Smith is here," she said. A series of sharp barks emanated from the receiver, to which she responded with a deferential,

"Yes, Mr Greenleaf," before replacing it and turning back to the newcomer. "Mr Greenleaf will see you right away, Mr Smith. Will you please come this way?" She lifted a flap at the end of the counter and ushered him through a door. There came a sound of heavy footsteps descending an uncarpeted staircase and a moment later Sukey heard Greenleaf greeting his visitor in an ingratiating manner quite unlike the bullying tactics he used on those he considered his underlings. An unpleasant man, she decided, and wondered why Gladys put up with him.

As if the woman read her thoughts, she gave a deprecating smile as she closed the door and returned to her position behind the counter. "He can be very charming, but he's easily upset. I suppose it's because he's got foreign blood," she added. "Foreigners do tend to get excited, don't they?"

"Yes, I suppose they do," Sukey agreed. "Is Mr Smith a regular customer?" she added casually.

"I don't remember seeing him before, but I only work here part-time." Gladys shot Sukey an enquiring glance. "Why do you ask?"

"No special reason – I just wondered. Well, I'd better be getting on to my next job."

"And I must start sweeping up the mess. If you wouldn't mind waiting there a second while I go out the back and fetch a broom – just in case someone comes in . . ."

"Of course."

Gladys disappeared through the door behind the counter and Sukey went over and stood by the shop entrance. Through the glass panel she saw a dark red Jaguar with two men in it pull in to the kerb in front of the BMW. The passenger, a sleek, dapper-looking man in a camel coat with a leather briefcase in one hand, got out of the front seat and turned to speak briefly to the driver before slamming the door and striding towards the shop. He stopped outside for a moment, eyeing the debris on the pavement, before entering. The jangle of the bell coincided with the reappearance of Gladys, carrying a heavy broom which she hastily put down at the sight of the new arrival. "Good morning sir," she said, looking slightly flustered. "Please go straight up, Mr Greenleaf is expecting you." She lifted the flap on the counter and stood aside; he brushed past her without returning her greeting or her polite smile of welcome, leaving behind a whiff of an expensive, musky body lotion.

"Another of nature's gentlemen – I don't think!" said Sukey to herself as she made her exit. Her van was parked a short distance in front of the Jaguar, which was the latest model and bore a personalised number plate. The newcomer was evidently a man of substance, the type whom one would not normally expect to patronise a scruffy business in a back street . . . unless of course police suspicions were correct and the scruffiness was just a facade.

The driver of the Jaguar, a youngish man with cropped hair and a heavy gold ring in his left ear, was leaning back in his seat, a cigarette in one hand and a magazine spread across the steering wheel. He appeared to take no notice of her as she passed, but when she had finished stowing her gear and was closing the rear door of the van she happened to glance back and noticed that he was sitting bolt upright, apparently gazing straight ahead. His eyes were completely screened behind dark glasses, yet she had the strong impression that he was staring at her. It was not the first time that a stranger, casually encountered, had shown an interest in her, yet something about this man's attitude, tense and immobile like an animal watching its prey, made her nerve-ends tingle.

She told herself not to be stupid, got into the van, settled in the driver's seat and clipped on her safety belt. She reached up to adjust her rear-view mirror and saw that the driver of the Jaguar was studying something that he held in his right hand, something that might have been a postcard or a photograph. As she drove away he looked up, smiled and raised whatever it was in a kind of mocking salute.

*   *   *

Copycat

The man calling himself John Smith sat in the dingy office above Henry Greenleaf's shop and waited with barely concealed excitement while the proprietor and the man introduced to him as Mr Wallis, after some preliminary polite exchanges over the coffee and chocolate biscuits provided by Gladys, bent over the small, gilt-framed picture that he unwrapped with meticulous care and laid almost reverently on the shabby mahogany desk. Neither man commented or showed any reaction; after a preliminary inspection Wallis took out a pocket magnifying glass and began moving it, inch by inch with tantalising slowness, over every detail of the canvas. Now and again he and Greenleaf exchanged glances; from the barely perceptible movements of the head, the pursing of lips and the twitching of eyebrows it was clear to the observer, trying to appear relaxed and confident but inwardly tense and impatient, that unspoken messages were passing between them. At one point, finding the prolonged silence all but unendurable, he remarked, "There's no doubt in my mind that it's genuine," and when there was no response, he added nervously, "The frame's original too." Both remarks dropped into the oppressive silence like pebbles into a bottomless well.

At last Wallis put the glass back in his pocket and helped himself to the last chocolate biscuit. Having eaten it, he wiped his fingers on a spotless white handkerchief before saying casually, "Would you mind telling us how you came by this painting, Mr, er, Smith?"

"It's from a private collection. The owner wishes to remain anonymous . . . for tax reasons, you understand." It was the carefully prepared and rehearsed reply to the anticipated question, yet he had the uneasy feeling that they did not believe him. He began to wonder if his informant had got it wrong. Were Greenleaf and his associate after all law-abiding citizens who would denounce him to the police? His stomach contracted in a sudden attack of panic, but it was too late to have second thoughts now.

After a further exchange of glances, Wallis spoke again and

for the first time his voice betrayed a hint of a foreign accent. "No doubt, this, er, anonymous owner has other items that he might consider selling?"

"It's possible. I can ask him. In the meantime, do I take it that you are interested in making an offer for the Turner?"

"We should like to see the rest of the collection first."

"So far as I know, this is the only item which my client wishes to sell."

The two men at the desk exchanged faintly amused glances. The visitor began to feel uneasy. This was not the reaction he had expected. Haggling over the price, yes; he was prepared for plenty of that before a deal was struck, but not this unexpected reference to a collection. What were they driving at?

A further unspoken message appeared to pass between the two dealers. After a moment, Wallis said, almost casually, "What about the Louis the Fourteenth ewer? Or the bust of Napoleon, attributed to Canova? Or perhaps the little Japanese lacquer cabinet . . . do I make myself clear?"

"I'm sure Mr Smith understands the situation pefectly," said Greenleaf while their victim sat trembling and open-mouthed, aghast at the realisation that his carefully laid scheme had been shot to pieces and desperately trying to figure out where he had gone wrong. "And in the meantime," Greenleaf continued, "we will take good care of this." He returned the painting to its wrappings, carried it across the room and opened an old-fashioned metal safe. He put the little parcel inside and relocked it with a heavy iron key. "You may tell your 'anonymous owner'," he said softly, "that his precious Turner is in good hands."

"Excellent," said Wallis. He too stood up. "Shall we go?"

The man who had so confidently introduced himself as John Smith passed his tongue over lips gone suddenly dry. "Go where?"

"To wherever you have stored the remainder of your haul, of course." The tone was no longer bland, but sharp and stinging as a whiplash, the narrowed eyes hard as granite.

He had walked into a trap. He had no idea on which side of the law these two men stood, how they had come to know the source of the painting or how they knew that he had stolen other items from the collection. In his confused state of mind his one thought was flight. As he rose to his feet, his knees almost buckling so that he had to steady himself with one hand on the desk, his eyes sought the door, measuring the distance and the time it would take him to reach it, realising that any attempt at escape would be futile.

The three men descended the uncarpeted staircase, Wallis leading the way with Greenleaf bringing up the rear. Sandwiched between them, Smith felt something hard pressing into the small of his back and heard a soft whisper in his ear. "No silly tricks, Mr Smith." As they passed through the shop, Greenleaf paused to inform Gladys, who was showing an elderly woman how to wind the clock she had just bought, that he would not be back until after lunch.

"You lead the way and we'll follow," said Wallis as they stepped outside, his tone as casual as if they were going on a normal business trip.

The street was empty. There was no one to whom he could appeal for help, even had he dared. He watched helplessly as the chauffeur held the door open for Wallis to get into the waiting Jaguar before strolling across to the BMW and standing guard behind him as he unlocked it and slid behind the wheel. Greenleaf took off his jacket and casually draped it across his lap, concealing his left hand as he settled into the seat beside him. As with shaking hands he buckled his seat belt and put the key in the ignition, he felt a momentary jab in the thigh.

"No silly tricks," Greenleaf repeated softly. "Just give us a nice quiet drive to where the stuff is hidden and you won't get hurt."

It was the end of a dream, the start of a nightmare. With despair in his heart, he started the engine and pulled away.

The chauffeur, whom the others addressed as Marty, kept

him covered with the gun while they stripped the cellar of its contents. He watched helplessly as a fortune slipped from his fingers. Precious items were taken from their wrappings, examined, exclaimed over, repacked and carefully transported up the stairs. He pictured them loading the waiting car and wondered if there was a faint chance that a passer-by would see them, become suspicious and raise the alarm. Not that it would be of much help; the spoils of his one attempt at burglary were irretrievably lost and discovery would merely lead to his own arrest and probable imprisonment.

When they had finished, there was a shout of "Marty!" through the open trap-door. The chauffeur lowered the gun and began to mount the stairs. Nervously, still fearing attack, the prisoner followed. No attempt was made to stop him, but he had taken only a few steps when he saw Greenleaf, who was waiting at the top, pull something from his pocket and toss it down towards him. It flew over his shoulder and he swung round to look as it landed on the floor behind him. He recognised it immediately: a little Victorian brooch in the shape of a love-knot, set with diamonds that glittered enticingly in the light from the ceiling.

"Give that to your girlfriend!" called Greenleaf. His voice echoed in mockery round the empty cellar. "Consolation prize!"

It was what he had been intending to do. At the sight of it lying there, all that remained of his vision of an idyllic future with the woman he loved, he let out a groan of mingled rage and misery. Half blinded with emotion, he bent to retrieve it, but before his fingers reached it something exploded inside his head and sent him spinning into eternal darkness.

Eighteen

The remainder of Monday passed comparatively uneventfully. Recalling DI Castle's request to be kept informed on the break-in at Henry Greenleaf's shop, Sukey attached to her report a brief message about the two well-heeled visitors and left it with Sergeant Barnes for him to note and pass on. She half expected Castle to follow it up later, but there was no further contact with him that day.

She was on the point of leaving for work on Tuesday morning when the telephone rang.

"Glad I caught you," said Jim. The lack of any greeting and a certain staccato harshness in his voice told her something serious had happened. "Do you know a village called Parkfield?"

"I've heard of it. Somewhere in the Stroud valley?"

"That's right. We've had another killing and I'd like you to come straight here."

"I'll need some directions."

"Fork right off the A46 between Painswick and Stroud. There's a No Through Road on the left just as you enter the village. It's the only house along there – Beacon Cottage. Man shot through the back of the head."

She grasped the significance immediately. "Same MO as—"

"Exactly. Get here as soon as you can. I've left a message for George Barnes so he'll know where you are."

"I'm on my way."

The clouds were beginning to lift after overnight rain and by the time Sukey turned into the steep, narrow lane signposted

Parkfield, the sun was beginning to break through. She felt a familiar feeling of apprehension as she approached her destination; since starting the job, she had attended several murder scenes and the sight of a corpse, however little disfigured, never failed to bring on a spasm of queasiness. Not that she was alone in that, she thought with a grim smile as, following Castle's directions, she took the even narrower turning on the outskirts of the village. She had seen hardened police officers throwing up with the best of them.

The cottage, named for its position at the foot of Painswick Beacon, could hardly have been more isolated. The tiny, two-storey dwelling was a good quarter of a mile from the village; at present it was partially visible through an as yet almost leafless hedge of ash and elder, but within a few weeks and throughout the summer it would be entirely hidden both from the lane and from other houses in the village.

The track ended in a wide, gravelled area which had evidently been laid out as a car park for ramblers; a printed notice requested visitors to take their rubbish home and a small green signpost beside a stile pointed to a footpath leading across a steeply rising field behind the cottage. This morning it was occupied by a police patrol car, DI Castle's maroon Montego, an ambulance and a 4WD vehicle which Sukey recognised as that belonging to a forensic pathologist, summoned to examine the body of yet another murder victim. She parked her van beside the ambulance, acknowledging the cheery wave of the crew, who were sitting in the cab sharing the contents of a flask and evidently prepared for a longish wait.

The heavy wooden gate bearing the carved name 'Beacon Cottage' stood open. Sukey ducked under the blue and white tape that had been strung between the posts and found herself in a small, neglected front garden where little grew but weeds and a few leggy roses still bearing the withered remains of last summer's blooms. An estate agent's board bearing the word 'Sold' lay on its side behind a silver-grey BMW tucked up in one corner. The sight of the car gave her a jolt, making her pulse quicken and banishing for the moment the incipient nausea as she picked her way gingerly along the uneven mossy path, muddied in places and slippery after the rain, to the front door.

"Where's the DI?" she asked the uniformed constable standing guard.

"In the cellar – the door's in the kitchen at the end of the passage. The medic's there as well, examining the body, and DS Radcliffe's in the living-room talking to the man who found it. Says he was out walking his dog, the hound was sniffing around in the front garden and then ran into the house through the open front door. Next thing he hears it alternately growling and whimpering so he goes in to investigate, finds it at the top of the cellar steps with its hackles up, glimpses what's lying at the bottom and rushes out to call us on his mobile. He's refused point blank to take a closer look at the victim, but he says the car belongs to the chap who bought the cottage a few weeks ago. Pretty shook up, he is. I daresay he could do with a cup of tea," the constable added hopefully.

"Then why don't you go and make one?" Sukey retorted as she entered the cottage. She found herself in a flagged passage with a door at the far end which stood open, revealing the kitchen. She heard a sudden sharp bark and DS Radcliffe emerged from a room on her left.

"Morning Sukey, glad to see you," he said with an ingratiating smile. "The gentleman who found the body is very shaken up – d'you think you could rustle up a cup of tea?"

"What is it about you men?" she demanded with an indignation that was not entirely feigned. "The minute a woman appears you pretend you don't know how to put a kettle on."

"I just thought—"

"Well think again. My first job is to report to the DI. I'll tell him what you said," she added over her shoulder as she headed for the kitchen.

Sunlight from an east-facing window streamed into the tiny room, which was simply, almost barely furnished and contained no modern appliances apart from a sink with a wooden draining-board and a cooker and refrigerator, both of which had seen better days. In the far corner was another door leading to a glass lean-to which, like the rest of the place, had a slightly ramshackle appearance.

Sukey gave a start as a disembodied voice that sounded as if it was coming from beneath her feet called, "That you, Sook?"

"Yes," she called back.

There was the sound of footsteps and the next moment DI Castle appeared from behind an old-fashioned wooden dresser which occupied almost the whole of one wall. "The victim's down there." He pointed to an open trap-door in the floor behind him. "Doctor Harding has completed his examination and I'd like you to have a quick look round and take some pictures before we move him." As he spoke, a grey-haired man carrying a black case appeared, gave Sukey a perfunctory nod, promised Castle to send his report as soon as possible and took his leave.

"Any idea when it happened?" Sukey asked.

"Harding won't commit himself – will they ever? – but probably within the last twenty-four hours."

Sukey nodded, her mind busy. "That car outside . . . I'm pretty sure I saw it yesterday, outside Henry Greenleaf's shop. I left a message for you . . ."

"Yes, I got it, but I haven't had time to follow it up. You reckon it's the same car?"

"I didn't make a note of the number, but it was certainly the same make and colour. I was in the shop when the driver came in; he said his name was John Smith and he had an appointment. He looked vaguely familiar . . ."

"The man who found the body, a Mr Henry Banfield, knows him as John Smith – assuming it is the new owner, that is," Castle interrupted. "He says some of the people in the village reckon it's an assumed name and that he's bought the place as a love nest."

"I had the same impression . . . about the name being assumed, I mean. And then another man turned up, a spivvy type in a flashy Jag. I assume he and John Smith were the important visitors Greenleaf said he was expecting. I think he said one of them was called Wallis—"

"Wallis?" Castle's voice was sharp with interest. "Are you sure?"

"That's what it sounded like."

"Don't you remember my telling you how Donna Hoskins heard Crowson refer to a man called Wallis?"

"I do, now you come to mention it, but I'm afraid it didn't ring a bell at the time," Sukey admitted ruefully.

"And he and this Smith character both have dealings with Henry Greenleaf," Castle mused. "Well, well, this is getting interesting. I take it you got a good look at them?"

"Enough to recognise them again, I think."

Castle gave a grim smile. "I doubt if you'll be able to recognise this one. I should warn you, he's not a pretty sight, but it's cool down there so at least he hasn't started to smell." He gave her arm a squeeze. "Sure you'll be okay?"

"I daresay I've seen worse," she responded bravely. "By the way, both Sergeant Radcliffe and the PC on the door seem to think it's every woman's mission in life to make cups of tea."

Castle's severe features relaxed in a momentary grin. "I guess we could all do with one when we've finished the preliminaries," he said. "We haven't any positive ID, but we'll go through his pockets when we get him to the morgue. I've asked for a check on the owner of the vehicle. Now, if you're ready . . . ?" He gave her a searching glance and she responded with a nod. "We might as well get this over with. Mind how you go, the steps are steep and a bit worn in places."

The kitchen was already beginning to warm up in the morning sun and the air in the cellar struck a chill contrast as, holding her bag of equipment in one hand and clinging to a metal rail attached to the wall with the other, Sukey gingerly followed Castle down the narrow flight. It led to a surprisingly large chamber lit by a fluorescent tube; from the freshly-swept appearance of the beaten earth floor and the brand-new cables running across the ceiling it was clear that the new owner had already made a start on the renovation of the property.

The body lay face down in a crumpled heap at the foot of the steps. At the sight of the hideous mess of blood, brains and bone that had once been a man's head, Sukey closed her eyes, swallowed hard and took several deep breaths.

"From bruising to the face – or what's left of it – the doctor reckons he went crashing down the steps after being shot," Castle explained. "What we'd like to know is, what was he doing in the cellar? As you can see, it's completely empty and there's no sign of anything that he might be intending to store down there."

"So maybe there was something there, and that's what the killer was after?"

"Exactly. I want you to go over every inch of it with a toothcomb to see if you can find anything useful."

"Will do."

At that moment the young officer descended the steps, averting his gaze from the bloodied heap at the bottom. "I've got the info on the car you asked for, Guv," he reported. "It's registered in the name of a Mrs Miriam Lockyer of Tewkesbury."

"It's probably her husband's, registered in her name for tax purposes," Castle observed. "I'll get someone round there straight away and find out whether hubby's at home or unaccountably absent." He turned to Sukey, who was unloading her camera. "You okay on your own for a moment? My radio won't function down here."

"Don't be too long," she pleaded, but he was already out of earshot.

There was only one way to deal with a stomach-churning situation such as this, she told herself as she settled down to her gruesome task. Treat the body as if it was a model, a waxwork. As a child she had been taken to the Chamber of Horrors at Madame Tussauds and some of the exhibits had haunted her dreams for nights. With hindsight, and a few years later, she had been able to laugh about it. Graveyard humour was a safety valve that had helped many an officer attending a death scene to overcome their normal feelings of shock and revulsion, and the thought came to her rescue now.

With her mind so occupied, she managed to keep the urge to throw up under control while she snapped away at the corpse and its blood-spattered surroundings. When she had finished she began an examination of the rest of the cellar, but apart from a few loose fragments of plaster and some discarded scraps of electric cable on the floor she found nothing of any significance.

"There's not much here to help us," she informed Castle when he reappeared a few moments later.

"What about shoe prints?"

"Not a hope. The floor's as hard as iron and whoever swept up after the workmen did a pretty thorough job."

"D'you reckon that is the guy you saw at Greenleaf's place?"

"The clothes are the same, that's all I can say. One thing, the soles of his shoes are clean. It was raining heavily by five o'clock yesterday and the front path is quite muddy, so it looks as if he got here before then."

"And the car's wet, so it's probably been here ever since." Castle pursed his lips as he considered the point. "Right," he said after a moment, "if you've finished, we'll hand him over to the ambulance crew. Constable Ray's just brewing up," he added and Sukey was surprised to find herself able to acknowledge his wink with a grin. She even chuckled aloud on learning that Henry Banfield, having recovered his nerve sufficiently to sign the statement DS Radcliffe wrote out for him, had declined the belated offer of tea and taken his leave.

When the pot had been drained and the mortal remains of the man known locally as John Smith had been removed by the visibly shaken ambulance crew, Castle began rapping out orders to Radcliffe while Sukey, bracing herself for a second – although considerably less harrowing – visit to the murder scene, prepared to resume her task. Half an hour later she emerged from the cellar to find Castle sitting alone at the plain deal table with his chin propped in his hands, his notebook open in front of him. He looked up with a tired smile as she put her case on the floor and sat down opposite him.

"Find anything?" he asked with a noticeable lack of optimism.

"A hell of a lot of blood," she answered with a shudder. "It's all over the walls and floor from about the fourth step from the bottom downwards, so at a guess that was where he was standing when he was shot. And I picked up this." She held up a transparent plastic sachet.

"What is it?"

"It's a brooch. It was lying under the body and it's covered in blood." She handed him the sachet and he studied it thoughtfully for several moments before handing it back.

"What d'you make of it?" he asked.

"I can't be sure, but I think it might be Victorian. It looks very much like one my grandmother used to wear."

"So what does that tell us, I wonder?"

"That it's possibly part of a larger haul that the victim had hidden in the cellar and that the killer dropped it while making off with the rest of the goodies?" she suggested.

"My first thoughts exactly. Now," – Castle referred to his notebook – "I've made a list of points that suggest a common factor between the disappearance of Miguel Rodriguez and the three shootings, i.e. this one and those of Crowson and Morris." He tapped the open pages with the end of his ballpoint pen as he went through them. "Point one: All three victims were shot in the back of the head. It's been established that the same weapon was used in the case of the first two and I'd be prepared to bet

140

that we'll find it was used to kill Smith – or whatever his real name is – as well."

"Which suggests we're looking for a professional hit-man," said Sukey with a shudder.

"Right. Point two: Smith has a rendezvous with Henry Greenleaf, who for all his squeaky-clean reputation has long been suspected of having dubious connections. Point three: also at that meeting is a guy called Wallis, and Donna Hoskins overheard a reference by Crowson to someone being 'shit-scared of Wallis'. It's not that unusual a name, but let's assume for the moment it's the same bloke. Point four: We're agreed that the trinket you picked up is probably part of a larger haul. Would you care to guess where it might have come from?"

"I think so." Sukey's brain suddenly went into overdrive as the conclusion he was leading up to became clear. "D'you mind if I have a shot at point five?" she said eagerly.

"Go ahead."

"When John Smith turned up in Greenleaf's shop, I thought there was something familiar about him but I couldn't place him. It's just come to me – he looked very like a man in a silver-grey BMW who turned up at Bussell Manor just as Mandy and I were leaving. And isn't Lockyer the name of the chap who advises Wilbur Patterson what items to add to his collection?"

"You're right!" Castle slapped his forehead. "How did I come to miss that?"

"You'd have spotted it sooner or later. You picked up the reference to Wallis that I missed," she added diplomatically, but she could tell from his expression that his mind had already moved on.

"I wonder what business he had with Greenleaf," he muttered.

"Maybe Greenleaf had offered to put him in the way of something of interest."

"Or he had something to offer, something he wanted fenced."

"Come to think of it," said Sukey, "he did have a parcel with him."

"What sort of parcel?"

She thought for a moment, trying to recall the scene. "Rectangular, done up in brown paper . . ."

"How big?"

"About the size of a standard pocket wallet, only thicker." Seeing the gleam of excitement that had appeared in Castle's greenish eyes, she added, "Is it important?"

"It might well be. It so happens that the most valuable item taken from Patterson's collection was a small painting by Turner in its original frame."

Sukey felt her mouth fall open. "Golly!" she exclaimed in an awed voice. "Do you really think—"

"I think it's time we had another chat with Henry Greenleaf, and his mysterious friend Mr Wallis. Of course," he went on, "each one of our five points on its own could be put down to coincidence – as no doubt Superintendent Sladden would take great pleasure in pointing out – but taken together they look pretty significant to me. There are still plenty of unanswered questions, though. The first one that comes to my mind is, is there a link between this killing and Roddy's disappearance?" He closed his notebook with a snap and stood up. "We won't find any answers hanging about here, Sook. As soon as Andy Radcliffe gets back from the village I'll be away from here, and I want you to go back to the office, write up your report and get everything over to forensics as quickly as possible."

"Right. And then what?"

She had become so involved in the exchange of ideas that she was beginning to think of herself as a fully-fledged member of the detection team. It came as a slight shock when he said, "Go to your next job, of course."

As she left the cottage a white police van drew up and a number of uniformed officers tumbled out. "Here to look for the weapon, I suppose," she said to herself as she drove away. "Fat chance!"

Nineteen

It was a little after nine o'clock when DS Radcliffe arrived at Parkfield Village Store and Post Office. A battered pick-up loaded with bales of hay was parked outside and an elderly bicycle was propped against the window. On either side of the street, cottages of Cotswold stone basked in the sun behind their tidy front gardens and a black and white cat sat grooming itself on a wall and pretending to ignore a blackbird that was sounding a staccato warning from a hawthorn bush. An air of peace and tranquillity – soon to be shattered when news of the crime became known – hung over the place. Radcliffe had seen it all before: the reporters, the photographers, the TV camera crews, all jostling for somewhere to park their vehicles and clamouring for interviews, quotes and statements from the police, while ghoulish sightseers hung around hoping to be caught in someone's lens and find their picture in the next day's paper. From the point of view of the media it would be a nine days' wonder, but for the inhabitants of this idyllic corner of the countryside the shock-waves would continue to reverberate long after the case was closed. If it ever *is* closed, he muttered to himself as he pushed open the door of the little shop. He was beginning to share DI Castle's pessimism.

Inside, a small knot of people were clustered round the counter, behind which stood a grey-haired, bespectacled woman. Her face bore the pattern of lines round the mouth and crow's-feet round the eyes normally associated with laughter, but there was nothing humorous in her expression now. As Radcliffe entered she was saying, in a voice that quavered, "I gave him a cup of tea with a dash of rum in it before he went home, the poor man's that shook up you wouldn't believe." It was evident that Banfield had made this his first port of call on leaving Beacon Cottage.

Radcliffe slid a hand in his pocket and brought out his identity card, but before he had a chance to show it a young man in green overalls, doubtless the driver of the pick-up, said, "I guess you'll be one of the detectives looking into it – can you tell us what's happened?"

"At this stage, all I can tell you is that we're investigating a very nasty murder," Radcliffe replied. "The reason I'm here is that I'm hoping some of you ladies and gentlemen will be able to help us with our enquiries."

"It's the gentleman who bought Beacon Cottage, isn't it?" said a ruddy-faced white-haired lady in a shabby anorak and tweed trousers, whom Radcliffe guessed to be the owner of the bicycle. She turned to the postmistress, who was leaning plump forearms on the array of magazines set out on the counter. "We always thought there was something fishy about him, didn't we?" She glanced round for confirmation and there was a general nodding of heads. Evidently, John Smith had been regarded by at least some of his new neighbours with a certain amount of reserve.

"What gave you that impression?" the detective asked.

"Hardly ever showed himself in the village, did he?" a small wisp of a woman with sharp features and a hairy upper lip piped up. "Typical weekender, come and go as they please, hardly bother to give the people who live here the time of day."

"We don't know he's – was – a weekender," the postmistress pointed out. "He's – was – having a lot of work done to the cottage. You never know, he and his wife might have been planning to live there once it's fit to live in."

"Wife!" snorted the white-haired lady. "If that po-faced little madam I saw outside the cottage when I walked past a couple of weeks ago is his wife, I'd be very surprised. A bottle blonde half his age with eyes the colour of lead shot and about as hard – practically looked through me when I said 'Good morning'."

"I've always thought there was something suspicious about anyone calling himself John Smith," the wispy lady interposed. "It's what these naughty men do when they stay at hotels with ladies who aren't their wives, isn't it?" She gave a little snigger and put a hand to her mouth, like a schoolgirl who has just told a dirty joke.

"When was the first time any of you saw him?" Radcliffe asked as the others exchanged covert, amused glances.

"That would be last October or thereabouts, soon after the cottage went on the market," said the postmistress. "Old Mr Hedges died and the family wanted a quick sale. Quite a lot of people were interested – Mr Smith was the first of several people who called in at the shop to ask for directions. And he's hardly set foot in here since," she added tartly.

"Would any of you happen to know what car he drove?"

The ladies shook their heads and exchanged helpless glances, but the young man, who had not spoken since his initial question, said without hesitation, "Silver-grey BMW. Brand new, T reg – the guy obviously wasn't short of a bob or two. He used to come down at odd times during the week, to see how the work was going on, I suppose. He was having the place done up."

"You saw him? Can you remember when?"

"Not exactly." The young man scratched his head. "I remember spotting the car once or twice when I was on my way to see to the sheep – I've got a flock of lambing ewes in a field behind Beacon Cottage. A local electrician has been doing some work there lately. He might be able to tell you a bit more about the chap."

"Thank you, that's very helpful," said Radcliffe when he had noted the name. "Now, if you ladies – and you sir – would be kind enough to give me your names and addresses, just in case we need to contact you again?" Everyone was more than ready to oblige and when he had written all the information in his notebook he gave each of them one of his cards. "If any of you should think of something, never mind how unimportant it might seem to you, anything at all to do with Mr Smith or the young lady you mentioned a moment ago, or anyone else you happen to have seen at Beacon Cottage . . ."

After receiving earnest assurances all round that they would do everything they could to help the police with their enquiries, Radcliffe left. He had undertaken the short journey on foot and had walked no more than a hundred yards on his way back to Beacon Cottage when the pick-up pulled up alongside and the young man, who had given his name as Tom Scully, leaned out of the open driver's window.

"A shooting, was it?" he asked.

Radcliffe looked at him in surprise. "What makes you think that?"

"Just a guess. Would it have happened around twelve o'clock yesterday?"

"We haven't yet been able to establish the time of death," said Radcliffe guardedly. "Do I take it you might have heard something?"

"Didn't hear anything, but I know Mr Smith got there around twelve because that's when I drove up to see to the sheep. His car wasn't there when I arrived, but it was there – with another one – when I left."

"Did you actually see Mr Smith, or the person in the other car?"

"Didn't see a soul, I'm afraid."

"Did you happen to notice what the other car was?"

"Only got a glimpse of it through the hedge, but it looked a big flashy job."

"What colour was it?"

"Sort of maroon." There was a brief pause before Scully continued, "You know what I reckon?" Without waiting for Radcliffe to reply, he said, "I reckon it's all to do with drugs."

For the second time, the detective asked, "What makes you think that?"

"Stands to reason, doesn't it? Two blokes in flashy cars meeting in an isolated spot . . . next thing one of 'em's dead . . . it's like that case we heard about the other day, innit . . . somewhere down in the West Country, two bodies in a Land Rover—"

"Just a minute," Radcliffe interrupted. "You mentioned two men, but I thought you didn't see anyone."

"No, well . . ." Scully looked abashed, but stuck to his guns. "I still reckon Smith had drugs stashed in the cottage and the other bloke was from a rival gang. If I were in charge, I'd get the sniffer dogs here. Well," he put the pick-up in gear and released the hand-brake, "I've given you my four penn'orth for what it's worth. I must get going."

"Did Sukey find anything significant?" Radcliffe asked when he got back to Beacon Cottage.

"A bit of jewellery." Briefly, Castle ran over the main points of his discussion with Sukey. "If it happens to have come from the Bussell Manor collection, and if John Smith turns out to be that fellow Lockyer that Wilbur Patterson spoke about, it could be a very useful lead. On the other hand, it might be something that belonged to the previous owner, something that got dropped when the cottage was cleared out." Castle picked up a dried cake of soap from the draining-board and began restlessly tossing it up and catching it. "Andy, I don't remember when I last had a case that was so full of ifs and buts."

"You're right, Guv. And here's something else to throw into the pot." He recounted his conversation in the shop and the theory put forward by Scully. "I was turning it over in my mind on my way back here, and although it's obviously nothing but surmise on his part, it seems a possibility that we should bear in mind. I mean, we've been so keen to see links between the Bussell Manor job and the killing of Crowson and Morris, but—"

"—we might be looking at nothing more than a string of coincidences," Castle interposed wearily, adding with a grimace, "as no doubt the great man himself will be quick to point out. At least, thanks to this chap Scully, I can assure him that no possibility is being overlooked." He put down the cake of soap and glanced out of the window where the odd glimpse of a dark blue uniform could be seen through gaps in the hedge. "They haven't found a weapon yet, and I very much doubt that they will, but we can't leave anything to chance. I'll have a quick word with the sergeant in charge and then we'll get back to the station."

Meanwhile, in the well-appointed sitting-room of a substantial detached house on the outskirts of Tewkesbury, Miriam Lockyer, an immaculately groomed woman whose age WPC Trudy Marshall put at around fifty, sat on a leather couch with her long, well-shaped legs elegantly crossed and a cigarette dangling from lacquered finger-tips.

"I haven't seen Stuart since Friday," she informed the young policewoman between leisurely draws on the cigarette. "I've been away and I only got back this morning." She gave a slightly brittle laugh and said, "What's he been up to anyway? Fiddling his clients' commission?"

"Have you a particular reason for thinking that?"

"Only that I've often wondered how a run-of-the-mill job with a local firm of auctioneers could support all this?" She made a languid circle with the cigarette before taking another draw.

"We don't know that he's been up to anything, Mrs Lockyer," said Trudy slowly. This sort of thing was never easy and although in this case she had the impression that the woman's attitude to her husband was not exactly that of the adoring wife, it was one thing to be told that your man had been arrested for embezzlement, quite another to learn that he had suffered a violent death.

"So what are you here for?"

"Has your husband recently purchased a property known as Beacon Cottage in Parkfield?"

"Where on earth is that?" The question was spoken in a casual drawl, but Trudy noticed a faint hardening of the carefully lipsticked mouth.

"It's a tiny village not far from Painswick."

Miriam Lockyer stubbed out her cigarette in a heavy glass ashtray. "I suppose he bought it as a love-nest," she said, and this time there was a waspish rasp to her voice.

"You suspect your husband of having an affair?"

"I *know* he's having an affair, and not for the first time either." She looked at Trudy with hard blue-grey eyes. "Look, why don't you come to the point? You say he hasn't done anything wrong, and you're not in the business of marriage guidance, so what are you doing here?" For the first time, a note of concern crept into the slightly husky voice. "Has something happened to him?"

Trudy braced herself for the moment of truth. "I'm afraid this is going to come as a shock," she said gently, "but I have to tell you that we found a body in the cellar of Beacon Cottage. The victim was known in the village as John Smith, but we have established that a grey BMW parked outside is registered in your name . . . and his wallet contained a driving licence and credit cards in the name of Stuart Lockyer."

There was a long silence, during which Miriam Lockyer sat staring ahead of her as if turned to stone. Then, with an almost studied calm, she uncrossed her legs and got to her feet. Without a trace of emotion in her voice, she said, "I suppose you'll want me to identify him."

Twenty

Sukey had just finished writing out her reports at the end of the afternoon when she received a call from DI Castle asking her to see him in his office. She found him seated at his desk, his brow furrowed, an open file in front of him. He looked up when she entered, waved her to a seat and said, "A bottle blonde with eyes the colour of lead shot and about as hard. Does that suggest anyone you've met recently?"

Sukey thought for a moment, frowning. Then she said, "I suppose that description could apply to . . . what was the woman's name? Fiona something or other . . . Wilbur Patterson's secretary. I noticed she did have rather unusual grey eyes. I didn't notice if the hair was natural or not . . . why do you ask?"

"Her name's Fiona Mackintosh. According to Radcliffe, that's how one of the residents of Parkfield described a woman seen at Beacon Cottage with Stuart Lockyer; alias John Smith."

"The dead man definitely was Lockyer, then?"

"Oh yes, the widow's identified the body from a hernia scar and a signet ring. She was spared a sight of his face, although Radcliffe says he seriously wonders whether it would have upset her that much. He doesn't think she's going to spend much time grieving over him."

"I suppose his relationship with his wife had gone sour and he found consolation with Fiona." In a sudden flash of memory, Sukey recalled the arrival at Bussell Manor the day of the robbery of the man she now believed to be Lockyer, and the fleeting glimpse of Fiona as she opened the door for him before he had a chance to ring the bell. "It occurred to me at the time that she must have been looking out for him," she told Castle after recounting the brief episode. "I guessed that Patterson had probably summoned him as a matter of urgency to discuss the robbery, so I didn't attach any particular significance to it at the time."

"No, I probably wouldn't have done either," Castle admitted, "but if the woman seen with him at the cottage was Fiona, then we're looking at a slightly different ball game. It's already occurred to me that Lockyer and Rodriguez might have been in cahoots – maybe the lovely Fiona was in on the scam as well."

"Are you saying that it could have been Lockyer who was given the job of passing on the proceeds of the robbery?"

"I think we have to consider that possibility. WPC Marshall said Mrs Lockyer seemed to imply that her husband wasn't above fiddling his clients' accounts. I suppose we'd better set about checking his record." Castle made a note while Sukey digested the latest twist to the case.

"If it's true that he's been cheating his clients, then could one of his victims have rumbled him and decided to pay him back?"

"And used the same method of execution as was used to dispose of Crowson and Morris? That would be an even more bizarre coincidence. No, I still believe that the same person killed all three and that the whole thing is tied up with the disappearance of Miguel Rodriguez."

"There's still no word about Rodriguez?"

"None whatsoever." Castle ran his thin, tapering fingers through his thick brown hair. "Sook, you remember I said a while ago that I had a bad feeling about this case?"

"I remember."

"Well for 'bad', read 'hopeless'," he said disconsolately. "Until today I had figured out a scenario that seemed to fit all the facts as we know them. Not that it brought us any closer to nailing the killer – or killers – of Crowson and Morris, or tracking down the elusive Mr Rodriguez, but at least it was something to go on, something that made sense. Now Stuart Lockyer has been thrown into the equation and I can't for the life of me see how he fits."

His downcast expression aroused in Sukey an all but overwhelming desire to reach out to him, take his hand and try to comfort him. Instead, she assumed her most businesslike manner and said, "I'm sure you'll get it sorted eventually, Guv."

"Oh, we'll solve it all right," he asserted, but with a certain lack of confidence. "It's just that I have this premonition . . ."

"I get premonitions from time to time, but they never come to anything." Glancing round to make sure there was no one within earshot, she dropped her voice and said, "Come round for supper tonight."

He sighed and shook his head. "I'd love to, but it looks as if I'll be working late. Now I'd better contact Wilbur Patterson and bring him up to date. Fiona's been on to us a couple of times enquiring about developments, and so far I've been stalling."

"You mean you haven't mentioned Roddy's disappearance, or the evidence we found in his car?"

"Remember how shirty Patterson got when it was hinted that Roddy might have been involved? I've been hanging on in the hope of turning up something a bit more concrete."

"Surely, he'll have to know now."

"Of course."

The phone on Castle's desk rang as Sukey got up to leave. He picked it up, listened for a few seconds, then said, "Tell him I'll be with him in a couple of minutes." He recradled the instrument and said, "Talk of the devil . . . Wilbur Patterson is in reception with a lady and he's in what the desk sergeant describes as 'a bit of a hurry'. In other words, breathing fire and baying for blood." With a mirthless laugh, Castle pushed his chair back and reached for his jacket. "Well, we've got some for him, haven't we? Not the kind he's expecting, though."

"I wonder if the lady is Fiona," said Sukey as the two of them made their way down to Reception. "If it is, she's in for a nasty shock."

Her question was soon answered; Patterson was waiting at the foot of the stairs with his secretary beside him. The minute he set eyes on DI Castle he said belligerently, "It's a fine thing when a man has to come to the police station to get information about an attack on his property instead of having it relayed to him." His voice reverberated round the reception area, causing heads to turn. "What is it with you English cops," he went on before the inspector had a chance to speak, "don't you believe in keeping the victims of crime informed?"

"Good afternoon Mr Patterson, Miss Mackintosh," said Castle in his most emollient manner. "It so happens, sir, that I was on the point of calling you when I received the information that you were here. Now, if you'd kindly step this way we can discuss the matter in private." He opened the door of an interview room and beckoned; Patterson, scowling and breathing heavily but momentarily silenced, moved towards it with Fiona at his elbow.

Sukey was about to slip out through the street door when Patterson caught sight of her and put out a hand like a boxing glove to bar her way. "Not so fast, young lady, I've one or two questions for you as well."

"Mrs Reynolds is not a member of the police force, she's a—" Castle began, but Patterson interrupted.

"Hell, I know what her function is. I left her and her partner giving my place the once-over and I want to know what they found there."

The DI cast a slightly helpless glance at Sukey and said, "Do you mind staying on for a few minutes?"

"No problem," she assured him, secretly delighted that she was about to witness part of the next act in the drama. She was particularly anxious to see how Fiona reacted to the news of Lockyer's death, and she had not long to wait.

Castle began by running over the events that had occurred during the days immediately following the break-in at Bussell Manor, beginning with the raid on the home of Crowson – an employee of Rodriguez – and the subsequent discovery not only of Crowson's body but of that of his close associate and colleague Jack Morris. During the recital Patterson, who appeared to be still simmering after his outburst in Reception, sat chewing his lower lip and glowering. After pausing for a few moments to allow time for what he had related so far to sink in, Castle said, "I'm afraid you won't like what I have to tell you next, sir, as I know you have complete faith in your friend's honesty, but we have reason to believe that Miguel Rodriguez was directly involved in the burglary at your home."

"Never!" Patterson exploded. "I can't believe it of him – you got evidence?"

Castle glanced at Sukey, inviting her to speak. "I found black fibres on the frame of the window in your office, a thumb print on the catch and the imprint of a trainer in the sand beneath that window," she said. "All have been subjected to very thorough tests and all have been traced back to Mr Rodriguez. We actually found the trainers and a black tracksuit in his car."

"And when we went to interview him, we found he had left home in a hurry, in rather peculiar circumstances." Castle took DC Hill's report of his visit to Miriam Prendergast from the file and read out the salient points before describing the fruitless attempts to locate Rodriguez at the clinic mentioned in the mysterious faxed message.

As he listened, Patterson's florid features registered mounting dismay. "Hell, you don't reckon he's been croaked, do you?" he said without a trace of his earlier truculence.

"For the moment, we have no reason to believe that he's come to any harm," said Castle.

Patterson sat back in his chair, shaking his head and wiping his face with a silk handkerchief. "And is that it?" he asked. "No sign of any of my property being recovered?"

"We found a fragment of a picture frame in Crowson's garage that we think may have come from your collection. It was our intention, after it had been subjected to tests in our laboratories, to ask Mr Lockyer for his opinion. Unfortunately, that has not been possible."

"I suppose you've not been able to reach him either," said Patterson irritably. "I've been trying his home and his office since yesterday and getting no joy."

Castle appeared to ignore the comment. Instead he turned to Fiona, who had been sitting a little behind her employer, her pale face expressionless. "Miss Mackintosh, do you happen to have with you the complete list of the stolen items?"

Fiona looked slightly taken aback. "I'm afraid not," she replied.

"But you can probably remember them – or most of them?" She did not reply, but merely waited. Sukey noticed that this time she had a slightly wary look in her lead-grey eyes. "Was there, for example," the detective continued, "a little Victorian brooch in the shape of a lovers' knot, set with amethysts?"

"There might have been something like that in that collection of Victoriana Stuart Lockyer persuaded me to buy a couple of months ago," Patterson interposed. "I don't recall seeing it; period jewellery isn't really my scene, but Stuart insisted there were several pieces there that would appreciate in value so I told him to go ahead. What about it anyway?"

"I found a brooch answering to that description this morning, on the floor in the cellar of an isolated cottage near Painswick Beacon," said Sukey in response to a glance from Castle. She wondered whether he had spotted the flicker of recognition that had passed over Fiona's face as he described the brooch; he could hardly have missed her nervous start at the reference to the cottage.

"So where is it?" Patterson demanded. "Fiona logs every

addition to the collection – she might recognise it even if I don't."

"It's at present undergoing tests in the laboratory—"

"What kind of tests? Why didn't you show it to me right away?"

"The brooch was covered in blood," said Castle quietly. "It was found beneath the body of a murder victim."

"Hell's teeth, another murder!" Patterson's gaze showed incredulity as it travelled between Castle and Sukey. "Who is it this time?"

"A man who was known in the village of Parkfield as John Smith," said the detective, and Sukey noticed that he was looking not at Patterson, but at Fiona. "However, we have now positively identified him as Stuart Lockyer. Catch her!" he shouted, as with a sigh that was almost a moan, Fiona slid sideways from her chair.

Twenty-One

"I tried to talk him out of it, but he wouldn't listen. He said it was a chance in a lifetime to lay our hands on some real money. He said there was no risk to us, we'd simply be riding on the back of that Spanish Casanova, as he called him—"

"I take it you're referring to Miguel Rodriguez?" DI Castle interrupted.

"That's right. Stuart hated his guts; he caught him once making a pass at me and said if it happened again he'd smash his face in." Fiona's voice faltered at the recollection and she wiped her eyes with a handkerchief that was already moist. "I told him not to be silly, there was nothing in it, but he said he couldn't bear the thought of anyone else so much as looking at me. Stuart thought the world of me, we thought the world of each other, we were going to be so happy in the cottage . . ." Her voice failed altogether as fresh tears poured down her cheeks.

After a night spent under observation in hospital following her collapse on hearing of the death of Stuart Lockyer, she was sitting, white-faced and trembling, in an interview room in Gloucester City police station. Opposite her sat DI Castle and DS Radcliffe and beside her was Wilbur Patterson, who had threatened to call in his lawyer and 'raise Cain' if he was not allowed to be present. "It's my property that's been hi-jacked and I've a right to hear straight from the horse's mouth exactly what went on," he had insisted and, after referring the matter to Superintendent Sladden, Castle had reluctantly agreed. "But I must ask you to remain silent during the interview, and to keep any questions of your own until later," Castle had warned, only partially reassured by Patterson's impatient, "Sure, sure, can we just get on with it?"

The two detectives allowed Fiona a few moments to collect herself before Radcliffe asked, "What exactly did you try to talk Lockyer out of?"

"Robbing Bussell Manor, of course." She looked vaguely surprised at the question.

"He told you he was planning to rob your employer?" She nodded without speaking. "Did he tell you how he planned to set about it?"

"Yes."

"How did he propose to get into the house without activating the alarm?"

"Isn't it obvious?" Patterson broke in. "She gave him the combination, the double-crossing little—"

"Please, Mr Patterson, you promised to leave the questioning to us," said Castle with a frown, and the big American sat back in his seat, muttering and glaring at the woman who had been his trusted secretary. The inspector turned back to her. "Is that what happened?" he asked.

"No." She shook her head violently. "That's what I thought he had in mind when he first mentioned it and I said straight away that I wouldn't do it because the police would know immediately that it was an inside job and we'd be found out in no time. 'I've worked out a much cleverer scheme than that,' he said. It *was* clever too," she added with a flash of pride. "And it worked, didn't it? You'd never have suspected—"

"But someone else obviously did," Castle pointed out grimly and then continued in a gentler tone as the young woman's eyes filled again. "You mentioned Mr Rodriguez a moment ago. Do I take it that he was part of the plan?"

"He was the most important part." A faint smile flickered over Fiona's wan features. "He was going to open up the place for us – he was to be our 'Open Sesame' as Stuart called him."

"Are you saying that in spite of Stuart's hostility towards him, he conspired with him to rob your employer?"

"Oh no! Roddy didn't have a clue about what we were planning. That was what made it so clever."

Castle felt his patience wearing thin. "I suggest you stop talking in riddles and tell us exactly what happened," he said.

It was a weary but quietly triumphant DI Jim Castle who parked outside the little semi in Brockworth and sank with a hefty sigh of relief into the comfortable sofa in Sukey's sitting-room. "Phew, what a day!" he exclaimed after drinking deeply from the glass of cold beer that she handed him. "Thanks love, I needed that."

"Have some crisps, Jim?" said Fergus.

"No thanks." Castle waved away the dish with a smile. "Something in the kitchen smells wonderful and I don't want to spoil my appetite."

"It's chicken casserole and raspberry trifle . . . and I made the trifle," Fergus said with a hint of pride.

"Wonderful."

"Never mind the food for the moment," said Sukey impatiently. "We want to know what's been happening since yesterday's drama at the station. I came straight home after you sent me to get medical help for Fiona and I haven't had a word from you since . . . you never called me yesterday evening, I've been out of the office all day and when I got in this afternoon there was no one in CID who could tell me anything. I know you've got a result – you've got that look about you, like a cat that's been at the cream," she added as he cocked an eyebrow at her over the rim of his glass.

"We got a partial result, yes," he said guardedly.

"Well go on, spill it."

"Okay." Jim put down the empty glass, declined with a gesture the offer of a refill and glanced across at Fergus. "All this in the strictest confidence, young man. Not a word to anyone, not even the girlfriend."

"My lips are sealed," the lad assured him solemnly.

"Okay. Well, for a start, we've recovered the Turner."

"Brilliant!" Sukey exclaimed. "Where was it? No, let me guess. Henry Greenleaf had it?"

"Clever girl. It was in his office safe."

"So that *was* what was in the parcel that Lockyer was carrying," she said reflectively. "Do I take it that Greenleaf hung on to it, maybe promising to find a buyer, and then advised the police?"

Jim gave an ironic chuckle. "That's what he'd have us believe, but we've made it quite clear that we're not buying that story."

Fergus looked puzzled. "I don't understand," he said. "Do you mean you just went to see this Greenleaf bloke and asked to see what was in the parcel that Lockyer brought him? Surely, if he owned up straight away, he must be on the level."

"It wasn't quite as simple as that. We had a warrant to search the place. Look, I'd better begin at the beginning. How long have we got before the food's ready?"

"About twenty minutes," said Sukey.

"That should be enough." Jim held out his glass. "I think I'll have that refill after all."

"I'll get it, but don't start till I get back."

As Fergus hurried from the room, Jim leaned across to Sukey and gave her a quick kiss. "All right, love?" he said gently.

She brushed his cheek with her fingers. "Fine," she whispered.

Fergus returned with a second can of beer which he opened and handed over before settling down in his chair again. "Carry on with the story, Jim," he urged.

"Right. Well, the FME – that's the Forensic Medical Examiner – happened to be at the station and we got her to attend to Fiona. It was quite a while before she came round, and when she did she started babbling something about having told him it wouldn't work and they'd be sure to be found out. The FME wouldn't let us question her, said she was in shock and insisted

160

on getting her into hospital for observation. We sent a WPC to keep an eye on her and when she woke up this morning she said something to the effect that with Lockyer dead she had nothing to live for and she might as well make a full statement about the robbery at Bussell Manor."

"Now I'm really baffled," said Sukey. "Are you saying it was Fiona and Stuart who did that job, and not Roddy?"

"In a way."

"But the evidence we found . . . the prints, the fibres from the tracksuit . . . and Roddy's disappearance . . ."

"Oh, Roddy was in it all right, but he wasn't responsible for the actual robbery. They simply used his expertise to get them into the place. It was a brilliant plan, and so breathtakingly simple. They'd almost certainly have got away with it if Lockyer had gone to any fence in the county but Henry Greenleaf."

"What made him choose Greenleaf?"

"Fiona didn't know, but she supposed it was because he reckoned he was the one with the contacts who'd know who was most likely to be interested in what was on offer."

"Lockyer would meet all sorts of people through his job with the auctioneers, wouldn't he?" said Sukey thoughtfully. "And I imagine there are some pretty dodgy characters in the art world."

Jim nodded. "It's well-known that not every dealer – or every collector, come to that – is over-fussy about the source of the stuff that's offered to them. Word soon gets around about who's likely to be interested in what. It seems that our Stuart had built up quite a thriving little business on the side, advising wealthy collectors when any items of particular interest were coming on the market. If a purchase was made on the strength of his advice, there'd be a commission for him."

"The way he did for Wilbur Patterson?"

"Exactly. So long as the stuff was clean it was perfectly legitimate, of course – there are probably any number of people in his position making a bit of extra cash in the same way.

Whether he fiddled the commission, as the widow hinted, is something that ought to be looked into. Some quite substantial sums could be involved that should be returned to—"

"Never mind that now," Sukey interrupted impatiently. "Tell us about this breathtakingly simple plan."

"Sorry, I was digressing. The plan was to lie in wait in the gardens – which contain several convenient little arbours that might have been designed especially for the purpose – for Roddy to come and open the place up for them. Once he was out of the way with whatever he was planning to steal from the collection, having deactivated the alarm so that all they had to do was let themselves in through the front door using Fiona's keys, they were to nip in and help themselves from whatever was left. Lockyer was familiar with the collection – after all, a lot of the items had been bought on his advice – and he knew exactly what would fetch the highest prices. And the best part of it from their point of view was that, to their astonishment, Roddy didn't take a thing. He was in and out in less than five minutes, empty-handed so far as they could make out – he certainly wasn't carrying anything. He even left the front door on the latch. They simply couldn't believe their luck; Lockyer reckoned the Turner alone was worth several million, even on the black market."

"A handy way to launder drug money?" suggested Fergus, who had been hanging on every word.

"It's possible. A chap DS Radcliffe spoke to in the village mentioned that he thought drugs might be involved."

"I'm having a job to take it all in," said Sukey. "I imagine that the plan – Roddy's plan, that is – was for Crowson and Morris to go in and pick up what they wanted later on during the night, after he'd opened the place up for them?"

"That seems to have been the way they'd operated in the past. I suspect that much of what our two amateurs got away with was on their shopping list. When they found out it had gone, they probably thought Roddy had double-crossed them."

"D'you reckon it was one of them who fingered Roddy, out of revenge?" Sukey suggested.

"It might have been – or maybe it was Lockyer, out of spite because he thought Roddy fancied his girl. We'll never know for sure, of course, but—"

"What I don't understand is, how did Stuart and Fiona know Roddy was planning the robbery . . . and when?"

"They didn't know for certain; it was a piece of inspired guesswork on Stuart's part after he'd observed certain factors common to a number of burglaries from private collections. I have to admit he was way ahead of the police from that point of view."

"But you spotted the connection as well," Sukey interposed. "That was why the undercover agent was brought in – the one who looks like me."

"Yes, but much later. To be fair, we were only working on the basis of similarities between break-ins within our own area. Lockyer had contacts, and Roddy's firm supplied customers, all over the country."

Sukey glanced at her watch. "Supper in five minutes," she warned.

"Right, it won't take long to tell the rest. It all started when Lockyer, who had several wealthy clients in Gloucestershire and the neighbouring counties, met Rodriguez at the home of one of them. He'd been supplying wine to the client for some time and like Lockyer was looked on almost as a personal friend. Shortly after that first encounter, the house was burgled in the owner's absence on holiday by someone who had the expertise to deactivate quite a sophisticated alarm system. It didn't occur to Lockyer at the time that Roddy might have been responsible – why should it? Then a similar robbery took place several months later at the home of another of his clients and he learned from a casual remark by the victim that he too bought wine from Roddy's firm."

"And that was enough to make Roddy a suspect?"

"Not immediately. That happened when Stuart bumped into

him again, this time at the home of a client in Warwickshire. He happened to notice Roddy apparently taking an interest in the security system. He commented on it and Roddy passed it off by saying something about the number of different systems on the market and wondering which were the most effective. He gave out that he was thinking of having his own home protected and Lockyer thought no more about it, but when that same client was robbed a couple of weeks later, it occurred to him that Roddy might be the 'Phantom Robber' as the media had dubbed him. By this time the police were getting a lot of flak because of the total lack of progress in tracking him down."

"I remember," said Sukey with a grin. "This is fascinating background stuff," she went on, "but you still haven't explained how Lockyer and Fiona knew that the Bussell Manor collection was on the gang's shopping list."

"They didn't know for certain; like I said, it was a piece of inspired guesswork. By coincidence – this case is full of them isn't it? – Lockyer had recently bumped into Roddy again during a visit to Wilbur Patterson and they both knew Patterson would be away playing golf the following weekend. It seemed an obvious opportunity for the Phantom Robber to do the place over."

"And all Stuart and Fiona stood to lose, if their guess was wrong, was a few hours' sleep," Sukey observed. "When they realised they had the entire collection to choose from, they must have thought their ship had come in."

"Instead of which, the grim reaper was lying in wait for poor old Stuart," said Castle sombrely.

"You said you had a bad feeling about this case," Sukey reminded him with a sigh. "And you were right, weren't you? . . . three deaths and one unexplained disappearance."

"I did, didn't I? Come to think of it, I still have. There's a long way to go before we wrap it up."

"At least, you've got a positive lead," Fergus pointed out. "You've got Greenleaf – has he been singing?"

Jim smiled at the lad's slightly self-conscious use of jargon.

164

"We arrested Greenleaf on the spot, of course, once we found the painting. He's at this moment in the cells, insisting that it was his intention to inform us about it at the earliest opportunity and denying all knowledge of the robbery."

"What about Wallis?"

"He swears he never saw the man before – claims it was Smith who set up the meeting."

"That's a lie for a start," said Sukey. "Wallis is a regular visitor – ask Gladys, his assistant. She has to buy special biscuits for him."

"We already have a statement from Gladys. We've told Greenleaf we know he's lying, but he's still sticking to his story. We've also pointed out to him that he's mixed up in at least one very nasty murder, but he seems to be more scared of Wallis than of going to prison. Does that remind you of anything?"

"What Donna Hoskins heard Crowson saying about Wallis in the pub?"

"Exactly. He's our next target . . . if we can get a lead on him. You saw him, Sook, so we'll be wanting a detailed statement from you as soon as possible."

"Of course . . . but in the meantime, let's go and eat."

Twenty-Two

"Everything about him looked prosperous," Sukey said reflectively. "The camel coat, the Jag – if he'd been sporting a pair of binoculars round his neck you'd have taken him for a wealthy racehorse owner down for Gold Cup Week in Cheltenham."

"Height? Build? Any distinguishing features?"

Sukey frowned and played with the handle of her coffee mug. The meal was over and the washing-up done, Fergus had slipped out to spend an hour or two at Anita's house and she and Jim were sitting at the kitchen table, their attention once more focused on the robbery at Henry Greenleaf Antiques and the possible connection with the killing of Stuart Lockyer at Beacon Cottage.

"About five-ten, I suppose," she said after a few moments' thought, "and fairly solidly built – not exactly fat, but sleek-looking, someone who enjoys good food and wine." Slowly, the image of the man took shape in her mind's eye.

"Did you catch any hint of an accent?"

"I never heard his voice – he spoke to his driver when he got out of the car, but of course I couldn't hear because I was inside the shop, looking out of the window. He never said a word when he came in, but he didn't need to – Gladys recognised him immediately and did everything but curtsey when he arrived so he's obviously a VIP. No manners," she added as she recalled the way he had so rudely pushed past the woman, ignoring her greeting.

"What about colouring?" asked Jim, busy making notes between mouthfuls of coffee.

166

"Short dark hair, and a slightly swarthy complexion, possibly Mediterranean. Or maybe he was tanned from a trip to the Bahamas – he certainly looked as if he could afford it."

"You said you thought you'd recognise him again."

"I've been thinking about that. I'm not sure . . . I mean, if I saw him in the street on his own I might, but I doubt if I could pick him out in a line-up. There wasn't anything particularly distinguishing about his features – he was clean-shaven with a slightly dark jowl and plumpish cheeks, but . . . I'm sorry, Jim, I really can't be more precise than that . . . no, there's one other thing. He uses a very distinctive after-shave or body lotion, sort of musky. I remember it because it reminded me of when Paul and I spent a holiday in Spain, years ago before Fergus was born. All the waiters in the hotel seemed to use it . . . Paul said the smell put him off his food, but I thought it was rather sexy."

"Oh, so you think Wallis is sexy, do you?" Jim demanded, feigning jealousy.

Sukey giggled and nestled against him. "Very, but since he's not available I'll have to make do with you."

"I'm not sure I'm prepared to play second fiddle to the mysterious Mr Wallis," he joked back, then turned serious again. "Mediterranean colouring and after-shave that reminds you of Spain. I'll make a note of that for what it's worth. Let's go back to the driver for a moment – you haven't mentioned him before."

"Haven't I?" she said evasively. It was true; knowing instinctively that Jim was likely to read something sinister into the man's motives in making that small, mocking gesture, she had deliberately kept it to herself. In any case, despite her momentary flash of unease at the time, she had all but dismissed the episode from her mind.

Jim gave her a searching look. "Sook, have you been keeping something from me?"

"Not really. It was just that he made a sort of pass at me

167

and I didn't want you to be jealous," she said demurely. "It was nothing, really."

"I daresay it was, but that's not what I'm concerned about."

"Really?" It was her turn to pretend to take offence.

He slipped an arm round her and gave her shoulder a squeeze. "You know what I mean. Would you recognise this chap again?"

"I doubt it. He looked like lots of other young men nowadays . . . cropped hair, dark glasses, black sweatshirt, earring. You know the type."

"Mm, it's not much to go on," Castle agreed reluctantly. "You said he made 'a sort of pass' at you. What exactly did he do?"

"He was staring at me quite hard while I was putting my stuff away in the van. Then, when I looked in my mirror before pulling away, I noticed him looking at something in his hand. As I drove off I saw him give a funny sort of smile and wave whatever it was . . . it looked like a piece of paper or card."

"Could it have been a photograph?"

"It might have been, I suppose. What of it?"

"Just a thought. I think we'll see if we can get a lead on this character as well. When you come in tomorrow I'll get you to look through some mug-shots to see if you can pick either of them out. I don't somehow think we'll find anything on Wallis – the name certainly doesn't mean anything, although the people at TRACE might possibly have heard of him – but the driver might be on our books."

"What about the personal number plate on the car? Have you done a check on that?"

"That was one of the first things we did, but it didn't help much. The vehicle's registered in the name of some obscure finance company with an accommodation address, which makes us suspect there might be something not quite legit about Wallis. I'm beginning to think Scully could be right and there's drug money involved in this." Jim glanced at his watch. "Look, love, I know it's only ten o'clock but I've had a heavy day and tomorrow's not going to be much easier, so if you don't mind . . ." He drained his mug and took it to the sink to rinse it, then returned to the table and pulled her gently to her feet. She slid happily into his embrace, her body tingling at the touch of his hands along her spine, her mouth responding eagerly to his. "See you tomorrow," he murmured as he released her.

"Sure."

At the door, he became suddenly serious. "I don't want to frighten you, but I think you should be particularly watchful for the next few days, or until we nail these unpleasant characters."

She looked at him in surprise. "What am I supposed to look out for?" she asked.

"Anything unusual, and especially any sighting of that driver. All right," he added, forestalling the dismissive retort she was about to make, "I know you think I'm over cautious, but maybe you've forgotten that little episode down at the nick when Roddy shouted 'Pepita!' at you."

"No, I haven't forgotten, but surely I don't represent any kind of threat to these people, whoever they are. They've taken Roddy out of your reach – at least, we presume that's what's happened. I take it there's no further news?"

"That's something I forgot to tell you. His cousin phoned to say they've had another fax, purporting to be from him and saying he's taking extended leave to recuperate from a nervous breakdown. Tomas is still not convinced it's genuine and neither are we. We'd all give a lot to know where that blighter has hidden himself – or been hidden."

"Just the same, I still don't see why Wallis and his gang should come after me," Sukey protested. "What harm can I do them?"

"It could be out of revenge. They think you're the woman who shopped Roddy, remember?"

"So what? The damage is done as far as they're concerned.

And surely, if they were going to target me, they'd have made some sort of move by now."

"That all sounds very logical, but I still have this uneasy feeling." Jim's arms tightened around Sukey and he pressed his cheek against hers. "Please, my love, be extra vigilant and let me know if anything unusual happens, no matter how trivial. Promise?"

She lifted her face for one more kiss. "Promise," she whispered.

By the time Fergus came home and mother and son had shared a nightcap of hot chocolate, it was gone midnight when Sukey got to bed. She read for a short time before switching out her light and settling down under the covers. She was just drifting off to sleep when the phone rang.

"Hullo!" she said, making no attempt to disguise the irritation she felt at being so rudely disturbed.

"Sorry, did I wake you up?" It was a man's voice, unfamiliar, with an unmistakable Home Counties accent.

"Who is this?" she demanded, wide awake now, her pulse quickening slightly.

"It's Susan Reynolds, isn't it? Or Sukey – I believe that's what your friends call you."

"I've a feeling you don't number among my friends," she said tartly. "And if this is some kind of practical joke, I'm not laughing."

"No joke, Sukey . . . or should I say . . . no, we'll discuss your other name next time I call. Sleep well."

A click followed by the dull drone of dialling tone told her the man had hung up. She immediately dialled 1471 and made a note of the number. It was almost certainly a public call-box and the nearest one was the best part of a mile away. Just the same, she got out of bed and peered out of the window; the little cul-de-sac was well lit and there was no sign of anyone lurking in the shadows. It was probably a waste of time reporting it, but remembering what Jim had said . . . she was on the point of calling him there and then, but decided that tomorrow would do. She assured herself that there was no immediate danger . . . the man had said he'd call again. She settled down once more, pulling the duvet closely around her because she was feeling suddenly cold. It was a long time before sleep eventually came.

A couple of hours or so after DI Castle expressed an interest in his whereabouts, Miguel Rodriguez was sipping a long cool drink as he reclined on a wide canopied day-bed after his evening swim. Consuela was still in the pool and his eyes followed her, his mind dwelling pleasurably on the lustful thoughts aroused by the sight of her supple body in its scanty bikini as it cut through the water, her black hair streaming behind her. She swam as she made love, with total dedication, giving meaning to each smooth, rhythmical, apparently effortless movement of her bronzed limbs.

After a couple more lengths of the pool she swam to the side immediately below where he was lying. Ignoring the steps a short distance away, she hoisted herself out of the water in one swift, athletic movement, dropped to her knees before him and kissed him with parted lips, her fingers knotted in his hair, her tongue exploring his mouth, water dripping from her body on to his own warm, responsive flesh. In response he seized her in his arms, unhooked the top of her bikini and flung it aside before pulling her on to the bed beside him and rolling on top of her. She gave a squeal of mingled protest and delight.

"No, no *caro*, not here. Isabella may be watching."

"Let her watch. It's probably the only chance she has of a bit of fun."

"That is cruel." Consuela pretended to be cross. "She is old now, but maybe in her day she—"

"—could never have been half the woman you are," Roddy murmured with his face buried between her breasts and his hands eagerly tearing at the lower half of her costume.

"No, no," she repeated, trying to wriggle out from under

171

him. "Not here . . . suppose Juan should suddenly appear?" she added as his hand grabbed at her crotch.

Abruptly, he stood up and scooped her into his arms. "All right then, we'll go indoors if it makes you feel better."

"Much better," she sighed. She wound her arms round his neck as he carried her across the patio towards the villa.

In the hall they met Isabella. "What time shall I serve dinner, Señor?" she asked, her face expressionless.

"What shall we say?" Roddy whispered in Consuela's ear. "One hour, two hours . . ."

"Whatever you say, my Roddy," she whispered back.

"Two hours then," said Isabella without waiting for his instructions. She turned and marched back to the kitchen, muttering – her whole body registering disapproval.

"She's probably miffed because we didn't do it where she could watch," said Roddy as he carried Consuela into his bedroom.

"You are so naughty, *caro mio*," she giggled as he laid her on the bed, removed the rest of her bikini and took off his trunks. This time she made no attempt to stop him.

Later, as they lay quietly in the cool, dimly lit room, Consuela reached across and brushed Roddy's face with her fingers. "The scars are healing so fast," she said sadly. "Soon, you will return to Europe and I shall lose you forever."

"It makes me sad too," he said, grasping her hand and kissing each finger in turn.

Had he been completely truthful, he would have added that the prospect filled him with dread.

Twenty-Three

W hen Sukey awoke early the following morning after a troubled night's sleep, the first thing that came into her mind was the anonymous telephone call. She went over it in her mind, trying to remember the details. The precise words eluded her; she should have made a detailed note there and then, but she had been half asleep when the phone rang and it had taken her several seconds to grasp that this was no ordinary nuisance call. At least, she had the number it had originated from. She glanced at her bedside clock; it was barely five. She had promised to let Jim know immediately if anything unusual happened and her hand reached out to grasp the phone, then hesitated at the memory of how tired he had been the previous evening. He badly needed an undisturbed night's rest – it could wait until she saw him at work in a few hours' time. She lay back on the pillow, recalling his words of warning and thinking how uncanny, almost prophetic, they seemed in the light of what had happened only a couple of hours or so after they were uttered.

She closed her eyes and tried without success to doze off again. An hour dragged past while the grey light filtering through the cutains changed gradually to pale gold and the events of the past few days went churning through her head in a ceaseless merry-go-round. Jim had warned her to be vigilant, to watch for anything unusual, particularly any sighting of the Jaguar or its driver. She had no way of telling whether last night's caller and the laddish-looking character who had scrutinised her so closely and made that half-mocking gesture were one and the same, but her instinct told her that they were. He knew her name and her phone number; almost certainly, he also knew where she lived. She slipped out of bed and peered out through a chink in the curtains, taking what she told herself was quite ridiculous care not to move them in case he should be keeping watch. Outside, everything appeared reassuringly normal; the little cul-de-sac with its ring of neat semis behind their tidy front gardens lay slumbering in the early morning sunlight.

The sudden hum of an electric motor made her heart leap in her chest and she stepped back in momentary alarm before the rattle of bottles told her that it was only the milkman on his round. Just the same, she waited, holding her breath, until the float drew up outside her house with the familiar whine of brakes and the driver jumped down and ran up to her front door with a bottle of milk in either hand. She let out an audible sigh of relief as she recognised the regular man and realised that she had half feared to see a tanned stranger in dark glasses with cropped hair and a gold earring. She turned away from the window and reached for her dressing-gown. "Pull yourself together, girl," she muttered and stole downstairs to make a cup of tea.

She drank her tea standing in front of the kitchen window, looking out at her little back garden. It was separated by a low hedge from the adjoining farmland that sloped gently away from the house and she found herself mentally assessing it from the security aspect. There was no public footpath across the field and the hedge was hawthorn, which was cattle-proof and would certainly provide a pretty formidable barrier to a prospective intruder – *but not to someone really determined*, added a warning voice in her ear.

She caught her breath and spun round in alarm at an unexpected movement behind her, then gave a shaky laugh at the sight of Fergus standing in the doorway in his pyjamas, his hair rumpled and his eyes bleary with sleep.

"Gus, you made me jump," she said reproachfully.

"Sorry," he said, yawning. "I was awake and I heard you moving about, so . . ." He wandered over to the teapot, peered inside and reached for a mug.

"You'll need to top that up," she told him. "I only made enough for one."

He nodded, switched on the electric kettle and waited for it to come to the boil. In silence, he added more water to the pot, filled the mug, added milk and sugar and stirred it before joining her at the window. "Who was that on the phone last night?" he asked.

"Some nutter." She tried to sound casual. "He didn't give a name."

"Nuisance call?"

"Something like that. I got the number – I'll report it when I get to work this morning."

"What did he say?"

"Nothing much. He did say he'd call again, though."

"D'you reckon it's anything to do with this case you've been working on?"

She turned to look at him and was moved by the concern in his face. "What makes you say that?" she asked.

"You obviously didn't sleep well and you nearly jumped out of your skin when I came in here just now." He stared down at his tea, avoiding her eye. "I've had a sort of feeling lately—"

"Oh, not you as well!" Sukey made a determined effort to lighten the direction the conversation was taking. "Jim's been going on like that for days – I can't think why – he's had far more difficult cases in the past."

"Not that you've been involved in. Mum, look at me . . . something's going on, isn't it? Please tell me . . . are you in some sort of danger?"

"What on earth makes you think that?" she countered, but she knew her voice lacked conviction.

He did not answer immediately. He drank his tea, went to the sink and spent several seconds rinsing out his mug with more than usual care. She noticed his colour rise and said curiously, "Gus, what are you trying to say?"

"I'm sorry, Mum," he said, his voice slightly thick with embarrassment. "The fact is . . . well, you remember that night when Jim was here for dinner just after the robbery at Bussell Manor?"

"Yes – what of it?"

"I was going on about how I was sure there was an under-cover agent involved and Jim practially admitted there was, and that it was a woman, but he wouldn't say any more."

"I remember."

"And then I went up to my room to do my homework."

"Go on," Sukey prompted as he hesitated, evidently searching for words.

"I . . . got thirsty after a while and came down to get a cold drink. You and Jim were in the kitchen and I was just about to come in when I heard him saying something about someone called Pepita who looks like you. I knew he'd shut up and change the subject the minute I appeared so I waited—"

"You mean, you were listening to our conversation?"

"I suppose so. Anyway, I heard him say he wanted you to go into a safe house, and you said you wouldn't . . . and then his phone went and there was the bit about the anonymous tip-off and Jim said he had to leave in a hurry, so I scarpered."

"I'm not surprised," Sukey said drily. "No one likes to be caught snooping."

"I didn't mean to, it just happened," he pleaded. "I thought about it for a long time, wondering whether I should say anything . . . I did feel worried, but I was afraid you'd think I'd been spying on you and Jim . . . and anyway I figured that if it was anything serious he'd take care of it. And when I got home after the weekend everything seemed all right, but I've been thinking about it on and off. Mum, this phone call – d'you reckon it's got anything to do with all these murders?"

"I can't be sure, Gus, but I have a nasty feeling it has."

"If you take Jim's advice and go into a safe house, will they let me go with you?"

"You don't imagine I'd agree to your being left here on your own, do you?" she said, touched by the almost desolate look on his young face. "If it came to that, you could go and stay with Dad . . . not that I've agreed to anything yet," she added. While they had been speaking, half of her mind had been racing ahead in a totally different direction.

"I'd rather stay with you, Mum." He took her hand and squeezed it.

She returned the pressure. "Try not to worry – Jim'll take care of things." She rinsed out her mug and put it on the draining-board. "We'll just have to see what he says when I tell him about the phone call. Anyway, we may be worrying about nothing she went on, more with the object of reassuring Fergus than with any belief that it was true. It's almost seven," she added briskly. "We'd better get on with the day."

Over his breakfast bowl of cornflakes, Gus remarked," If this was a thriller on the telly, the police would probably use you as a bait to lure the killer into a trap."

"Funny you should say that," Sukey replied without thinking as she transferred bacon and tomatoes from the grill to hot plates, added an egg to each from the frying pan and put them on the table.

Her son looked at her in horror. "Mum, you wouldn't . . . ?"

"It's crossed my mind," she admitted. In fact, she had thought of little else since the idea first came to her. "Jim believes there are some powerful and ruthless people organising the robberies and the killings and if they're behind these calls it means that for some reason they think I'm a serious threat to their operations. If that's the case, they're going to come after me wherever I go."

Fergus put the empty cereal bowl to one side and reached mechanically for his bacon and egg, but made no attempt to eat. "Are you saying you'd rather stay here under police protection and wait for this chap to . . ." He swallowed hard and pushed the plate away again as if suddenly nauseated.

"I agree it's terrifying, but what's the alternative? Spending weeks, months perhaps in hiding, unable to go out, do my job or see any of my friends? The police haven't got any positive leads – without some sort of break they might never manage to lay their hands on this gang."

"Don't do it, Mum, please!" The lad's eyes were full of tears and Sukey reached across the table and put a hand on his arm.

"Let's not talk about it any more for the moment," she said gently. "It was just an idea, but try not to worry. If the worst comes to the worst, Jim will see that we're given protection. Come on, eat your breakfast."

They were just clearing the table when the phone rang, making them both jump and exchange apprehensive glances. Sukey felt her voice tremble as she picked up the receiver and said a cautious, "Hullo."

"I hope you slept well, Susan," said the caller. The voice and accent were unmistakable and she shivered, despite the warmth of the kitchen. "Or do you prefer Sukey?" he went on, taunting her. "Or how about—"

"I prefer neither from you," she interrupted defiantly. "Please stop bothering me with these stupid calls." She slammed down the handset and looked across at Fergus. "It was him again," she said shakily.

"Quick – get the number!"

"Yes, of course." Once again she tapped out the code and noted the information. "It's different from last night's . . . he's obviously moving around," she said, frowning.

Seconds later, the phone rang again. In an effort to steady herself she took several deep breaths before answering. "Now look here—" she began. It was his turn to interrupt.

"You hung up on me, Sukey," he said. "That wasn't nice."

"It's not nice to be pestered with anonymous phone calls. It happens to be a criminal offence and if it happens again I'll—"

"Inform the police?" he broke in mockingly. "That's rich, coming from you . . . *Pepita!*"

Sukey felt her knees buckle and she grabbed the edge of the table. "What did you call me?" she said in a hoarse whisper.

"Don't you like me using Roddy's pet name for you?" A hint of sympathy, heavily laced with irony, crept into his voice. "Don't tell me you miss him."

"I don't know what you're talking about," she said, trying desperately not to betray her agitation. "My name isn't Pepita and I don't know anyone called Roddy."

"And I'm the Duke of Edinburgh," he jeered.

At the sound of the name 'Pepita' she saw her son's eyes widen with alarm. Seeing him about to speak, she put a warning finger to her lips.

"It's true," she insisted into the phone. "You're making a mistake . . . you've got the wrong person."

His dismissive laugh had an unpleasant, chilling undertone. "No, it was you who got the wrong person, when you betrayed Roddy. There's a price to pay for treachery, Pepita."

"For the last time—"

"No, this isn't the last time . . . but it will be soon. Goodbye for now." A sharp click was followed by the whirr of dial tone. With a hand that shook, she replaced the receiver.

"Him again?" Fergus whispered and she nodded.

"Gus, I'm scared," she said shakily.

"You must tell Jim right away."

"Yes, of course. Give me a moment to calm down."

"Shall I make some coffee?"

"Yes please."

When the phone rang for the third time, Fergus made a grab at it. "Let me take it," he said eagerly.

Sukey snatched it out of his reach. "No!" she said sharply. "He may not realise you're here . . . he may not even know about you." A new, hideous fear swept over her as she picked up the receiver and almost screamed into it, "Look here, I told you—"

179

"Sukey? Is something wrong?"

"Oh Jim, thank God it's you!" She could have wept with relief.

"What is it?"

"I've been getting these phone calls, three of them, one last night and two more just now. I thought it was him again."

"Stay where you are. I'll be with you in twenty minutes."

"She's a plucky lass, your Mrs Reynolds," said Superintendent Sladden. "If she's really willing to go ahead, we stand a good chance of nicking one of the key figures in this mob."

DI Castle stared at his senior office in consternation. "You mean you're prepared to go along with it, sir?"

"Can you think of a better idea?"

"I suggested getting the real 'Pepita' to stand in for her, but she turned it down flat, said the hit man would smell a rat straight away if a different voice answered the phone."

"Smart as well as plucky," commented Sladden with a nod of approval.

"I was hoping you'd help me talk her out of it."

"Why ever would I do that?" Sladden fixed Castle with a penetrating stare. "If it was one of the other SOCOs – anyone else, in fact – you wouldn't be objecting, would you? Come on, be honest," he went on as Castle remained silent.

"No, sir, but—"

"But nothing. We'll plan the operation very carefully. From what this character said to Mrs Reynolds, he doesn't seem to be in any great hurry to move in."

"I had that impression as well," Castle agreed. "It sounds as if he enjoys playing cat and mouse."

"Perhaps she can play the cat and mouse game as well. Let's get her to string him along if she can while we get everything in place. Some external security lights – that should discourage him from striking at night – and a phone with an instant tracer button. I'll get on to Special Branch and ask for an armed officer to be on duty round the clock. We'd better ask for a woman – we don't want to give the neighbours anything to gossip about, do we?" Sladden made notes while he was speaking. "Now, what about the lad? Didn't you mention something about packing him off to his father until this is sorted?"

"He says he won't go . . . insists on staying with his mother."

"Can't have that. Make sure he's out of the way as soon as possible. After that . . ." The Superintendent put down his pen and leaned forward on his elbows. "I know you aren't going to like this, Castle, but from then on you're to keep right out of this operation."

"But sir—"

"No buts, Castle. I know you're emotionally involved with Mrs Reynolds and this has got to be one hundred per cent professionally handled, no risk of personal feelings interfering with anyone's judgement at a crucial moment."

"I assure you, sir, you can trust me not to—" Castle began, but Sladden made an impatient gesture.

"Stay out of it – that's an order," he said, adding more gently, "Don't worry, Jim, we'll take care of her."

Twenty-Four

As Sukey pulled on to her own drive, the car that had been discreetly following her on the last part of her journey home slid past, circled the rest of the little cul-de-sac and parked a short distance from the junction with the main road. A woman passenger got out, a slim, bespectacled figure with collar-length blond hair wearing a dark blue coat and skirt. A handbag dangled from her left shoulder and she held a clipboard in her right hand.

As Sukey got out of her car to open the garage, the front door of the adjoining house opened and her neighbour appeared. He gave her a friendly wave as he put a couple of milk bottles on his doorstep and then gestured at the newly installed security light on her front wall. The police hadn't wasted any time. "Expecting burglars, are you?" he said with a grin.

"Not especially, but there have been a few break-ins not far away," she explained, repeating the story she had been given. "My boyfriend thought it mightn't be a bad idea . . . he says it's quite an effective deterrent."

He nodded agreement. "I've often thought of it. Cost a lot, did it?"

"Enough." She nodded and smiled as she got back into the car, drove into the garage and switched off the engine. In the act of closing the up-and-over door she saw the woman on the opposite side of the road. She appeared to be scanning the house numbers and consulting information on her clipboard, eventually stopping outside the fourth house along. Sukey watched her open the gate, walk briskly up to the front door and ring the bell.

A personal door at the side of Sukey's garage gave on to a narrow passage that ran between her drive and her back garden and was enclosed at the front end by a solid wooden gate secured by metal bolts which she checked before unlocking the back door and entering the house. As she opened it, a high-pitched bleep sounded; she had been expecting it, but just the same it gave her a start. Dumping her handbag on the kitchen table, she hurried to the front room, on her way dropping in the hall the suitcase she had been given on leaving the police station. Peering through the curtains, she was just in time to see the woman with the clipboard disappearing through the open front door of Number Eight.

"So far, so good," she said aloud. It was a little after half-past six and she calculated that it would be at least an hour before her own doorbell rang – plenty of time for a shower and a change of clothes. An afternoon spent closeted at the station being briefed by a Special Branch officer, coupled with the fact that the weather was exceptionally mild for April, had left her feeling uncomfortably warm and sticky. She was apprehensive too, asking herself for the hundredth time whether she was doing the right thing. There was a sick feeling in her stomach that refused to go away despite the repeated assurances she had been given about the measures that had been and would continue to be taken to ensure her safety.

After her shower she went into Fergus's room, stripped the bed, remade it with clean sheets and tidied up some of the litter that he had left lying around. Her throat contracted as she put some jeans and an old pair of trainers in the wardrobe and saw it denuded of most of his everyday clothes. All the arrangements for his removal had been made by the police; she had been allowed a brief word with him once he was safely ensconced in Paul's flat and it had been an effort to control her tears as she did her best to reassure him that they were both in good hands, that it would be all right, that once the danger was over everything would be back to normal in no time. Thank goodness Paul had risen to the occasion splendidly; they had had their differences in the past, but she could not fault him now.

The sky had become overcast and the light was already fading by the time she went downstairs and into the kitchen to unpack the provisions that she had picked up at a corner shop – the supermarket had been declared a potential danger zone – on the way home. She had just put the last items away when the bleeper sounded again from a tiny illuminated panel beside the back door that she had not noticed until now; seconds later the front doorbell rang. Acting on instructions, she took a quick peek through the front room window. As she expected, the woman with the clipboard was standing on the step wearing the half-doubtful, half-expectant expression of someone making a cold call, uncertain of finding the householder at home.

"Good evening," she said briskly when Sukey opened the door. "I'm from Premier Market Research; we're conducting a survey on the extent of public interest in organic food and environmentally friendly products. I wonder if you can spare me a little of your time to answer a few questions?"

While she was speaking, the newcomer held up an identity card which Sukey affected to scrutinise carefully before saying, "Yes, I suppose so. Come in."

"That went all right," said the newcomer as the door closed behind her. "You'll be interested to know that a representative sample of the residents of Woodbine Close have a strong interest in protecting the environment and are dead against GM food."

"Well, good for them," Sukey said. Something about the tone of voice and the wry hint of humour struck an immediate chord and she held out her hand saying, "I'm Sukey Reynolds."

The newcomer put her clipboard on the hall table and took Sukey's hand in hers. "Hi Sukey, I'm Nina Barratt," she said. Her voice was warm and friendly, her grasp strong and reassuring. "Any more calls since you got home?"

"No."

"Fine. Hang on a minute while I check in." Nina took a mobile phone from her handbag, tapped out a number and waited a few seconds before saying, "Stage one completed, no problems so far."

"I'm so relieved you're here," said Sukey fervently as Nina switched off the phone and put it away. "Everything's moved a bit fast today, but that doesn't mean I haven't had time to look over my shoulder every few minutes."

"I'm not surprised. Everything okay this end?"

"I think so. My son is with his father and the security lights have been installed. That bleep sets my teeth on edge," Sukey added with a grimace.

"You'll get used to it. What about the phone?"

"I haven't checked. It's in the kitchen—" She was about to add, "and there's an extension upstairs," but Nina interrupted.

"Then that's where the new instrument will be. Which way?"

"Straight ahead." Sukey took a step forward, intending to lead the way, but Nina moved swiftly ahead of her and opened the kitchen door.

While they were talking, the light had been fading fast and Sukey reached for the light switch. Her hand froze as Nina said sharply, "No lights till the curtains are drawn!"

"Well, pardon me," Sukey muttered. She felt a stab of resentment as it dawned on her that while Nina was there she was no longer in charge in her own home. She stood in the doorway, watching while her bodyguard moved swiftly to the window, keeping out of sight as she peered out into the twilit garden and the field beyond.

"Right, okay, close the curtains before you switch on and make sure your shadow doesn't fall on them," she commanded and Sukey, rather sulkily, obeyed. It had been a stressful day and she was beginning to feel the strain.

Meanwhile, Nina was inspecting the phone. "Yes, that's okay. Look," – she beckoned to Sukey, who was still standing by the window – "every time you answer a call, be ready to operate this button." She pointed with her forefinger. "As soon as you're sure it's him, go ahead and press it."

"What happens then?"

"The moment the source is identified a call goes out for a rapid response team to check it."

"The calls have come from public call boxes so far. Supposing he's hung up and gone by the time they get there?"

"It's up to you to keep him on the line as long as you can." Nina's grin held a spark of mischief as she added, "He's been playing cat and mouse with you so far. It's time for you to play the cat as well . . . or shall we say, copycat?"

"I'll do my best." With an effort, Sukey threw her ill-humour aside. "I suppose we'd better think about some food . . . and what about a drink? Would you like a glass of wine?"

"Nothing alcoholic for me; I'm on duty remember? A soft drink would be fine and some food even better – I'm starving. I'd like to use the bathroom first, though."

"Of course. I'll show you where you're sleeping – your case is in the hall."

Having installed her guest in her temporary quarters, Sukey returned to the kitchen, poured herself a drink and began preparing vegetables for their supper. She had just put the pan on the stove for a stir-fry when a voice behind her said, "Don't be alarmed, it's still me!" She swung round and gave a gasp of mingled shock and astonishment at the sight of the figure in the doorway. The collar-length blond wig had disappeared, revealing short, neatly trimmed dark hair. Gone too were the spectacles and the heavy make-up; the smart business suit had been replaced by a checked, long-sleeved shirt worn outside loose cotton trousers. For a moment, as she stood gaping at her own living double, Sukey thought she was hallucinating. Then the extraordinary truth dawned on her.

"You're Pepita!" she exclaimed.

"Ironic isn't it?" Nina said drily. It might have been imagination, but Sukey thought she detected a momentary flicker of
pain in the other woman's eyes at the mention of the name. For
a few seconds the two studied each other in an slightly bemused
silence. Then Nina said, in a voice that was not quite steady,
"We really are remarkably alike, aren't we? Our trigger-happy
friend's in for a shock – he's getting two copycats for the price
of one!"

Sukey blinked as if trying to clear temporarily distorted
vision. Until now, she had only half believed in the notion of a
doppelgänger and it was taking time to adjust to the reality.
"Is that why they selected you for this job?" she asked.

Nina shook her head. "Pure chance – I just happened to
be the only suitable officer available." Her eye fell on the
bottle of chilled chardonnay that Sukey had left on the table.
"I think, if you don't mind, I'll have that drink after all – a
very small one, and don't tell on me, will you?" she added
with a faint smile.

"Of course I won't. Help yourself." Sukey gave her a
glass. She noticed that Nina's hand shook slightly as she
poured out the wine. "I guess you know the background to
this pantomime, then?"

"I know that you're under threat because Roddy – Miguel
Rodriguez – mistook you for me when he saw you one day at
the nick. They wouldn't tell me why he was there, or anything
else at all. Incidentally, have you any idea what's become
of him?"

Sukey had been on the point of relating the bizarre circumstances of Roddy's disappearance and the subsequent trail
of untraceable faxes, then remembered that Jim had told her
everything in the strictest confidence. "All I can tell you is
that he did a runner before the police had a chance to pull
him in for questioning."

"That's what they told me, but I believe there's more to it
than that. I think he's being protected by the people behind all
the robberies, probably because they want to use him again."

"How can they? If he shows up again he'll risk being recognised and arrested."

Nina shrugged. "Plastic surgery and disguise are pretty sophisticated nowadays. It wouldn't be difficult to alter his appearance, give him a new identity."

"Did you tell the police that?"

"No. They weren't interested in my theories. They simply told me that they reckon a professional hit man has been given the job of killing you because they think you're me, gave me a rough description of a possible suspect who favours shooting his victims in the back of the head and said in effect that was all I needed to know."

"Would that description include dark glasses, cropped hair and a gold earring?"

"Yes – does it mean something to you?"

"It applies to the driver of a car connected with the case, but it could equally apply to any number of young wannabees. The hit man may be someone entirely different."

While she was cooking, Sukey told Nina about the episode outside Henry Greenleaf Antiques. "Jim Castle's convinced there's a connection between the killings and the art robberies, and that Rodriguez is the missing link." She dished up the food and set it out on the table. "I hope you don't mind eating in the kitchen."

"Not a bit."

For a few minutes they ate in silence. Then a thought struck Sukey. "Jim – and presumably the Super as well – thinks that the motive for wanting to kill Pepita is revenge for betraying Roddy. Do you believe that?"

Nina shook her head. "Funny you should say that." She played with the stem of her empty glass, waving aside Sukey's offer of a refill, her expression abstracted. "Motive was hardly mentioned during my briefing," she said after a pause. "I suppose they reckon it's the intention that counts, not the motive."

Sukey waited a few moments before saying quietly, "You haven't answered my question."

188

"No, I haven't, have I?" To Sukey's consternation, Nina's voice wavered on the final words and she laid down her fork and put her hands over her eyes.

"Look, I didn't mean to upset you . . ."

"It's all right . . . you have a right to know why you're being targeted." Nina brushed the back of her hand across her eyes and made a valiant attempt at a smile. "I'd be grateful if you'd keep this to yourself if possible."

"Of course." Because she seemed at a loss how to go on, Sukey said gently, "You care for him, don't you?"

"I kept telling myself it was just a temporary thing, I'd forget about it as soon as the operation was over. And I never intended to let it go as far as it did, but a couple of nights before that robbery, things got out of hand and for the moment I just forgot why I was there with him . . ."

"Look, there's no need to go on if it hurts."

"No, I have to tell you because I think I can explain why the people behind all these robberies want you – me, that is – out of the way. I mentioned disguise and plastic surgery and so on, but there are some things it would be difficult to alter without doing a man permanent injury, and, well, without going into details, I'd be in a position to describe a certain feature which would make identification more or less certain." As she spoke, Nina's voice lost its tremor and became almost clinically detached.

"I shouldn't have let it happen," she went on. "It was very foolish, very unprofessional. No one will ever know how close I came to chickening out of the whole operation. It would have meant the end of my career and the waste of hundreds of hours of police time, but the thought of turning Roddy in, of being the cause of his being banged up . . ."

Once again, her voice wobbled and Sukey picked up the wine bottle. "Are you sure—?" she began.

"Quite sure." Nina's mouth was set in a determined line; the moment of weakness had passed. "I'm here to protect you, remember? I wouldn't be much good in a shoot-out if I was half cut."

"Shoot-out!" Sukey had temporarily forgotten the reason for Nina's presence. "Have you got a gun on you now?"

"Of course – it never leaves me." Nina finished what was left of her meal and pushed back the empty plate. "Thanks Sukey, that was delicious."

"There's fruit crumble to follow."

"Sounds super."

They had just finished their meal and were clearing the table when the bleeper sounded, making Sukey freeze in sudden terror, then leap sideways and shrink against the wall as Nina hissed, "Keep away from the window!" before diving for the light switch. The interior darkness revealed that the outside light above the kitchen window had been activated. Nina cautiously lifted one corner of the curtain and looked out, then gave a little chuckle. "Come here and see your intruder," she said.

Sukey looked where she was pointing. A hedgehog was crossing the back lawn, moving like a little clockwork toy. It was not until she released her breath that she realised she had been holding it until her lungs were almost bursting. "I can see we're going to have quite a few false alarms," she said, with a feeble attempt at a laugh.

"Don't ever get too relaxed," Nina warned. "I don't think our man will make his move in darkness, but we're taking no chances. Every time that thing sounds, treat it as if it's the real thing, okay?"

Twenty-Five

By mutual consent, they turned in early, leaving their bedroom doors ajar so that they would hear the warning signal. After a long period of wakefulness Sukey fell into an uneasy sleep; some time in the small hours she sat up in bed with a start, feeling as if an electric needle was being driven into her skull. Something – or someone – had been detected by one of the sensors. Still only half awake, she threw off the bedclothes, lurched to the window and peered out. The one street lamp that illuminated the cul-de-sac was switched off at midnight, but a ring of brilliant light fell on the front garden, fading on the perimeter to penumbra and then to deep shadow. It lent an air of unreality to the familiar scene, as if the curtain had risen in a theatre where the final act of a melodrama waited to be played out. But there were no actors; the stage was silent and deserted.

Something moved behind her and she spun round with a cry of alarm on seeing a dim figure framed in the doorway.

"Get away from the window!" The voice was a harsh, urgent whisper.

"Nina! You scared the life out of me!"

Without replying, Nina crossed the room and stood against the wall, peering obliquely round the curtains. Sukey slumped down on the edge of her bed, her heart thumping and her head spinning after the sudden leap from slumber into wakefulness. Nina's right hand was concealed, but from her stance and the angle of her elbow, it was easy to surmise that she was holding a gun. She was still fully dressed; evidently, she had gone to bed prepared for something like this.

"Can you see anyone?" Sukey whispered.

"Not from here. Don't move or make a sound – I'll check from the other windows." Like a shadow, Nina slipped out of the room and padded across the landing, while Sukey sat shivering in her nightdress. The figures on her digital clock glowed red in the semi-darkness, ticking off the seconds.

At last Nina came back. "After all that, it was only a cat." As she spoke, the exterior light went out, leaving them in darkness. "I daresay we shall get a few more false alarms," she went on in a matter-of-fact voice, "but please remember what I said about never standing directly in front of the window, especially just after the alarm has sounded."

"I'm sorry," said Sukey humbly. "I was so startled, I forgot all about it. Is it okay to put my light on now?"

"If you want to. It's only three o'clock."

"I don't know about you, but I could use a hot drink. I'm frozen."

"Not a bad idea. You put on something warm and I'll go and put the kettle on."

It was clear that even though the moment of crisis had passed, Nina still considered herself in charge. Reflecting that if this was likely to be a regular occurrence it might be a good idea to follow her example and sleep in something more practical, Sukey pulled joggers and a sweatshirt over her nightdress before going downstairs.

After drinking a cup of tea, they went back to bed. To Sukey's surprise, she awoke the following morning to find that she had had several hours of restful sleep. The smell of fresh coffee wafted upwards as she crossed the landing on her way to the bathroom. She went downstairs to find Nina in the kitchen, reading the morning paper with a mug of coffee in her hand. A used glass and cereal bowl stood on the draining-board.

"I've made myself at home – I hope you don't mind," she

said as Sukey entered. "I put my head round the door before I came down, but you were dead to the world. You needed that sleep; the stress was getting to you."

"No problem," said Sukey as convincingly as she could. "I hope you found everything you wanted."

"Yes, thanks. Can I get you anything? I only made enough coffee for one, by the way – I thought you'd prefer yours fresh."

"That was very thoughtful of you," said Sukey drily as she took orange juice and milk from the refrigerator.

Nina gave her a sharp glance over the rim of her mug. "Look," she said, "I know it must be hard, being bossed around by a stranger in your own home . . ."

"It's all right, I didn't mean to sound sarky. I know you've got a job to do."

"Let me make a fresh pot of coffee while you eat your cereal."

"Thanks."

After a short silence, Nina said, "I've been thinking, trying to get some sort of feel for the psychology of this joker. I reckon he's a bit of a sadist who enjoys making his victims squirm before he kills them – hence the phone calls."

"How long d'you reckon he'll keep it up?"

"Hard to say. It depends on how long he's got to finish the job. If he's not been given any other assignments, I suppose he can spin things out and have his fun for several days before making his move."

Sukey shivered and put down her spoon, her appetite gone. "Several days!" she exclaimed in horror. "I'll be a nervous wreck."

"No you won't . . . but in any case, if you box clever, you might be able to hurry things along."

Nina put two mugs of fresh coffee on the table and sat down again. Sukey picked hers up and wrapped both hands round it, grateful for its warmth. "How do you mean?" she asked.

"Like I said, I think he gets his kicks giving his victims the jitters, so next time he calls, try and act scared, plead with him . . . and of course, tell him it's all a mistake, that you're not Pepita but someone who looks like her. He won't believe it, of course – in fact, we don't want him to—"

"Oh, thanks very much!" This time the sarcasm was intended. "I do believe you *want* him to take a pot at me."

"Of course I don't, I simply want to flush him out into the open."

"Yes, I see." Once again, Sukey found herself questioning the wisdom of the entire enterprise. "Just the same, I'm beginning to wonder whether I should have taken Jim's advice."

"Gone into hiding, you mean? No, I reckon you made the right decision." Nina sounded as casual as if they had been discussing a change of wallpaper.

"I hope so." Sukey finished her coffee and stood up. "I think I'll have a shower."

At that moment the telephone rang and the two women exchanged glances. "If it's him, wait a few seconds before you say anything, try and sound scared, and keep him talking as long as possible." Nina took off her wristwatch and put it on the table in front of her. "Okay, answer now."

Sounding scared won't be a problem, thought Sukey as she picked up the receiver. Her lips felt stiff and her mouth was dry; her cautious "Hullo!" was a feeble croak.

"Good morning, Pepita." He sounded genuinely cordial, like someone greeting an old friend.

Sukey's hand shook as she pressed the tracer button. She cleared her throat and licked her lips. "Why do you keep phoning me? What do you want with me?" she asked. There was nothing simulated in the way her voice trembled.

"I thought it'd be nice if we got to know one another a little better," he said. Despite the metallic, slightly nasal accent, the voice had an oily quality that sent a shiver down her back.

"Why should I want to get to know you?" she quavered. "I never asked you to phone me and I don't want to talk to you – please leave me alone."

"Oh, but we must talk. I like to be on friendly terms with the people I work with . . . or should I say, work on?" He gave a low, drawn-out chuckle. "Did you sleep well, Pepita?"

"Do stop calling me that!" Sukey almost shouted into the phone. "Can't you get it into your head that I'm not Pepita, I don't know anyone called Pepita, you've got me mixed up with someone else—"

"You think I'd fall for that story? You must think I'm stupid."

"It's true – please believe me! You're making a dreadful mistake—"

"You're the one who made the mistake, Pepita, when you betrayed Roddy." The voice sank to a menacing whisper. "A woman who betrays her man can be dangerous, very dangerous. You're dangerous, Pepita, and you must pay the price."

"What price? What are you going to do?"

"You'll find out when I'm good and ready."

"There must be some way we can sort this out."

"Oh don't worry, it'll be sorted out very soon. Goodbye for now."

"No please, don't go away."

His only response was a chilling laugh before the receiver at the other end was replaced.

"Well done, you sounded petrified," said Nina approvingly as Sukey too hung up.

"I *am* petrified," said Sukey grimly. She went back to her chair on legs that had turned to jelly. "D'you think I kept him talking long enough?"

"Two and a half minutes from picking up the phone," said Nina calmly as she clipped her watch back on her wrist.

"What happens now?"

"The source of the call should have been located the moment you pressed that button and the police will home in and throw a cordon round the area. That's the theory, at any rate. We'll just have to wait and see how quick off the mark they've been. Whereabouts did the earlier calls come from?"

"They were all fairly local."

"Let's say, on average, within half-an-hour's drive from here. If you want to have that shower it might be as well to get on with it. If there's anything to report, the police will get through to me on the mobile."

Sukey hurried through her shower, got dressed, dried her hair and went back downstairs to find Nina once more reading the newspaper.

"Any news?" she asked.

"Not yet. D'you want this?"

Nina offered the paper, but Sukey waved it away. "No thanks, I couldn't concentrate. How long d'you think it'll be before we get news?"

"Impossible to say. We could be in for a long, boring wait."

It was over two hours before Nina's mobile rang. Sukey waited, itching with nerves, while the undercover policewoman calmly listened with only the occasional "Yes", "Right", or "Okay" in response to whatever was being said at the other end. When the call was over she put down the phone and said quietly, "They've got him."

"Thank God!" Sukey could have wept with relief. "What happened?"

"He was in a callbox about five miles away. By a lucky chance a police patrol was quite near, on their way back to the station at the end of a shift. He'd gone by the time they arrived, but a woman who was about to use the phone had seen him, told them which direction he'd taken and actually went with them in the car to look for him. She was able to point him out and they went after him, but he saw them coming and bolted. I didn't get all the details, but it ended up with him taking refuge in some woods and they had to scramble the helicopter."

"Brilliant!" Spontaneously, Sukey flung her arms round Nina and gave her a hug. Her hand encountered something hard and she froze for a second before releasing her. "Gosh, is that your gun?" she asked.

"Sure." Nina patted the spot beneath the loose shirt where the weapon lay concealed.

"Have you ever actually shot anyone?"

Nina smiled and shook her head. "I had to show it a couple of times, but thank goodness I've never had to fire it – except in practice of course."

"What happens now?" asked Sukey.

"We stay in touch and wait for instructions." Nina glanced at her watch, then flexed her arms and shoulders. "I get a bit tense during these operations and the muscles tend to seize up," she explained. "You must be pretty uptight yourself – how about a short run to wind down?"

Sukey shook her head. "No thanks. I work out at a fitness club, but I'm not into road running. Besides, Jim might get in touch so I'd rather stay here. You go – I'll be fine now."

"You're sure?"

"Of course."

"Right. I'll only be fifteen minutes or so." Nina picked up her mobile, clipped it on to her waistband and let herself out by the back door. The bleeper screeched a warning and Sukey reached up and switched off the system.

"Am I glad I've heard the last of that thing," she declared fervently.

She was upstairs making her bed when, less than ten minutes later, the front doorbell rang. Glancing out of the window she saw a British Telecom van parked outside her gate and a figure in blue overalls on the doorstep. Assuming that he had been sent to remove the specially adapted telephone, she ran down and opened the door.

"You haven't wasted any time," she said cheerfully, then froze in terror as the man turned to face her. Dark glasses, cropped hair, gold earring.

White teeth flashed against tanned skin as he gave a slow, wolfish smile. "Hi, Pepita!" he said. "We meet at last."

Twenty-Six

For a moment, Sukey stood like a statue, paralysed with shock and disbelief. It was impossible: he was under arrest after having been cornered during an elaborate police operation. How could they have let him get away and why had she and Nina not been warned? Her heart seemed to stop and her lungs would barely admit enough breath for her to gasp, "How did you get here – how did you escape?"

"Escape? Where from?"

"From the police . . . they said you'd been caught."

"They got it wrong, didn't they? What a joke!" His smile was mirthless, mocking her. He moved forward, lifting his right arm, which until then had been hanging at his side. A casual observer, seeing from a distance a man in BT overalls holding something in his hand, would assume it was a mobile telephone and think nothing of it. But it was not a telephone that she felt pressed against her stomach as he said, "This will only take a moment. Let's go indoors."

On legs that felt on the point of collapse, Sukey backed into the hallway. He followed, casually closing the front door behind him with his free hand while keeping the gun pointing steadily at his intended victim.

"That's better," he said in the harsh, nasal accent she had come to dread hearing. "We don't want to frighten the neighbours, do we?"

"What do you care about frightening people?" she faltered. "I believe you enjoy it!"

"I have to admit I do . . . sometimes . . . in certain cases, and this is one of them," he taunted her. "In fact, Pepita, you're a *very* special case. You've given us all a lot of trouble, especially Roddy."

"I'm not Pepita! How many times do I have to tell you?" she pleaded. "This man Roddy you keep talking about . . . I don't know him, I've never met him, so how could I betray him?"

"Save your breath, Pepita – you've come to the end of the road. From now on, the filth will have to find someone else to do their dirty work for them, won't they?" He glanced down at the gun, shifting it slightly between his fingers, almost fondling it.

"You're a fine one to talk about dirty work!" Sukey snapped in a sudden surge of spirit. If she was going to die, she wasn't going to cringe to this vermin. "What do you call your paymasters – philanthropists?"

"Big words, Pepita."

"You're really getting a kick out of this, aren't you?" She could hear her voice rising, thin and hysterical. Fear had her once more in its claws. Nina was out and powerless to defend her; somewhere the police were frantically seeking an escaped prisoner. Would it occur to them that her house would be the first place he would head for, to carry out his assignment and make his getaway? Even if it did, could they get here before her life was blanked out in a searing flame of agony? If she managed to keep him talking until Nina got back there might be a chance . . . she'd said fifteen minutes or so and it must be ten since she left . . . another five minutes would be an eternity, but it was her only hope. A desperate wish to survive stung her brain into life. "You want to see me grovel, don't you?" she said defiantly. "I'm sorry to disappoint you, but I'm not going to."

"Pity – it would add to the fun," he acknowledged with a sneer.

"Well, I'm not going to indulge your perverted idea of fun."

"Have it your way. I'm a bit pressed for time, so I think

we'll get on with it. Turn round!" The change of tone was like a whiplash. He raised the gun and levelled it at her head. "Turn round . . . now!"

"No!" A sudden recollection of the way Crowson, Morris and Lockyer had died flashed into her mind. Their executioner had shot his victims in the back of the head. A whim . . . or a weakness, an inability to meet their gaze as he pressed the trigger? "If you're going to shoot me, you'll have to look me in the eye!" She heard him exhale sharply, saw his jaw tighten . . . and knew she had found his weakness. Her one chance now was to play on it. "You have a problem with that, don't you?" she said softly.

"Cut out the bullshit – turn round!" he repeated, but some of the sting had gone out of the command. He was wavering; a muscle at the corner of his mouth had begun to twitch and the hand that held the gun was shaking slightly.

"You really do have a problem, don't you?" she repeated. "What is it – some traumatic experience that makes it easier to blow someone's brains out from behind so that you don't have to face them . . . is that it? Why don't you tell me about it?" she rushed on. "Remember what they say about a trouble shared?" To her astonishment she even managed a smile on the last words.

"Do as you're told, you fucking bitch!" His voice was hoarse and unsteady; now he was really rattled. "Turn round!"

"And make it easy for you? Why should I?" Looking him defiantly in the eye, she began to move backwards along the passage. Almost as if mesmerised by her gaze he followed her, step by step, as she inched towards the kitchen. If she could move quickly enough, there might be a chance of escape through the back door. She felt the door frame pressing against her spine, then an arm grabbed her from behind, dragging her sideways; simultaneously a voice – Nina's – shouted, "Armed police! Drop the gun!"

There were two reports. Something whizzed past Sukey's ear and shattered the kitchen window. The gunman dropped his weapon with a howl of pain, clutched his right shoulder and slid to the floor, landing in a crumpled heap against the wall, his face contorted with pain, his eyes closed and blood pouring down his arm. Shaking in every part of her body, Sukey watched in bewilderment as Nina leapt forward to retrieve the gun.

"You're nicked," she said coolly. Keeping him covered, she unhooked her mobile phone from her belt and manipulated it one-handed.

"Target disarmed and arrested at Number Twelve, Woodbine Close," she reported. "He's winged in the shoulder and bleeding so we'd better have an ambulance. No other casualties." She snapped off the phone, returned it to her belt and studied her prisoner with almost clinical detachment. "We've got to keep you in good condition, haven't we? You're going to be very useful to us."

He gave a groan and opened his eyes, then blinked in disbelief as his gaze moved from Nina to Sukey and back again. "Jesus, I'm seeing double," he said weakly.

"No, there really are two of us," Nina assured him. "But you might be interested to know that my friend was telling the truth. She isn't Pepita – I am."

"What a fucking cock-up!" he muttered. "When Wallis finds out he'll do his nut."

"Tell us where to find him and we'll break the news for you," Nina promised.

He shot her a look of sheer hatred. "Get stuffed!" he snarled.

The telephone rang. "You get it, Sukey," Nina ordered without taking her eyes off the would-be assassin.

Sukey stumbled into the kitchen and picked up the receiver. "Who is it?" she asked in a shaky whisper.

"Sukey?" It was Jim, his voice unnaturally loud, rough with anxiety. "I've just been told . . . there's been a shoot-out at your house . . . are you all right?

"Yes, I'm fine. Nina arrested the hit-man and we're waiting for the police and an ambulance."

"You're not hurt?"

"No, I'm all right, truly, but . . ." The tears were streaming down her face; delayed shock made her voice thick, almost unintelligible. "Get here, Jim, please . . . just get here!"

"It was the most unbelievable cock-up," said Jim.

"Funny, that's what the hitman said when he saw Sukey and me together – or words to that effect!" Nina observed.

"I couldn't believe what was happening," said Sukey. "One minute we hear he's safely banged up in the nick and the next he appears on my doorstep waving a gun. How on earth did he do it?"

"He didn't – that's where the cock-up comes in," said Jim. A trace of harshness in his voice told Sukey that beneath his cool, reassuring exterior he was seething with anger.

"Tell us exactly what happened, Jim," Fergus begged.

It was seven o'clock in the evening and the four of them were sitting at the table in the dining-room of Number Twelve Woodbine Close amid the debris of a takeaway meal. Despite Sukey's protests that she was perfectly all right, Jim had insisted on calling a doctor, who had given her a sedative and ordered her to bed. She had slept until six and awoke to find that the kitchen window had been repaired, Fergus brought home and Jim and Nina in charge of the catering arrangements.

"It was another case of mistaken identity, of course," Jim began. "The guy they arrested wasn't the one who made the call to you, but another one answering the rough description which was all we had to go on. He must have been waiting to use the phone and nipped into the box the minute our man left."

"So the woman identified the wrong man?" Sukey closed her eyes, thinking how close to death the blunder had brought her.

"Exactly. The mistake would have been realised straight away if the chap hadn't made a bolt for it the minute he saw the police car."

"I suppose he was a criminal too," said Fergus.

"He'd escaped from a youth detention centre earlier in the day, nicked a car and had just phoned his girlfriend in London to check that she was home."

"And meanwhile the hitman was heading in my direction," said Sukey with a shudder.

Under the table, Fergus gave his mother's hand a squeeze. "You did brilliantly, Mum," he said proudly. "I reckon you ought to get a commendation." He turned to Jim and said, "Wasn't it a bit premature to give the all clear the minute the guy was arrested? I'll bet if you'd still been on the case . . ."

"It certainly was premature," said the detective. "It put your mother's life in danger. Someone who shall be nameless was so pleased with himself on getting what he saw as a result so soon after taking over the case that he couldn't wait to spread the glad tidings. He's got a lot of egg on his face over this one," Jim added, not without a certain relish.

"What a bit of luck that Nina got home in time." Fergus shot a grateful smile at the woman who had saved his mother's life.

"Not luck. As soon as the mistake was realised I got a call on my mobile," Nina explained. "You see, although we'd been told an arrest had been made, I hadn't been officially taken off the case, so I kept the mobile and my gun at the ready."

"Thank God for that!" said Sukey fervently. "I reckon you're the one who deserves the commendation."

"It was providential that you'd turned off the bleeper," said Nina. "If our friend had heard that, things might have turned out differently."

"What happens now, Jim?" asked Sukey.

"We're hoping this character – he says his name's Martin Goreman, but whether it's genuine or not we've yet to find out – will lead us to Wallis and his mob. There might even be a chance of recovering some of Patterson's art treasures. The case isn't closed yet, not by a long way."

"There's Roddy to track down as well," Fergus pointed

out. "Or do you think his body will turn up one of these days?"

"I doubt it. From the trouble they took to take him out of our reach, I reckon his masters have an interest in keeping him alive – so long as he agrees to dance to their tune."

"And carry out more robberies, you mean?" Fergus looked puzzled. "I don't see how . . . wouldn't he be recognised?"

"In England, yes – but there are plenty of art collections in other countries. Interpol has been alerted so with luck he'll get his come-uppance before too long. Anyway, that's enough talk about villains." Jim laid down his knife and fork and glanced round at the others. If he had seen the momentary flicker of pain on Nina's face, he gave no sign. "I believe there's fruit salad to follow," he said. "Shall I get it?"

"I'll clear this lot away," said Fergus. He stood up and began stacking the used plates. "Mum, d'you mind if I go round to Anita's when we've finished? She was a bit miffed when I wouldn't tell her why I had to cancel our date yesterday." He glanced at Jim, who had just re-entered carrying a bowl of fruit salad. "Is it okay to tell her what's happened?"

Jim put down the bowl and thought for a moment before saying, "I'd prefer you not to go into any details until it's been decided how much of this morning's events are going to be released to the press. You can just say that a police operation was mounted at your house, an arrest was made and your mother's a heroine," he added. The love and pride in the smile that he gave Sukey made her heart glow, yet at the same time she felt a pang of sadness on Nina's behalf.

Shortly after Fergus left, Jim said, "Sook, I'd like to stay a bit longer, but I'm on duty over the weekend so if you don't mind I'll go home now. What about you, Nina? I believe you left your car in the multi-storey . . . would you like a lift into Gloucester?"

Nina hesitated. Sensing a reluctance to accept the offer, Sukey said quickly, "Why don't you stay here till tomorrow and keep me company? The spare room's full of junk, but you'd be quite comfortable on the couch."

"Thanks, I'd like that," said Nina gratefully.

When Jim had gone, the two women settled in armchairs in the sitting-room with cups of coffee. After a moment, Nina said, "Thanks so much for the offer of a bed. I wasn't looking forward to a night on my own."

"I guessed as much. Was it because of all that chat about Roddy? I thought it must have hurt, knowing how you feel about him."

"It did, a bit."

"You haven't told me how you made contact with him."

"As you know, I'm with the Regional Crime Squad. We had a request for a volunteer to infiltrate Roddy's circle and I was picked for the job because before I joined the police I worked for a firm of sherry importers and knew something about the wine trade. Roddy was a known womaniser; he and his friends used to meet in a wine bar in Soho and chat up the birds. I made contact with him there; he was with two men who I later got to know as Crowson and Morris. I pretended we'd met briefly – he didn't remember, of course, but he was very polite and friendly and bought me a drink. I asked him if there was any chance of a job with his firm and he said unfortunately there wasn't, which was a bit of a blow because we understood they were looking for a PA, but there was no reason why we shouldn't see one another again. I'd given him my cover story . . . I was married to a man who was always off on business trips and it all went like a dream. We wined and dined and partied . . . and I managed to keep his interest by not jumping into bed with him straight away. He wasn't used to that." Nina's face lit up for a moment, as if the words brought pleasurable memories, then darkened again as she added, "I really believe he came to care for me . . . almost as much as I care for him."

"What do you think will happen to him now?" asked Sukey.

"He'll have to play along with whoever's running the show, whether he likes it or not. Once he realises what he's got mixed up in, he'll loathe every minute of it."

"He could refuse to co-operate."

"You think so?" Nina shook her head decisively. "It would be suicide – he'll have no choice if he wants to stay alive." Her eyes were brimming with tears. "Sukey, I'm so afraid for him – and the worst part of it is, I'll never know what becomes of him."

Twenty-Seven

O n Saturday morning Sukey drove Nina into Gloucester. "I guess it'll be a relief to get back to normal duties after all the excitement," she remarked as she pulled up a short distance from the entrance to the multi-storey park where Nina had left her car.

"It will in a way." There was a touch of wistfulness in the policewoman's voice and Sukey stole a sideways glance at her. She was looking straight ahead, making no attempt to get out of the car.

Impulsively, Sukey put a hand on her arm. "It's been great knowing you," she said warmly. "I owe you my life – I'll never forget that."

Nina gave a faint smile, but did not turn her head. "All part of the job."

"It's strange, isn't it – we were constantly together for two days, but I know hardly anything about you. I don't even know where you live."

"There's no secret about that. I share a flat in Oxford with my brother. His wife died a couple of years ago and he's got no children, so as we're both on our own it seemed to make sense for him to move in with me. He's away quite a bit, so I have the flat to myself most of the time. He'd have a fit if he knew what I've been up to," she added with a wry grin. "I've never let on about the firearms training."

Despite the lightness of her manner, Sukey detected an underlying sadness. She sensed that it would be a long time before she got over Roddy. "Why don't we keep in touch?"

she suggested. "Oxford's only an hour or so's drive from Gloucester. Maybe we could get together some time when Jim's on weekend duty and Fergus is out with Anita or staying with his Dad—" She broke off in some embarrassment; the suggestion had been well intentioned, but it had only served to underline the difference in their circumstances.

There was no trace of self-pity in Nina's manner as she replied, "That would be lovely." She rummaged in her handbag. "Here's my card – call me when you have some free time." She got out of the car and grabbed her case from the back seat. "Take care, hope to see you soon," she said.

Fergus had offered to cancel his plans for the weekend to stay at home with his mother, but she insisted that she was all right on her own. She managed to keep herself busy with household and gardening tasks, but they had never seemed more wearisome or arduous. The time dragged and the telephone remained infuriatingly silent until early on Sunday evening, more than forty-eight hours after Goreman's dramatic arrest.

Jim was on the line; he sounded weary but triumphant as, without any preamble, he declared, "We got a result! Wallis was picked up early this morning off the Isle of Wight on an ocean-going yacht laden with stolen antiques and art treasures, including most of the stuff from Bussell Manor."

"Brilliant! How did you get on to him?"

"Goreham. It was a long time before we could get a word out of him, but in the end we got him to talk." Jim gave a hoarse chuckle. "You'll never guess how we managed to persuade him!"

"Tell me."

"Later, love. I'm all in and I haven't washed or shaved or had a proper meal for twenty-four hours. I'm going back to the flat for a shower and a change of clothes—"

"You can have a shower here," she interrupted. "Gus can fix you up with a clean shirt and I'm sure he'll be delighted to lend you the electric shaver his father gave him for Christmas. And then you can tell us all about it over supper."

"I'll be with you in half an hour."

"I imagine it's going to keep the lawyers busy arguing for quite a while," said Jim when he laid down his knife and fork after demolishing a plate of chicken and chips. "All I can say is, I'm glad it's not my problem."

"Don't start talking in riddles," said Sukey severely. "We've been very patient, but you won't get your coffee and cake until you tell us what's happened."

"Yes, come on Jim," Fergus urged. "We're dying to know how you got Goreham to talk. We thought perhaps he'd be too scared, like that other guy, the one whose antique shop got done over—"

"Greenleaf. Yes, it'll be interesting to see how that joker reacts when he learns we've got his pal Wallis and busted the whole operation . . . at least, this end of it. Whether it'll lead to the big fish is another matter. That part of it's right out of our hands."

"Never mind that – just get on with your end of the story," said Sukey. She cut a large slice of fruit cake and put it on the table just out of Jim's reach. "Talk!" she ordered with mock ferocity.

"Okay." He put up his hands in surrender. "It was Patterson's idea, as a matter of fact. He's been on our backs ever since Fiona spilled the beans about the way she and Stuart Lockyer planned their robbery at Bussell Manor. We let him know we'd made an arrest, but were having trouble getting information out of the prisoner. You'll never guess what he came up with."

"I'm not going to try. You jolly well tell us," said Sukey in exasperation, but Fergus gave a sudden squeak of excitement.

"I know!" he declared. "He suggested that you do a deal with Goreham – let him know he might be in line for a big reward!"

"Well done, lad." Jim reached across and gave Fergus a pat

on the shoulder, then swung his hand round to snatch the plate of cake from Sukey's grasp.

"That strikes me as highly unethical," she said, making no attempt to stop him as she considered the latest revelation. "Isn't there some law that says a criminal can't profit from his crime?"

"That was our first reaction, but Patterson pointed out that the insurance company was offering the reward for information leading to the recovery of the stolen property. Goreham had nothing to do with the robbery so he'll claim that he's perfectly entitled to the money. He'll go down for a good long stretch for attempted murder, of course, which as things stand might be all we'll be able to charge him with because the gun he threatened you with isn't the one used to kill the other victims. At the moment there's nothing to link him with those murders—"

"—and when he comes out of prison he'll have a nice little nest-egg waiting for him," Fergus finished with an air of triumph.

"That's what he's hoping for. Whether he'll get away with it remains to be seen. As I said, it should keep the lawyers happily arguing the toss for quite a while."

"What you're saying is, you told Goreham that he'd be in line for the reward if he'd tell you where to find Wallis," said Sukey. "That sounds suspiciously like bribery to me."

"Oh, we used a much more subtle approach than that. We managed to let his brief overhear a reference to the fact that Patterson's insurance company was increasing the reward. His ears nearly touched the ceiling," Jim added with a chuckle. "He couldn't wait to report that little gem to his client."

"So officially it was Goreham's own idea – that was really smart!" said Fergus in admiration.

"I'm glad someone appreciates our cleverness," said Jim with a sly grin in Sukey's direction. "What the outcome will be I've no idea, but the point is, it worked. Wallis is behind bars – incidentally, Sook, you'll be amused to know that one of the arresting officers complained about his excessive use of a very pungent body lotion. Patterson's got his property back, including one picture with a damaged frame that he said he never liked much anyway, so everyone's happy except the villains."

"Not everyone," said Sukey thoughtfully.

"Well, everyone who deserves to be. If Fiona hadn't gone along with Lockyer's plan to rob her employer she might not be grieving for him now. There's Donna Hoskins, of course. It'll take her a while to get over Crowson, but at least she's got her mother to take care of her."

"Yes, I suppose so," Sukey agreed, her thoughts momentarily far away. She had not been thinking of either Fiona or Donna.

He had not known a moment's peace of mind since the final interview with El Dueño. Waking and sleeping, he was haunted by the memory of the cold eyes and the cruel, mirthless smile. He was tormented by the trail of death that he had unwittingly set in motion – first old Mrs Frampton, then Crowson and Morris and finally the brutal slaying of Stuart Lockyer. But the final blow had been the almost casual revelation about the woman who, in spite of her betrayal, was still the only one he had ever truly cared for.

His mind went back to the final briefing, the handing over of passport and airline tickets together with documents and letters of introduction to support his claim to be Señor Ramon Alvarez, rightful heir to his late uncle's business in Madrid. Only when he had stowed everything in his briefcase and was about to take his leave did the bombshell fall.

"I forgot to mention, *amigo*," his tormentor had said with an urbane smile, "that your little English *chica* has been causing us a great deal of trouble. She shot the agent sent to eliminate her."

He remembered how thin and reedy his voice had sounded, as if shock had all but paralysed his vocal chords. "Pepita armed – a killer?"

"Killer – no, at least not this time. Unfortunately."

"Why unfortunately?"

"She only wounded our man and he has talked, which has caused us a great deal of inconvenience. It will take a while to repair the damage to our organisation, but we shall find time to deal with your Pepita eventually."

"What do you mean – deal with her?" The question had been asked mechanically; he knew only too well what the man meant.

Once again had come that cruel smile. "I am not a fool, *amigo*. It is clear to me that despite her treachery you are still in love with her. That makes you a weak link in the chain; so long as she lives, you are not safe from detection. Have no fear – I shall see that you are informed when she has ceased to be a threat to your freedom. Now, I wish you a safe journey and good luck. I expect much of you. So long as you obey instructions to the letter, you have nothing to fear."

He would never forget the implied threat in the final words, nor the sense of revulsion at the contact with the smooth, well-manicured hand, tainted with the blood of countless victims, that El Dueño extended. The memory filled him with self-disgust and despair.

The drive to the airport, the plane journey, the arrival in Madrid where he had been met by the secretary of his late 'uncle' had all been part of the waking nightmare. He had checked into his hotel and later rejoined the secretary – a middle-aged, severely dressed woman with mournful eyes, jet-black hair and skin the colour of wax – for an informal dinner. After the weeks of preparation, he had played his part mechanically, perfectly. Now, after arranging to be in the company's office at eight o'clock the following morning, he was at last alone.

He went into the bathroom and stared at his reflection in the mirror above the washbasin. His new reflection, one that he still had difficulty in identifying as himself. It was uncanny, the difference a few small changes could make. Gundlach had

212

done his work well. Even his own cousin would not recognise
him . . . but Pepita would know him immediately, if ever they
had a chance to make love again. At the memory of the light
touch of her fingers on that tiny, ineradicable mark, he broke
down and wept.

When he was calm again he finished undressing, switched
off the lights and got into bed. He lay for a long time with his
eyes closed, but sleep would not come. Like a recorded message, endlessly repeated, El Dueño's words echoed monoto-
nously, mercilessly, in his brain. *So long as she lives, you are
not safe.* He got up and went to the window, where he stood
for a long time staring down at the people in the street, the
passing traffic, the lights in the shop windows. Among them
was the illuminated green sign of an all-night *Farmacia*. He
could buy something there to help him sleep.

He dressed and went out. On his return he wrote two letters
which he put in the same envelope, thankful for the foresight
that had prompted him to buy stamps before leaving for the
evening's rendezvous. No doubt he could have obtained them
at the front desk, but for all he knew the hotel might be part
of El Dueño's organisation. For the same reason, instead of
using the mailbox in the hotel, he went back into the street
and found one a short distance away. Then he returned to his
room. As he lay in bed, waiting for sleep, a different message
was running through his head. This time it was saying, 'So
long as you live, her life is in danger.'

The chambermaid who serviced the third floor was a phleg-
matic woman who had worked in the hotel for many years. She
knew the importance attached by the owners to keeping intact
its reputation as a well-run establishment, untouched by any
whiff of disturbance or scandal. When, on entering room 307
the following morning, she found the occupant apparently fast
asleep with an empty bottle labelled 'Paracetamol' on the table
beside him, she quietly informed the manager, who called the
room on the internal telephone. Receiving no reply, he sent for
a doctor. When it was established that Señor Ramon Alvarez

was beyond mortal help, the manager contacted a friend at police headquarters on whose discretion he knew he could rely. Thus it was that the staff of Alvarez y Cia were advised that, tragically, their new employer had died in his sleep from natural causes, and this information was duly relayed to the man known throughout the organisation as El Dueño.

Three days later, Superintendent Sladden found a letter bearing a Spanish postmark on his desk. When he had examined the contents, he sent for DI Castle.

"What d'you make of that, Jim?" he said, tossing a single sheet of paper across the desk.

Castle studied the letter in silence for several minutes. At last he said quietly, "If it's all true – and I see no reason at this stage to think otherwise – it contains some valuable leads. Taken along with what we can get out of Wallis and Greenleaf, it might well lead to the break-up of a combined smuggling and money-laundering organisation, most likely linked to the drugs trade."

"It will have to be dealt with at the highest level." Sladden's voice held a note of regret at the thought that such a high-profile operation would pass out of his hands. "Let's hope that in due course our part in bringing it about will be recognised. I'll be sure to mention your contribution in my report, Jim."

"Thank you sir. Perhaps Mrs Reynolds too . . . ?"

"Yes, of course. Now, there's one other small matter to see to. There was this enclosure with the letter." He held up a sealed envelope. "It's addressed to someone called Pepita – perhaps you would arrange for it to be delivered."

"Of course, sir."

Epilogue

"Roddy's dead, isn't he?" said Nina.

"Yes," Sukey replied. She held out the envelope she had been asked to deliver. "This was enclosed with a long letter he wrote to the police in Gloucester. Superintendent Sladden asked Jim to see that it reached you and we – Jim and I – thought it would be easier for you this way."

"That was kind." Nina took the envelope in both hands as if it was something precious and liable to break if carelessly handled, but made no move to open it. "What did the other letter say?" she asked unexpectedly.

"I haven't actually seen it, but Jim told me the gist of it. You were absolutely right; he was taken to a clinic in South America and underwent plastic surgery before being given a false identity and sent back to Europe to carry on where he left off. He obviously felt he couldn't go through with it, realised there was only one way to escape from the people who were manipulating him and decided to blow the whistle on them before he—"

"Bowed out," Nina finished in a surprisingly calm voice as Sukey broke off in embarrassment. "How did it happen?"

"I don't know any details – all I can tell you is that he was found in a room in a Madrid hotel after having apparently taken an overdose. The letter he sent to the police – or a copy of it – has been passed to the Spanish authorities and I gather it contains some valuable information about people they've had their eye on for a long time but haven't been able to touch for lack of evidence."

215

Nina's eyes dropped to the envelope in her hand. "Well, good for Roddy," she said softly.

"Would you like me to go?" Sukey offered. "I expect you'd like to be alone when you read that."

"No, please don't go yet," said Nina quickly. "You've come all this way . . . the least I can do is offer you a cup of tea."

For the first time, Sukey detected a tremor in Nina's voice and guessed that to be left alone was the last thing she wanted. "Never mind the tea, but I'll stay a bit longer if you like," she said quickly. "Why don't I go and sit out there while you read your letter?" she went on, nodding across the little sitting-room of Nina's Oxford flat towards the open French window, which gave on to a balcony just wide enough to accommodate a couple of garden chairs.

"Yes, all right."

In ordinary circumstances it would have been very pleasant to relax in the late spring sunshine and enjoy the view while thinking of nothing in particular. The balcony overlooked a small, well-tended communal garden bright with early roses and bordered by a stream where a pair of swans paddled majestically up and down, stopping now and again to dip their beaks into the gently flowing water or preen their snow-white feathers. The light was strong; after a few minutes Sukey closed her eyes and reflected sombrely on the contrast: outside, all was peace and tranquillity; in the room behind her the curtain was falling on the final act of a human tragedy.

The sun was warm on her skin; there was no sound but the drone of a distant aeroplane; she felt herself drifting away. She was aroused by the rattle of china as Nina deposited a tray on a small table beside her and sat down in the other chair. "I often drop off when I'm sitting out here," she said. "It's surprisingly quiet in spite of being so close to the main road."

"I'm sorry, I didn't mean to—"

"There's no need to apologise." Nina poured tea, handed a cup to Sukey and pointed to a plate of biscuits. "Help yourself."

For a few moments they drank their tea and nibbled biscuits without speaking. At last, Nina put down her empty cup and said, "There's one bit of information in Roddy's letter to me that might help with the police enquiry."

"Oh?"

"It's the answer to a question I was always dying to ask him – but of course I never could because I wasn't supposed to know he was up to anything criminal – which is, how did he get mixed up with that mob in the first place?"

"That's something I've often wondered."

"It was so typical of him . . . I'm afraid he was a bit big-headed in some ways." Nina gave a gentle, almost indulgent smile, like a mother excusing a harmless shortcoming on the part of a favourite child. "He was at a reception being held in some stately home; the owner was holding forth about his 'impregnable' security system and Roddy remarked to someone standing nearby that anyone with the right knowledge of electronics could easily get past it. Then he got a phone call from a man who claimed to represent the firm that installed the system and asked him if it was true. Knowing Roddy, I suspect he boasted a bit about how he could do it; anyway, this guy asked for a demonstration – so that steps could be taken to rectify possible weaknesses in the system, he said. Roddy couldn't resist a challenge like that, so he did it . . . and was then asked to repeat the performance at a private house while the owner was away. The next day he read that the house had been robbed and realised that he'd got himself mixed up in a scam."

"So why didn't he go to the police?"

"He admits he should have done, but he was afraid he might end up in gaol himself and anyway he reckoned that so long as no one got hurt, it was okay. As I told the police in my report, part of him lived in a fantasy world and I can imagine how he must have seen himself . . . a kind of romantic, Raffles-type figure, always one jump ahead of the law. He got a cut from every job, but he didn't need the money, it was the thrill of the thing that appealed to him. Then he found out what he'd really become involved with – the drugs, the murders, the utter ruthlessness of the people running the show – and the knowledge was just too much for him." Nina's voice, which had been strong and steady throughout the recital, suddenly cracked, her face crumpled and tears welled up in her eyes. "The final straw was the knowledge that, so long as he was alive, my life would be in danger. I could have identified him, you see, despite the plastic surgery, so I had to be eliminated. And he would have tried to find me, they knew that . . ." This time, her voice failed completely.

"I'm so very sorry," said Sukey gently.

After a few moments, Nina wiped away the tears. "Don't be sorry," she said. "I'm thankful it's over, and proud that he had the courage to end it the way he did. I can grieve for him in peace now." She put a hand on Sukey's arm. "Thank you for coming. It would have been much harder to face it alone."